MAGIC SOURCE

MAGIC SOURCE

THE EVERMORES CHRONICLES™ BOOK 3

MARTHA CARR

MICHAEL ANDERLE

DISRUPTIVE IMAGINATION

LMBPN Publishing
PMB 196, 2540 South Maryland Pkwy
Las Vegas, NV 89109

Version 1.01, January 2022
ebook ISBN: 978-1-68500-606-8
Print ISBN: 978-1-68500-607-5

THE MAGIC SOURCE TEAM

Thanks to our JIT Readers

Dave Hicks
Diane L. Smith
Dorothy Lloyd
Zacc Pelter

Editor

SkyHunter Editing Team

CHAPTER ONE

A coffee maker flew, trailing a rainbow of magical and electrical sparks behind it. It knocked a monitor off a desk, left a scratch on the basement office's wall, and sailed over the partition into the workshop area beyond.

Fran Berryman ran after the coffee maker, frantically waving. She'd tried all sorts of spells to catch it or bring it back to Earth, but the magical machine was determinedly resistant to the effects of her light and sound magic. It was all very well wielding the power of the Evermores, but some days she wished she was a more conventional witch. The flexibility of modern spellcraft had some advantages over ancient cosmic powers from the dawn of humanity.

A flying toaster joined the coffee maker. The two devices circled each other in a sort of dance, the toaster spinning on its corner while the coffee maker billowed steam like a cloud of dry ice all around them. Professional dancers could hardly have put on a better show.

Fran dashed around the partition to see Bart Trumbling standing under the devices, also waving. Magic gently emerged between the gray-haired gnome's fingers and drifted up to form a mist around the appliances. As the magic condensed into a net to capture them, the coffee maker and toaster flew clear, dropped behind another partition, and disappeared.

"This isn't quite what I expected when you said we should liven up breakfast," Bart said.

Singar Twitchtail grinned and wriggled her rat-like nose. The Willen's whiskers twitched. "Look on the bright side. We know the batteries last."

"Because we've been chasing them for an hour!"

"Imagine how much worse fully charged versions would be."

"Time for a change of tactics." Fran pressed a finger to her lips, then pointed past Singar's workbench, around one side of the partition. Bart crept that way while Fran went around the other side, back toward the part of the basement where Mana Wave Industries' staff did their admin work.

The rogue appliances were sitting on the floor. The coffee maker leaned against the toaster with their power leads tangled together as if holding hands. It was almost cute to look at, and for a moment Fran was tempted to leave them to it. She didn't have anyone to hold her close. Could she begrudge a toaster its happiness?

Still, these weren't living things. They were prototypes that she and Singar had been working on, options for the next Mana Wave product. If she wanted her business to succeed, she needed to get them under control.

She crept toward the appliances while Bart came from the other side. A classic pincer movement, except that instead of trapping an army between the advancing columns of its enemies, they were trapping two lumps of magically infused plastic and metal between the advancing fronts of a pair of startup executives.

Fran and Bart both raised their hands and magic rippled between their fingers. The devices stirred, shifted as if looking around, and tried to take flight again. This time, Fran hit them with a sound wave as they lifted.

Its energy knocked them back into a magical net that Bart had summoned. He closed its mouth quickly, then tightened the glowing strands around the wriggling appliances. They battered against their restraints but eventually went still.

Carefully carrying the magical net between them, Fran and Bart walked back into the workshop area. Singar held a screwdriver with a glowing tip ready between clawed fingers. She poked it through the net, touching each device in turn. Each time, there was a flash of expended energy and the appliance fell still.

"That should do it," Singar said. "You can let go of the spell."

The strands of the magical net faded. Bart sat at the end of the workbench, watching the coffee maker with suspicion. Fran took out her screwdriver and joined Singar in disassembling the devices.

"What do you think?" Fran asked. "Adjust the power level, or connect something differently?"

"I think it's time to give up on your dreams for the Brilliant Breakfast brand and instead focus on something that works." Singar pulled wires, crystals, and circuit boards from the coffee maker's base.

"But it's breakfast, and it's brilliant." Fran waved her arms in the air. "Who wouldn't want that?"

"People who don't want their kitchen to run away."

"Maybe if we changed the control software."

"For that, we'd need Smokey to turn up for work."

"He does turn up for work."

"Not today."

"I could do the programming."

Singar raised an eyebrow. "Isn't that how we got to this point?"

At the far end of the basement, a door opened. The sound of footsteps coming downstairs followed it. A moment later, Gruffbar Steelstrike and Elethin Tannerin walked in.

Gruffbar's beard was full of half-cooked fragments of waffle and streaks of batter dripped from his leather jacket. Even by dwarf standards, his scowl was impressive. He slammed the twisted remains of a Wi-Fi-enabled smart waffle iron down on the workbench. One last light glowed on its front panel, only to snuff out when Gruffbar wrenched a magical crystal from the device's base.

"How far did it get this time?" Fran asked.

"Too far," Gruffbar growled.

"And the batter reservoir…"

"Wouldn't have been a problem if someone hadn't let it get the jump on me."

Gruffbar scowled at Elethin. The elf seemed completely unperturbed. There was laughter in her eyes as she looked at Gruffbar, and Fran knew that she was letting him see her amusement. Elethin was a PR professional and an expert in her work. If anyone saw what she felt, it was because she wanted them to.

"I'm sorry, I didn't see it coming," she said with half-hearted sincerity. "It's a good thing you had your ax with you."

Gruffbar unslung the ax hanging from his shoulder. Its shaft was a shotgun, and batter had gotten into the barrel.

"I think you should clean this." He thrust it at Elethin.

"Oh, no. I never touch a man's weapon unless I'm sure it's clean."

The waffle maker joined the other devices on the workbench, where Singar and Fran stripped them for parts. Their contract to make a containment unit for the FBI, together with the investors they'd found, meant that the business was no longer broke, but they still couldn't afford to let anything go to waste. Every penny counted, which was why they needed to get a new product ready soon.

"So we're giving up on breakfast, then?" Bart picked up a marker pen and went to a whiteboard in the corner of the room. "I mean, it was a fun idea, but…"

Fran sighed. "You're right. We should move on."

Bart crossed the letters "BB" off a list. They'd crossed off a lot of the list already, and several of the remaining ideas had big red question marks next to them.

"Next idea," he said, "the device for teaching sign language."

Singar took a box from the corner of the room and opened it on the workbench. Inside was a device with a pair of mannequin hands sticking from the top. "I'm still proud of this one."

"It's a wonderful idea, but it's not going to work," Elethin said.

"Of course it is." Singar pressed a button on the side. The hands started making signs. Then they moved faster, slapping dangerously against each other and rocking the device from side to side. Singar hastily switched it off. "Just needs some work."

"I mean there's no market for it." Elethin had perched on a stool in the corner of the room with her legs elegantly crossed and one high-heeled shoe dangling. "Not enough customers want something like this for us to make a profit."

"Technology's not only about profit."

"That's what you should say once we're all millionaires and you can manufacture this as your philanthropic contribution to the world. You can set up a charitable foundation for it while I'm drinking champagne in the private pool of my new rural retreat. Right now, we need to make something profitable, and this isn't it."

Singar scowled. One of the hands on the device rotated and raised its middle finger at Elethin.

"Very mature." The elf shook her head. "I've done the market research. While this device could be lovely PR further down the line, it's no use to us now."

The distant door opened again. This time, there was a padding of small feet. A mottled black and gray cat strolled in and leaped up onto the workbench. He sniffed the broken waffle maker, then the batter dripping from Gruffbar. A crow fluttered in behind him and landed on Fran's shoulder.

"Good of you to join us, Smokey," Elethin said.

The cat twitched his tail.

"I told you all I had a thing this morning," he said. "We were protesting at the city council meeting."

"How did it go?" Fran asked.

"They're still refusing to rewire public buildings so different-sized creatures can operate the elevators," Smokey said. "They said they might put in ramps up to the controls instead, which is a complete cop-out, but at least it's better than nothing."

"Like drilling a good mine shaft, progress is seldom fast," Gruffbar noted. "At least you got something out of them this time."

"Yeah, I suppose." Smokey paced in a circle, then curled up on the corner of the workbench. "How are the proto-types going?"

Fran walked over to the whiteboard. As founder and CEO of Mana Wave Industries, it was her job to take control when things weren't going great, to keep people motivated despite the ups and downs. Bart had taught her that and now grinned at her and gave a big thumbs-up.

"It's time to come up with some new ideas again. We've gone through everything we plausibly could on this list. We need to get creative again."

She picked up a cloth and wiped the board clean. Weeks of failed work vanished in moments.

"How about a variation on what we've already made?" Bart asked. "That's usually a safe option."

"What we have is a containment unit for trapping magical beings," Fran pointed out. "I'm not sure there are a lot of variations to make on that."

"We shouldn't do any more with it," Smokey said. "We

7

needed the work before, but I don't want to give the man more ways to oppress us."

"You didn't mind it when we were getting started," Elethin said sharply.

"Yeah, well, I've been arrested a few times since then. Seeing the inside of a jail cell will change your perspective."

"It doesn't matter anyway," Gruffbar said. "Our contract with the FBI is clear. If they advance past the initial unit to buying these from us in mass numbers, we can't sell any related products to other customers. There's too much risk that they might supply people with ways around the containment technology."

"Sounds like monopolistic practices to me. This isn't how markets are supposed to work."

"Take it up with the authorities." Gruffbar wiped batter from his ax. "For now, we need other options."

"Do we?" Singar asked. "As soon as they finish the field tests, the feds will be coming to us for refinements and mass production. That'll put us in plenty of profit."

"If the tests go well."

"They will. We made a solid product."

"Too solid," Smokey muttered.

"None of that matters." Fran tapped her pen against the board. "I didn't found this company so that we could only make a boring old containment cage for the FBI. I founded it to make extraordinary things, so we could brighten and transform people's lives.

"We don't only need ideas so we can make a profit. We need to come up with new ideas because it's fun and cool and makes all of this worth the effort." She grinned. On her shoulder, the crow flapped its wings. "So, throw your ideas at me. The wilder and weirder, the better. We can think about practicality later. For now, it's time to let our imaginations run wild."

She looked around the room. There was an awkward silence.

"Come on. Somebody must have something."

"How about…" Elethin waved. "I don't know, a hot tub that can tell when I want the temperature changed, and that has a champagne tap."

"You think that's worth putting magic into?" Singar sounded incredulous.

"Absolutely. I don't see you giving us better ideas."

"Oh, I will!" Singar drummed her fingers against the workbench. "Give me a moment to think. I've burned through a lot of ideas lately…"

Fran wrote "magic hot tub" on the board.

"Ooh, I've got it!" Bart raised his hand.

Fran grinned and stood ready to write the next idea down. It was going to be a fun day. Then her phone buzzed. She looked down and saw a reminder from her calendar.

"Got to dash." She threw the pen to Gruffbar. "You're in charge. I want to see a hundred great ideas when I get back."

CHAPTER TWO

Fran stepped out of the workshop into the office area of Mana Wave Industries. It was all part of the same basement, underneath a former mirror factory that was now a carpet shop. One day soon, she would have a proper office, like the magitech giants that dominated the rest of Mana Valley. Until then, she was quite happy with their quirky headquarters.

She grabbed her backpack and roller skates from under her desk and hurried up the stairs into Worn Threads. There were a couple of customers around, and Gail talked to one of them about underlay, but she smiled and waved as Fran hurried past.

Out in the street, Fran strapped on her skates, then set off along the sidewalk, out toward the edge of Mana Valley. As she passed the Blazing Bean coffee shop, she waved through the window. She would've liked to stop by, not only for cake and coffee but for a chance to talk with Cam, but people were waiting for her, and she didn't want to be late.

The city changed around her as she moved through it. The area where Mana Wave Industries was based was once rundown but recovering. Old buildings were becoming converted apartments and offices for people who couldn't afford the downtown office blocks or the riverfront apartments, which was almost everyone. The city was expanding as the magitech sector grew, thanks to Oriceran's contact with Earth. Areas that had come close to collapse showed signs of revitalization. It was splendid to see.

Past her neighborhood was one with more shops and businesses that had sprung up on relatively cheap, previously untouched land. She whizzed past supermarkets, bulk food retailers, and a steam wagon showroom, where a Kilomea considered the four-wheel-drive on the forecourt. Then her wheels carried her through a quiet residential suburb and out into the foothills.

Skating uphill was a pain and giving herself a magical assist wasn't worth the effort, so Fran switched back to her sneakers with the rainbow of glittering sequins across the front. Carrying her skates, she walked up past individual houses with expansive lawns and stepped yards or the sort of acreage that could plausibly be called "grounds" instead of a garden. At last, she reached the one she was after, set back from the road by a long driveway with trees planted all around the perimeter to shelter it from view.

She knocked on the door, and a blond guy wearing a tight t-shirt and a serious expression answered it quickly. He looked like he was about her age, somewhere in his early to mid-twenties, but Fran knew that Enfield was older than that. She hoped that she looked this good when she had a couple of hundred years under her belt, or a couple of thousand, like some of the other Evermores.

"You're just in time." Enfield held the door open for her.

"I am? I mean, there's no need to sound so surprised. I must turn up on schedule, like, at least half the time."

Enfield shook his head. "Not in my experience."

"Well, life's full of cool distractions. You can't expect me to ignore them all the time. I'm here now, and I'm ready to help move the Source."

"Good. We need to get this finished so we can go home."

Enfield led her through the house to a large room next to the kitchen. There, they'd pushed aside a dining table, making space to hold a prisoner.

In the middle of the room was the containment unit that Fran and her colleagues had created. It consisted of a mirror, less than two feet across, with runes carved along its edges and an assortment of magical and mundane technology fixed underneath. A framework of extending metal rods rose from the mirror's corners. Small crystals gleamed at their joins, forming the framework for a magical field that *crackled* and flashed as the unit's inmate struggled against confinement.

The Source itself looked different from when Fran had last seen it. It still glowed with the magical energy that gave it form, but it had settled and shrunk as if to fit its cage's confines. Instead of a towering, muscular monster that changed shape with every passing moment, it was now human-sized and roughly humanoid in shape. It was an uncanny imitation of what an intelligent magical would look like with its smooth body and featureless face.

It was a blank space on which to write countless possibilities, letting Fran's imagination project all kinds of options for how it could look if it wanted to. In some ways, it was as full of potential and variety as before. Only now, Fran had to imagine different forms onto it.

"That's really him?" Fran asked, gazing at the Source.

"It," Winslow corrected, emerging from the kitchen. "Not him."

The leader of the Evermores expedition looked stern, an expression that brought out the wrinkles at the corners of his eyes. His movements were fluid and efficient, calm as a still summer's day, but there was an intensity beneath it all as he looked at the Source.

"Sorry, yes," Fran said. "I got distracted by the shape, you know?"

"Of course. Don't let this fool you. The Source is an energy, not a magical person like us, and we need to return it to secure the magic on Earth. Speaking of which, have you come prepared?"

"Totally." Fran set down her backpack, took out an electronic box with a screen on the top, and wired it up to the containment unit. "We've been working on this for the past couple of weeks, in between the prototyping. Once you open a portal, I'll extend the containment field into it. As long as you have someone on the far side to take the Source, everything should be peachy."

"We still can't carry it through in the containment unit?"

"Too many uncertainties. Magical fields from the portal, the unit, and the Source. If you were transporting a witch or wizard, I'd say risk it, but this…" Fran shook her head. "No way."

She watched the Source, that shining pillar of magical power. It was a shame they couldn't keep it here in Mana Valley. She could've studied it properly and looked for other ways to tap into its energy. Maybe she could've used it in her batteries as an alternative to the part of her power that went into making them work.

Her energy wasn't going to be enough forever, not once they started scaling up the business, but the Source was something else. The readings on the control panel told her what extraordinary power it was putting out for the unit to reflect at it. It was something that could've changed the world.

Perhaps it had. After all, wasn't that the whole point of this? From what Winslow had told her, the kemanas on Earth were reliant on what the Source put out. Without it, the magic over there would fail, as it had started to do when the Source was loose. They needed to return it to where it came from. That was why the Evermores had come out of hiding and why she was working with them now.

She tapped an icon on the screen of the new device. The field around the Source flickered.

"Ready when you are," Fran said.

Winslow spread his hands wide. A portal appeared against the wall at the side of the room. It wasn't like the portals that most people summoned to cross between worlds. The glow was different, and when Fran paid attention, it almost seemed like the circle of power was singing.

It was like the types of portals she could summon with her traveling mirror, except more so. Through it, there lay a vast underground cavern with a web of knotted roots stretching across its floor and stone houses carved up its walls, the home kemana of the Evermores.

"Can't you put the portal a little closer?" Fran asked. "Just to be on the safe side."

"It will be fine," Winslow said.

Half a dozen Evermores gathered around, watching and waiting. They smiled proudly. The most important mission of their lives was coming to an end. Through the portal, more of their kind had gathered, ready to receive the Source, to contain it on the far side and bind it again.

Fran tapped another icon. The rods on the containment unit shifted, separated, extended. They couldn't reach the portal, but they formed the base of a magical funnel that pointed into the opening. The funnel lengthened, a field of magical light and power. Then there was pulsing from the mirror base. The Source shifted on its feet and stumbled down the tunnel as unseen forces pushed it.

A light flashed on Fran's controller. She frowned. Something was wrong with the fields. They hadn't designed the feedback loop that took the Source's energy and turned it back into containment to go far beyond the mirror base. Something was wrong with it.

No, that wasn't the problem. Something else was amiss. Another factor was interfering with the magical field, possibly the portal. She couldn't work out what without time to examine the data.

"We need to shut this down," she said.

"We're nearly there," Winslow replied.

"But it's going to—"

The Source flung its arms wide. There was a roar and a flash. The field rippled and strained. The Evermores staggered back. The portal swirled.

"It's breaking loose!" Fran exclaimed.

The Source flung itself against one side of the magical funnel. The field strained and bent but didn't break yet. Strands of power grew thinner and the framework rods buckled.

"Everybody, quick!" Winslow said. "Hold it in."

The Evermores started to chant. Magic flowed from them, forming a cord woven from light and sound that closed around the Source.

"Steer it into the portal," Winslow shouted above the discordant noise of the Source and the more tuneful sounds coming from the Evermores. The cord threaded through the containment field, tightened around the Source, and dragged it toward the portal.

Fran tapped her screen, calling up data from the containment unit and its extension, desperately trying to work out what was happening and what had gone wrong. She'd made this device. She should be able to make it work. She could save this situation.

The Source screeched and thrashed. The cord bound around it stretched and snapped, letting out a burst of light and sound that left everyone else temporarily stunned.

Fran blinked the flashing from her eyes. When she could see again, the containment field strained to its limits as the Source tried to push out. This shouldn't be happening. The field was supposed to feed off the prisoner's energy so however hard they pushed, it pushed back equally hard.

"Again!" Winslow shouted.

Once more, the Evermores started chanting, calling the magic to them. A net shimmered in the air and closed on the Source, then pushed it toward the portal.

"We've got it," Winslow said. "Just a little further."

The Source was almost at the opening. It stretched out a hand, and the net strained around it. The Evermores kept pushing. Sweat ran from their brows. Fran tapped her screen.

The Source slammed a hand against the wall and grabbed the portal's edge with its other fingers. It strained and pushed back. Raw power streamed from the portal, and the net disintegrated around it. Collapsing magic ran through the containment field, which wavered, distorted, and rippled like the surface of a pond in the wind.

The Source screeched a triumphant sound.

"Harder!" Winslow said. "Stop it!"

"It's not working," Enfield called. "It's going to break free."

"No it isn't." Fran's fingers danced across the keys. She dashed over to the base of the containment unit and kicked it across the floor, underneath the Source. "Shut the portal down, now!"

"We need to get the Source through," Winslow bellowed.

"More than you need to stop it escaping?"

For a moment, there was doubt in his expression, then calm certainty returned. He waved, and the portal vanished.

Fran hit an icon on her screen. The containment field shrank back to its previous size, dragging the Source in above the mirror. For a moment, its arm stretched out for where the portal had been, and she thought the field would collapse. Then the field pulled that arm back inside, and the Source fell silent.

With a sigh of relief, Fran sat on the floor and checked her readings. Winslow laid a hand on her shoulder.

"Well done," he said. "Sometimes I forget that you are one of us and how capable that makes you."

"Thanks," Fran said. "Although this wasn't about being an Evermore, so much as it was about all my years in tech."

"Of course, of course."

"Are you all right?" She looked up at him. His expression wasn't the calm she had at first assumed. It was something else, a more chilling sort of stillness.

"I am concerned. About what this means, about how it came so close to escaping."

"I won't let it happen again." Fran pulled components out of her backpack. "We can reinforce the containment unit, make it into something more permanent to hold the Source here in case the field gets disrupted again."

"Thank you."

"What about transporting it over?" Enfield asked.

"One problem at a time," Winslow said quietly.

Fran ran wires from the containment unit and contemplated what else they could add. She would call Singar up here, of course, and Smokey. Between them, they'd find a way to make a stronger, more stable containment unit to ensure there weren't more escape attempts.

For her, this looked less like a problem and more like an

opportunity. If the Source wasn't leaving the Valley yet, maybe she could tap into its power. Maybe she could work out what it could do for her and magitech.

Winslow looked worried, but she was excited. Played right, this could go better than any of their prototypes.

CHAPTER THREE

Something like night hung across the nightmare realm. Not the night of Earth or Oriceran, with moonlight and scattered stars, nor the pitch dark found in caverns and locked cells. This was a darkness shot through with the red of embers and the green of the sickroom. The edges of objects caught fragments of that light, enough to make their blackness stand out even more.

The Darkness Between Dreams sat in that twisted night with its minions around it. Nightmare hounds prowled a desolate, broken landscape. Warped creatures of fangs and tentacles stumbled between them, grunting, growling, and thrashing at each other. The Darkness Between Dreams loved them all, these followers it had, these creations, its true people. It loved them, and soon it would free them.

Soon.

A point of light appeared in the air in front of it, an alert sent across the chasm between worlds, a message from a device in its Mana Valley office. It needed to return.

Reluctantly, it stopped running its tentacles down the

flank of its favorite hound. The hound looked at the Darkness Between Dreams and bared its teeth, which flashed in the red light.

"I must go," the Darkness Between Dreams said. "But don't worry. I will return. Soon, you'll come with me. Soon."

It twisted two of its tentacles in a circle. A portal appeared. The Darkness Between Dreams slid through, and the portal closed behind it. There was a sadness to moments like this, severing itself from its home realm. Soon, it would make a whole world its own, the greater nightmare realm that its creatures deserved. Not long, now. Not by the timescales it worked with.

It emerged into its office. On the phone on the desk, a light was blinking. The Darkness Between Dreams moved over to it, black tentacles rippling across the floor, and hit the button.

"Is it that time already, Julia?" It put on the voice of Howard Phillips, CEO of Philgard Technologies.

"Yes, Mr. Phillips," his PA said from the other end of the intercom. "He's in the building and on his way up."

"Keep him for a few minutes when he arrives. I need time to prepare."

"Of course."

The Darkness Between Dreams let go of the intercom button and headed for the back of the room. At a wave of its tentacles, a concealed wardrobe opened in the wall. It took out two suits: a skin suit, to disguise it as human, and a business suit, to armor that human against the world.

With a ripple of black flesh, it slid into first one suit, then the other, sealing the gaps in the skin before it buttoned up the shirt and vest. It slipped on leather-soled shoes, slid cuff-links through their holes, and fastened a gold watch around its wrist.

At last, Howard Phillips took his seat behind the desk. He smiled and cleared his throat. The disguise was complete.

With a human finger, Phillips pressed the intercom button that he'd operated with a tentacle only minutes before.

"I'm ready, Julia," he said.

The door opened and Julia Lacy walked in. She was short and slender for a witch, but had long ago demonstrated to Phillips that she was entirely human. Any semblance to the smaller magical folk was pure chance. With one hand, she clutched the tablet that was her constant weapon in the battle to manage Philgard's staff. The fingers of her other hand toyed with her silver necklace.

"Liam Wade of Prestige Craft is here to see you, sir," she said.

He'd known who was coming. After all, he was the one who'd summoned Wade here and told him to arrive through the building's back entrance to keep the matter quiet. Still, it was important to maintain the rituals, to pretend that this wasn't the most important meeting of his week. He didn't want to give others the advantage of knowing how important they were to him.

"Thank you, Julia. I'd like you to sit in on this one. While you're about it, why don't you call Handar in?"

"Yes, sir."

As if this too wasn't part of the performance. As if he'd

ever intended to take this meeting without his PA and bodyguard, his two most capable mortal lieutenants.

While Julia stepped out, a wizard walked into the room. He was six feet tall, with dark hair and blue eyes. He wore a tailored suit, silk tie, a gold watch, and he had the sort of build that came from a personal trainer and a home gym.

"Liam." Phillips stood and extended his hand. " Thanks for coming in like this. It's so good to see you again."

"And you." Liam Wade shook the hand and smiled with a warmth that could almost have been genuine. "I've been saying to the guys that we haven't seen you at the club enough recently."

"You know how it is." Phillips gestured at the chair across from him, then settled into his seat. "Sometimes the demands of the board can be unrelenting."

"Oh, I know. Some of my shareholders are real tyrants." Wade winked.

"What can I say? I wouldn't have bought a controlling interest in Prestige Craft if I didn't think you were worth controlling."

Wade laughed. "You make me sound almost like a serf."

"I do, don't I?" Phillips said those words stony-faced, without a hint of warmth, and for a moment, Wade recoiled from him. Phillips enjoyed that. Then he smiled, the fake warmth returning. "Of course, I don't need serfs or drones. I need people with real skills and initiative. This is why I called you here."

The door clicked shut. Julia took a seat to one side of Wade and gave him a welcoming glance for a moment before she looked away. Handar Ennis sat on his other side. The seat *creaked* beneath the Kilomea's muscular bulk.

He didn't smile, and if he had, it wouldn't have been a comforting thing. Whatever his expression, his tusks added a menacing element to his face.

"You've brought the whole team to meet with me," Wade said. "At least the team that matters, huh?" He smiled again. "This must be serious."

"Isn't it always?" Phillips asked. "Have you heard of a company called Mana Wave Industries?"

"Mana Wave?" Wade's expression became an ostentatious show of thought as if he was delving deep into his memories and it was straining his whole face. "I don't think so. Should I have?"

"Probably not. They're small fish, a magitech startup working out of a basement in the Valley."

"Ah, the old classic. How many entrepreneurs tell stories about the glory days of their youth, when they were working in loft conversions or dusty back rooms, getting their first products to work?"

"Far more than ever really did it." Phillips snorted. "This place is full of phonies."

"Of course it is. Fakery is how we get business done." Wade raised an eyebrow. "Or is that a little too honest for you?"

"This is why I chose you, Wade." Phillips suppressed the urge to laugh. If only Wade knew how fake he was. "That playful charm of yours is going to come in handy."

"Chose me?"

"I have a task for you."

"I have a business to run."

"Only as long as I let you keep running it." Phillips

leaned forward. "You do want to keep running it, don't you?"

Wade stiffened, then gave a hollow laugh.

"Of course, Howard. I'm always happy to help out a good friend and colleague."

"Good." Phillips stood and walked over to the window. He waved Wade over to stand beside him. "Quite a view, isn't it?"

"Very impressive, Howard. You must be proud."

"Oh, I am. I've put a lot of effort into getting to where I am. Still, there are always opportunities to do better, and I want you to help me seize one of them."

"You want me to take over this Mana Wave Industries, then sell it to you?"

Phillips considered that option for a moment. Perhaps a possibility for later, but right now, he was trying for something more subtle.

"No, I want a more indirect approach. I want you to find a way to work with them. I trust you to work out how. Don't do it through your minions. Get hands-on. Tell them whatever's needed to make that convincing."

"You want me to infiltrate a startup?" Wade laughed. "Really, Howard, is this the best use of my time?"

"There are some very ambitious people on your board. Perhaps one of them would be more cooperative…"

"I'm joking, of course. Ha, ha, ha! Please, tell me more about this Mana Wave."

"They're a means to an end. I'm looking for signs of another organization that I believe has connections with them, a group known as the Evermores."

"Evermores…" Wade had that thoughtful look again. He shook his head. "Don't know them either, I don't think."

"You wouldn't. They keep quiet. Have done so for a very long time. We believe that at least one of them has a connection to Mana Wave. Handar will provide you with the little we know about this individual.

"Your job will be to get close to the people at Mana Wave, listen, look, and learn anything you can. Slowly and carefully. I don't want you alerting them to my interest."

"A little corporate espionage? It's been a while, but that could be quite fun." Wade chuckled. "Then what?"

"Then whatever you want. You're free to pursue other business deals with these people, to seize whatever opportunities they provide. I hear they have potential, so I'm sure you'll find compensation for your time."

"At some grubby little tech startup?"

"We all began as grubby startups, remember?"

"Only in our portfolio statements."

"Then think of it as a chance to see the details, to develop a more convincing story for next time someone writes your profile."

"Fine, fine, fine…" Wade sighed. "Is there anything else while I'm here? Want me to move into an apartment above a takeout and start doing my laundry?"

"Don't be ridiculous. Even I have limits." Phillips raised an eyebrow. "That really would be the nightmare for you, wouldn't it? To live like everybody else?"

"Gods, yes. Can you think of anything worse?" Wade shuddered. "This business is going to be bad enough." He turned and caught Handar's eye. "Email me the details, will you?"

Handar shook his head. "No data trail."

He held out a cardboard folder. Wade drew a deep breath, then accepted it from him. He flicked it open and saw a surveillance photo of a blond man in his twenties running down the street.

"This is him? Doesn't seem all that special to me."

"Trust me, he's special," Handar said. "You want to get yourself messed up? Take him on."

"Don't worry. I'm not the sort for back alley fistfights. Not everybody likes a bit of rough." He looked past Handar at Julia with a smile. "Though of course, I don't have to be a perfect gentleman."

She smiled too. "I'd hope not, for this."

"We're done here." Phillips returned to his desk. "Wade, if you have any questions, contact Handar. If I need an update, I'll contact you."

"Of course, Howard." Wade headed for the door. "I'll show myself out, shall I?"

"I can show you out." Julia rose from her chair.

"No, we need to talk." Phillips nodded at Wade. "One of Handar's people will escort you."

His expression stiff, Wade left the room, closing the door a little too loudly behind him.

"You didn't have to humiliate him like that," Julia said. "Practically saying that he's beneath us. I thought you wanted to keep him cooperative."

"You didn't have to make eyes at him," Handar growled. "I mean, seriously, that guy?"

"He's hot, and it's not like I have a lot of time for dating. You take the opportunities you can."

"Don't take that one," Phillips said. "I need to keep him

in his place. Liam Wade is a man best dealt with like that—some flattery here, a put-down there. He's never learned healthy emotions. It's one of the things I find pleasing about him."

"Whatever you say, Howard." Julia smiled. Any disappointment she felt was negligible compared with her satisfaction at serving her boss. She was in this for the long haul. "What else did you want to talk about?"

"Many things." Phillips switched on his computer. "The world isn't going to conquer itself, even through the crude mechanisms of the market. We have a busy week ahead."

CHAPTER FOUR

Fran and her roommate Josie sat in the bucket of a flying cab, being carried over Mana Valley by a giant eagle. Below them, the early evening traffic drifted along streets that the authorities had recently started to widen, to keep up with the growing congestion that the city's economic prosperity brought.

There were almost constant road works now, with teams of magicals in high visibility jackets working through each night to shift buildings a few feet over and make space for the addition of extra lanes. Some of it was done manually by dwarf mining clans, with their expert engineering knowledge. Magic moved other buildings, spells weaving together to shift not only the visible parts but the foundations beneath them.

"Hey, look, the old drive-in movie theater's gone." Josie pointed at a spot that had become a complex junction and fueling station.

"Aw, that's so sad," Fran said. "How are cars going to go see movies now?"

"Not much of a surprise, though. That thing was old-fashioned before they built it. Like those 2020s-themed restaurants or the crenelations on Victorian buildings."

"Fake old can be fun, especially once it starts to get properly old. You know, when there's this mixture of deliberate and fake falling apart, and it's hard to tell what's supposed to be the way it is. I love that stuff."

"Did you ever go to the drive-in?"

"No." Fran shook her head. "Never had a car or a wagon over here, and I don't think they'd have liked my flying carpet. Still, it's a shame to see it go."

They descended onto the roof of an apartment block not far from the new junction. Josie paid the eagle, and it soared away.

"Are you sure I can't pay half?" Fran asked.

"I was the one who insisted on getting a cab," Josie said. "Besides, I got my first pay packet as a team leader, so I have a bit of cash to spare."

"I'm so proud of you." Fran squeezed her friend's arm. "Rising through the ranks at Philgard."

"You're proud of me?" Josie laughed. "You've set up your own business!"

They headed down the stairs into the building. Fran compared door numbers with the back of her hand, where she'd written her mom's new address.

"It was cool of Irene to invite us round for dinner," Josie said.

"I think it's a guilt thing," Fran said. "After staying on our sofa all that time, she feels like she has to pay us back."

"On the one hand, it was a bit of a pain," Josie admitted. "On the other hand, that's what family's for, right?"

"To drive you nuts?"

"To help each other out!"

"OK, that too. Ooh, this is it."

Fran knocked and a few moments later the door opened.

"Francesca!" Irene Berryman hugged her daughter, then moved on to Josie. "And Josie. Come in, both of you. Dinner's cooking."

They followed her directly into the apartment's living room. It was bigger than Fran had expected, with wide windows, thick rugs scattered over varnished wood floors, and a kitchen area with a small dining table off to one side.

"Wow, Mom." Fran looked around. "This is way nicer than I expected."

"Really?" Irene looked around. "I suppose it's not bad. I'm used to having more space back on Earth."

"It's more space than we have, and there are two of us."

"No! Well, all right, maybe a little larger." Irene led them to a pair of nicely padded sofas. "Here, take a seat. The lasagna needs a little longer."

She opened a bottle of wine while her guests sank onto one of the sofas. The cushions were soft and comfortable, with a clean new furniture smell. After a hard day's work, Fran felt the risk of falling asleep.

Irene sat on the edge of the other sofa, her glass in her hands.

"Well, here it is..." She waved to encompass the area. "My new abode. And I'm not getting in anybody's way."

Fran wanted to reassure her mother that she hadn't been in their way before, but they all knew that wasn't true. Instead, she looked for a change of topic.

"How's the job hunting going?"

"Not bad. I've been doing some temporary admin work while I look for something more in line with my skill set. How about you two? Josie, how's the new job?"

"Funny you should ask…" Josie opened her handbag and took out a phone. She placed it carefully on the coffee table. "I brought this to show you both."

"A cellphone?" Irene sounded a little uncertain. "Is it one of those new ones that have magical features?"

"Oh my God!" Fran grabbed it and turned it over in her hands, eagerly examining every inch of its surface. "Is this the new Manaphone prototype?" She waved it sternly at Josie. "Are you allowed to take this out of the office? I don't want you getting fired to entertain us."

"Yes, I'm allowed." Josie carefully pried the phone out of her friend's hand. "I have to follow some rules and procedures." She took a couple of forms from her handbag and handed them to Irene and Fran, along with corporate-branded ballpoint pens. "You are now an informal focus group, helping me to test the phone and gather public feedback. Sign the NDA on the top sheet, and you can play with this thing as much as you want."

Fran hurriedly scribbled her name in the box, then grabbed the phone again. Irene took her time reading through the paragraphs above.

"Francesca, dear," she said. "You shouldn't sign something like that without reading it first."

"I trust Josie," Fran replied.

"That's lovely, but still…" Irene finally signed her form. "You need to be careful. The law can be crushing if you're on the wrong end of it."

"I have a good lawyer." Fran scrolled through apps. "Gruffbar can get me out of any trouble a phone lands me in."

"Josie, dear, please tell her. She listens to you."

Josie laughed. "Fran barely listens to anyone."

"Do too!" Fran tapped an icon. "Ooh, what does this do?"

Patterns swirled on the screen, spinning colored disks that drew the eye. Fran watched them, entranced.

"Self-hypnosis app." Josie hurriedly switched it off. "It's to help you relax. You're supposed to set a time limit before it'll start." She made a note on her phone. "What else has your attention?"

Fran leaned forward so Irene could see the screen.

"Is that the email application?" Irene asked. "Open that."

"That's boring!" Fran protested. "Every phone has email."

"It's important. The main point of a phone is to communicate. You need to know that it'll do it right."

"Fine." Fran rolled her eyes but opened the app.

Josie leaned back and watched as the two Berryman women played with the phone. Every so often, she noted something they said or did. This was as valuable to her as talking about the apps themselves. Knowing how customers worked out the phone and how they navigated it once they'd mastered the controls would tell her a lot about what would happen once it was released.

After ten minutes, there was a *beeping* from the kitchen. Irene hurried over, pulled a pan of lasagna out of the oven, and set it on the dining table next to a big bowl of salad.

"That smells delicious, Mom," Fran said.

"Thank you, dear." Irene waved them to seats and poured more wine. "Do eat, but maybe put Josie's new phone away first."

Fran hesitated, then went and set the Manaphone down on the coffee table.

"You're right. I shouldn't get sauce on it."

The food was delicious, and the conversation was good, but still, Fran's attention wasn't on the meal. She kept glancing over at the coffee table and the phone on it. This was the road less traveled, the way Josie had gone, getting advance access to the latest big tech gadgets by working for the big companies. Fran was immensely proud of what she was doing, but she couldn't help feeling a little envious of what her friend had.

"Sorry, Irene," Josie said as the dessert came out and Fran paid hardly any attention. "I should never have brought that phone with me."

She gave Fran a knowing look.

"I can behave myself," Fran said. "Cross my heart. This is a delicious cobbler, Mom."

"Thank you, dear. Josie, I'm glad that you brought the phone with you. These things always seem to get tested on young people. It's nice to have someone ask my opinion."

"Well, if you want to give your opinion, there's a whole load of score sheets attached to the back of the NDA."

"I saw. Do you think those are the best way to get people's opinions?"

"What do you mean?"

Irene took a spoonful of cobbler and chewed on it thoughtfully before answering.

"In my experience, asking people to rate anything on a

scale of one to ten doesn't give you helpful information. It's like when I used to use dating apps when I was younger—"

"Mom!" Fran's eyes went wide with alarm. "Am I about to hear things I can never un-hear?"

Irene laughed. "Don't worry. All I'm trying to say is that it wasn't the scores of how well we matched that helped me find the right people. It was the details in their profiles. Qualitative data trumps quantitative for me every time."

Fran hesitated. In mentioning dating, her mom had opened the door to another topic, just a little, and she wondered if she could open that door wider to see whether her father lay behind. Before she could ask, Josie spoke, and the moment was gone.

"I agree with you, Irene. I'd much rather have substantial ideas I can work with than a bunch of digits. So, what can you tell me about what's good and bad with this phone?"

She put her phone on the table and set it to record the conversation.

"I think some useful things are missing," Irene said. "For example, there's no controller app to link up to my domestic devices. These days, I want to be able to switch on the oven or the heating on my way home, and a phone that can't do so is missing out."

"For magical devices, too," Fran said. "What if you could, like, find your wand using your phone, or even control the wand that way, trigger preset spells at a distance?"

"I'm sure no one would abuse that." Josie flashed her a sarcastic grin. "Still, neat idea, carry on."

"I like that idea about finding the wand," Irene said.

"How about a magical detector so you can sense other spells and devices too."

"We've been working on something like that," Josie said. "Just not for the phone. I'll see if we can simplify and integrate it. What else?"

"An aura filter," Fran said, "so you can take pictures of magic with your phone."

"And videos as well," Irene added. "Sometimes watching a video is the easiest way to remember how a new spell works."

"Could you integrate a spell for controlling the phone from a distance? Like, a sort of a magical link between you and the phone?"

"Ooh yes, so you could use your magic like a remote control. So handy for changing the music or the video if you've plugged into a screen to watch something."

"Ooh, ooh, ooh, a projector that plays videos onto walls! I bet that with a spell to enhance the brightness, you could get enough light to do that without external equipment."

"Could it project them into the air? I don't have any blank walls in here."

"Or something for music, like…"

They kept on talking while Josie sat back and listened. People in the office had plenty of opinions about what the phone should do, but they mostly fitted within the patterns established by previous models. Fran didn't limit herself like that, and once she got going, neither did her mother.

This might not be the type of feedback that more senior managers had asked Josie to collect, but it was the best sort of feedback she could find. If they really wanted, she could get the surveys filled in later. For now, she was happy to sit back, listen, and devour the cobbler that the others were too busy to eat.

All in all, she had a pretty good job.

CHAPTER FIVE

Morning sunlight shone off the ancient wizarding tower, giving a luminous sheen to its pale marble walls. It fractured off the crystal window frames, refracting in bright colors that made a rainbow of the fountain in the courtyard. On its roof, a wyvern hung from the brass spire, watching the world below with heavily lidded eyes.

"Whoa," Fran said as she approached the looming oak doors with a crow perched on her shoulder. "This place is amazing!"

A troll stood beside the doors. Instead of the doll-like size that trolls habitually spent their time in, she'd expanded to eight feet of muscle that loomed over any visitors. It was an unspoken warning from the building's owners—don't mess with us and we won't leave you flat.

It seemed a little unnecessary after the electric fence topped with barbed wire and being buzzed in through the main gate, but Fran supposed that tradition was important. In fairness, the fence wasn't much use against any magical who could fly.

"I'm here to see Gabriella Daigle," Fran said in a voice that felt all the smaller in comparison to the door guard. She pulled out her phone, hoping the email from Gabriella might provide some verification.

"Name?" the troll bellowed. Her hot breath washed over Fran, flapped the crow's feathers, and sent Fran's hair into disarray.

"Fran Berryman. I'm from—"

"In." The troll pushed one of the doors, which swung back, grinding and creaking on ancient hinges.

"You should probably oil that," Fran observed. "It can't be good for the door."

"In," the troll repeated, pointing inside with a thick finger. "Names at back."

"Thanks!" Fran turned to the crow on her shoulder. "Sorry, but I'm leaving you out here. Got to be professional."

The crow cawed resentfully but flew off to examine the fountain.

Fran walked through the huge doors, then stopped to gaze around in amazement. The inside of the tower was bigger than the outside, a vast tiled hall like the ballroom from a Disney take on a fairytale. The pillars holding up the vaulted ceiling were more marble, rising like a forest of cold, still trees. Her footsteps echoed and re-echoed as she walked toward the back wall, where a great carved slab of black stone stood between a pair of curving staircases.

Carved names showed in that black stone. The stone-mason's chisel had chipped away the top layer of black to reveal a pale gray underneath. Fran scanned it from the bottom up and found Gabriella Daigle's name, listed on the seventh floor. There was no sign of an elevator, so she started up one of the staircases, with its polished steps that smelled of ancient forests.

"This can't be very accessible," Fran panted as she passed the fifth floor.

The air shimmered and a brightly colored bird appeared, hovering a foot away from Fran's face.

"We provide magical transportation for any guests with mobility issues," it twittered in a shrill yet tuneful voice. "Do you have any accessibility issues you would like to share?"

"I'm okay." Fran paused to catch her breath. "It's a lot of stairs, you know?"

"The tower contains an infinite number of stairs to allow for the addition of new floors. Would you like to know more?"

It was incredibly tempting to say yes, both to learn more about this amazing tower and spend more time with the spectacular bird, but Fran was painfully aware that she had an important appointment to keep.

"Next time," she said. "I'll come early."

"Very good." The bird shimmered and vanished.

Fran reached the seventh floor and found the door with "DAIGLE" carved into it. She knocked.

"Enter," came the response.

Before Fran could touch the handle, the door swung open, and she stepped inside. The room's decorations were the same traditional aesthetic that marked the rest of the building, with shelves full of ancient books, patterned rugs spread across oak floorboards, and a set of ornately carved chairs around a mahogany table in the large window alcove facing the door.

An antique globe stood on a pedestal a few feet from the table, and Gabriella Daigle stood next to it. The gray-haired witch was wearing a dark suit and pearl necklace, similar to the outfit she'd worn for Fran's investor event. She tapped the globe sharply, and the top swung back, revealing a collection of glasses and crystal decanters.

"Martini?" she asked.

It was tempting. It would certainly take the edge off Fran's nerves, but she had to keep her wits about her. "No, thank you, Ms. Daigle."

"I've given you too much money for us to stay formal. You can call me Gabriella."

She waved a wand and ice cubes appeared in a cocktail glass. She poured in spirits from a couple of the bottles, added a twist of lemon peel and an olive, then sat at the table, her legs stretched out in front of her.

"If you change your mind, you can help yourself." She waved toward the globe. "In the meantime, take a seat."

"Thank you, Gabriella." Fran sat. The chair was far more comfortable than it looked. "Thank you again for your investment. It's going to make a huge difference to Mana Wave Industries."

"That's rather the point. I have high hopes for what you'll achieve with it."

Fran looked around her. The grandeur of this place fit what she'd expected, but after her previous encounters with Mana Valley business leaders, she felt like something was missing.

"Don't you have a personal assistant?" she asked. "Or a secretary?"

"If a job's worth doing, it's worth doing yourself." Gabriella sipped her drink. "I know my money can be intimidating, but I've always made sure to manage it in a way that I can personally control. That's how I ensure I make the right choices."

"You mean everything you invest in succeeds?" That was a thought to brighten Fran's spirits.

"Of course not. Even good ideas sometimes don't work out. Even good businesses fold in bad circumstances. But I take the right risks. That's how I can afford this place. It's how I can afford to take a risk on wild cards like you."

"Oh." Fran deflated a little. "Well, do you want to hear about the products we're currently working on?"

"No." Gabriella shook her head. "I'm not interested in that sort of micromanagement or in how it would influence your decision-making. What I want is to provide you with another opportunity."

"An opportunity?"

"There's a company I have a small investment in, Prestige Craft. Mid-level magitech, not as dynamic or interesting as you but more established. Old money and traditional leadership, with the advantages those bring. They've heard about you somehow and heard that I invested. They're interested in working together."

"Oh!" Fran smiled. It was great to hear that people were interested in them. "What on?"

"Something entertainment-related. Beyond that, I think it's your opportunity to shape." Gabriella glanced at her slender silver watch.

"Their man will be here any minute. He's pleasant enough, but remember, he's in sales, so there's some bluster there. I'm not using my influence here to say that you have to work with him. This might not be the right opportunity for you. Just have a chat, test the waters, see what you think."

"Okay, sure."

"If it works out, this could be profitable for both of us, but it's your call. If I didn't trust your judgment, I wouldn't have invested in you."

There was a knock on the door.

"Enter!" Gabriella called.

The door swung open, and a wizard walked in. He was tall and well-built, dressed in a blue suit that perfectly fitted his body. He smiled at them, and there was a twinkle in his eyes that called on Fran to smile back.

"Hi, Gabriella." He walked into the room. "How are you today?"

"Good enough." Gabriella waved her cocktail glass. "Liam Wade, this is Fran Berryman, CEO of Mana Wave Industries. Fran, this is Liam Wade, head of sales at Prestige Craft."

"Delighted to meet you." Liam gave Fran a handshake that was firm enough to be reassuring without being too forceful. "I've heard great things about what you're doing."

"Really?" Fran blushed. "Thanks, that's super to hear."

"You know where the drinks are, Liam," Gabriella said.

"Well, if you insist." Liam went to the globe and made himself a drink. "Can I get you something, Fran?"

"Um, I guess a small one? Like, nothing too strong."

"Good thinking. It's too early in the day for proper

43

drinking." He handed Fran a glass of something sweet and fizzy, probably a million miles from what Gabriella was drinking. "So, what terrible lies has Gabriella told you about me?"

He winked at the older witch, who smiled a little as she rolled her eyes.

"Not much," Fran admitted. "She said that you're interested in working with my company, but, um, that's it."

"Cool, well, let me tell you a bit about Prestige Craft. We've been in the magical artifacts business for generations. As I'm sure you know, companies like ours have to shift into magitech if we want to survive these days. Only way to keep up with the bright hotshots like yourself."

"Oh, yeah, sure," Fran said as if she knew this already. She took another sip of her drink to cover any hesitation. It was really good. "That's why you want to work with us?"

"Exactly!" Liam had taken a seat across from her. Now he looked at her with an intensity that said she was the most important thing in the world. No, better than that, it said that her business was the most important. "Word's starting to get around about Mana Wave. You're dynamic, imaginative, doing novel things with a skilled team. That's the sort of company we at Prestige want to partner with."

"What do you want to make together?" Fran asked.

Liam laughed. It was a rich laugh, friendly and warming.

"That's the million-dollar question, isn't it? I have a few ideas, but I'd like to scope you guys out first, spend some time exploring what you do, what we do, and how we could combine the two. For example, I hear that you don't have a sales team yet, while that's one of our big strengths.

We can provide that side of any shared projects or help you to develop your own sales force."

Fran licked her lips. The drink, combined with a recent lack of sleep, was making her brain a little fuzzy, and something was bothering her here that she couldn't quite grasp. She set her glass down and slid it away from her. Liam did the same, and his face became serious.

"You'd come and look at what we're doing?" Fran asked.

"Absolutely. I'm really interested to see what makes Mana Wave tick and how we can help you."

"So you'd see everything we're doing?" This sounded risky to Fran. However well her team crafted their products, they wouldn't sell well if another company stole their ideas and made them first, using their bigger resources, and as Liam had admitted, strong sales team.

"I see your concern," Liam said. "We both have secrets to protect, and while I suspect yours are more interesting, I have shareholders who would lynch me if I let you get away with ours. We'll sign watertight non-disclosure agreements before we go anywhere near each other's business and agreements around non-competition on products currently under production. I don't want either of us to be left at a disadvantage if this partnership doesn't work out."

When he put it like that, it all seemed very reasonable and well thought out. Without that flashing smile, she saw a man who was serious about his business and who took her seriously too. Still, better safe than sorry.

"My legal director will want to look over the agreements in detail before we sign anything. Knowing Gruffbar, he'll want to add some clauses."

"Of course. I can put him in contact with my legal team. But in principle?"

"In principle, it sounds like a good opportunity." Fran grinned. "It sounds like it could even be fun, seeing how your business works, learning from each other. It would be awesome to get an outsider's perspective on some of our ideas. You know how it is when you've been talking about the same things with the same people for a month, and you need to see it in a different way."

"Oh, I'm all too familiar with that." Liam laughed. "That sort of turned-in thinking is exactly what I'm looking to break out of." He reached across the table, and this time his handshake was businesslike. Then he raised his glass. "Here's to a fruitful collaboration."

"To working together." Fran raised her glass too, then finished the drink.

"Splendid." Gabriella, who had sat silently through their conversation, got out of her seat. "You two exchange numbers, then get out of here. I'm pleased with this, but I have more important people to meet with this morning."

Giddy with excitement, Fran scribbled her number down for Liam, then headed for the door. People had heard about her company. People wanted to work with them.

CHAPTER SIX

Giddy with excitement from her successful meeting, Fran called a flying cab for her trip up to the foothills. A smaller and paler wyvern than the one wrapped around the roof of Gabriella's tower carried this one. The large winged lizard was friendly and talkative, and they had a good chat about cartoons as it carried Fran across the city in a basket hanging from its claws. A pair of crows flew beside them, forming a tiny flock with the wyvern.

"Doesn't this thing get cold in winter?" Fran asked as the wind whipped her hair.

"I have an enclosed container for that." The wyvern shifted its talons on the basket handle. "I find that customers prefer the exposure at this time of year. To feel the wind and the sun. The sensation of flying is part of why they hire me. That and avoiding the traffic."

Fran looked down. Sure enough, the streets below were packed, traffic trailing in every direction. If it were still like this when she came back from the Evermores, she would enjoy skating past the slow-moving vehicles, relishing the freedom her wheels gave her.

She didn't want to draw too much attention to the Evermores' house, so she had the wyvern drop her off a little distance away, at the end of the driveway up to one of the grander houses. The crows settled in a nearby tree and watched while she paid her fare.

"Wow." The wyvern scratched its scales as it looked around. "You have some rich friends."

"Oh, their house isn't this big," Fran said.

"If it's up here at all, they're doing well for themselves. You can barely get an unfurnished cave in this area without paying a prince's ransom."

It hadn't struck Fran before, but the wyvern was right. The Evermores must have plenty of money to afford somewhere so comfortable and secure. She wondered if it was all hoarded wealth that they'd piled up over the millennia, the interest on centuries-old investments, or if they had gainful employment in the modern world. If they did, they'd kept it well-hidden from her.

She waved the wyvern goodbye, then headed up the road to the Evermores' house with the crows circling above her head.

Enfield met her at the door and led her to the dining room. The Source stood in the middle of the room, still confined within the containment unit. It glowed more brightly than Fran remembered, and looking at it for any length of time hurt her eyes.

The runes on the containment unit's mirror base glowed brightly too, reflecting the power that the device was dealing with. They'd designed it to take the strain of holding the Source, but even so, this was impressive.

"We did well, didn't we?" Fran said.

"Of course," Singar said. She was already at work with her toolbox opened beside her and crates full of components spread around. Wires trailed from the containment unit to a laptop in front of her, on which diagnostic software was running. "We're good at what we do."

"Then why did the Source nearly escape?" Enfield asked.

"Probably because of your lousy portal magic." The Willen rolled up the sleeves of her flannel shirt as if preparing for a fight. "Or something you haven't told us about what's happening here."

"It's not our job to fill the gaps left by your ignorance."

"Oh, real helpful, magic boy."

"Guys, guys." Fran waved to quiet them. "Chill out. The Source didn't get away, and now we're working to keep it contained. So, Enfield, is there anything we don't know about the Source that we should if we want to strengthen the field?"

He shrugged. "You'd better talk to Winslow. He's the most experienced one of us."

"Then could you get him?"

"Sure."

Enfield headed out of the room, leaving Fran and Singar to their work.

"Is something the matter between you two?" Fran took a laptop out of her bag.

"I don't trust anyone that wholesome," Singar said. "For dung's sake, he goes running every day. That's not right."

"Some people like exercise."

"No one likes exercise that much, except maybe Puritans and sadists, who are basically one and the same."

Fran connected her computer to the containment unit and set up some extra sensors. She wanted to gather more readings on the Source while she had the chance, in hopes that they would help with holding it in the long term.

"Is it really just about running?" she asked. "You don't mind when I go skating with Bart or when Elethin talks about the gym."

"I do mind." Singar toyed with one of her whiskers. "Maybe it's not only about him. It's these people."

"The Evermores?"

"Exactly. I don't trust them."

"I'm sure they're fine. After all, I'm related to them."

"Trust me, you can't always trust your relatives. I've learned that one the hard way."

Fran waited to see if more was coming. She didn't know much about Singar's background, but anyone who habitually carried a switchblade in the folds of her skin had probably seen some bad things.

"Are they paying us yet?" Singar asked.

It wasn't the sort of thing that Fran had been interested to hear, but it was a valid point and one that connected to her earlier thoughts. Wherever the Evermores' money came from, if they could afford this place, they could afford to pay for Mana Wave's services. There was no need for her to treat this as a favor to her extended family anymore. She should talk about that with Winslow.

As if on cue, the senior Evermore walked in with Enfield trailing him.

"Fran." Winslow nodded at her. "It's good of you to help us out again."

"Yeah, about that." She drew a deep breath. "I think we're going to have to start charging you for our services soon."

"Now, in fact," Singar interjected, without looking up from her screen.

"Right, yes." Fran drew another deep breath. She could do this. She could explain herself, get what they needed, and—

"Of course," Winslow said. "Get Bart to send me a bill. I'll make arrangements to have it paid."

Fran blinked. That had felt too easy.

"Don't you need to talk about how much it is first?" she asked. "Like, I don't know, haggle or something?"

"Fran, the man's offering to pay us," Singar growled. "Don't mess with it."

Winslow chuckled.

"Your whiskered friend is right," he said. "I trust you not to cheat your kin, Fran. Was that all you wanted to talk with me about?"

"Oh, no, that wasn't it at all." Fran laughed. "I got, like, totally distracted from the point there." She waved at the Source. "I hoped you could tell us more about him."

"About it, you mean."

"Right, yes, it." Fran looked at the figure inside the magical containment field. "It's like looking at a statue, you know, you can't help starting to think about them in human terms, but I guess that's a habit from what shape they are."

"External appearances can be deceptive. Not many

people would look at a young woman in a unicorn t-shirt and think they were meeting a CEO."

Fran looked down at her t-shirt, with a rainbow running from the unicorn's horn, and laughed.

"I guess you're right."

"Why don't we go and have a cup of coffee," Winslow said. "I know Singar likes to work in peace, and it will be a more comfortable way to talk."

"Sure, make this about me," Singar muttered. "Not about splitting us up."

"What was that?"

"Nothing. I could do with the quiet. Clear off, all of you." Singar glared at Enfield. "That includes you, marathon man."

Fran followed the two Evermores into the kitchen. Winslow poured them all coffee from a pot on the counter, and Fran added cream and sugar to hers. Then they headed out into the back garden. A set of chairs surrounded a garden table on the patio. They took seats there, looking out across a wide lawn to the mountains that flanked Mana Valley. At one side of the garden, Fran spotted her familiar crow companions perched in a densely grown tree, peering out between its leaves like a pair of tiny spies.

"I like it here," Winslow said. "There's a peace to seeing nature in its grandeur every morning."

"Do you get that back home?" Fran asked.

"No, but I've stayed in places like this before, from time to time. I will make the most of it while we're here."

"I'm sorry that you can't go home yet. It must be frustrating, having to wait until we can safely move the Source."

"I'm far too old to be frustrated by a matter of mere days or weeks." He patted her on the arm. "Thank you for the thought and your efforts. Are you any closer to making the Source movable?"

Fran shook her head.

"I don't know whether something's changed with the Source or the containment field, or whether something else is interfering, but right now, we have to focus on containment. It shouldn't be possible, but the Source is, like, straining the seams of what we've made. We have to stabilize it first to make sure it doesn't escape. Transport can wait."

"I understand. Does this have implications for the unit's other use, for your contract with the FBI?"

"Not unless they're containing something else with energy on this scale."

"Then you need not worry. There is nothing in either world that can compare to the Source."

It was as good an opening as Fran was going to get, so she dove straight in. "What is the Source? It would help if we understood it better."

For a long moment, Winslow just drummed his fingers against the table and stared at the mountains, those looming figures of eons-old stone. Even his millennia of life were nothing compared with them. At least, Fran assumed so, but maybe he was even older than she realized.

"I don't know if anything I tell you will truly bring understanding," Winslow said. "The gap between the forces we're talking about here and your everyday life is a staggering one. But I will do what I can to bridge it.

"The Source is an embodiment of ancient magic, a thing far older than any civilization that Earth has ever seen, and stretches into the ancient depths of even Oriceran lore. Think of it not as a creature or an object but as a set of interactions, like the laws of physics—of instincts so deep that the reality contained within them cannot help but follow their will. Does that make sense?"

"Not really."

"That is the challenge of explaining this." Winslow sipped his coffee. "Perhaps I should focus on the history of the Source rather than its nature. That will be easier for you to wrap your young mind around.

"Long ago, when the connections between Earth and Oriceran were parting, we Evermores bound the Source to the Earth. We did it in such a way to ensure that magic would continue on Earth, even without the connection to Oriceran. Though the root of magic would be separate from Earth for thousands of years, this offshoot would remain. Its power would flow through the kemanas, allowing magicals to continue as they had done before."

"So the Source provides the power to the kemanas?"

"Exactly. And through them, to all magicals on Earth."

"But it's not there now."

"No, and that is a problem."

"People can still cast magic over there."

"For now. Remember, the Source is not a creature. It is a set of principles. The power that can be created by drawing upon those laws is huge, and some of it remains in the magical kemana network on Earth, even in its absence. While the Source was loose, the magic it had provided became destabilized by its actions. With the Source trapped, that power has become more stable, but over time, it will drain away. Unless the Source returns, magic will fade from that world."

"Can't they draw on Oriceran magic again?" Fran thought of all the magicals she knew who lived on Earth and how much they would struggle if they had no power. The idea that they might be dependent on what she was doing with the Source, that she might have so much responsibility, was so daunting that she found herself wishing it was untrue.

"For now," Winslow said. "The magic won't be as strong, and when the cycle of the worlds turns, and the portals close again, Earth's magicals will be left bereft. We have time to fix this, but that time is not infinite, and the longer the Source is held here, the more power Oricerans will have over Earth's inhabitants. That is a situation bad people could abuse."

"Gosh!" Fran stared down at her coffee. Unlike the vastness of the mountains or of what Winslow told her, that cup of steaming brown liquid was something whose limits she could comprehend. "We really need to get this right."

"Absolutely. I think there is a useful lesson in it all, something about the Source's nature. Remember what I've told you, that the Source is a set of complex and tangled rules. That might make it sound rational, but we don't follow the rules of physics rationally. They simply control us, as the Source's instincts control it. Because of the tangled way those rules interact and how erratically they touch the world, that can make the Source seem irrational, a force of nature. You can't reason with it. It has to be controlled and contained."

"Like you keep saying, it's not a person." Fran nodded. "I get that." She gulped down the last of her coffee and set her cup on the table. There was a tightness in her forehead, and she didn't think it was only her morning cocktail wearing off. "I'd better get back to work. The world is depending on me."

CHAPTER SEVEN

That evening, Fran rolled around the outdoor skate track, occasionally looking back to check that Bart was keeping up with her. Part of her wanted to speed up, to race around the track and let her concerns fall away. In Bart's defense, he was going faster than he used to, and she wanted to encourage him.

"You're doing so much better!" she called.

"What?" Bart turned his attention from his feet to her. For a moment, he skated with more speed and confidence than she'd seen from him before. Then an alarmed look crossed his face as if he'd suddenly remembered how bad he was at this. He wobbled, waved his arms, and his feet shot away from each other. He hit the ground with a *thud* that made Fran wince and made her glad the gray-haired gnome wore so much padding.

She skated back and crouched by Bart. A crow landed beside them and peered at Bart, its head tipped to one side.

"Are you all right?" Fran asked.

"I'll live." Bart pushed himself into a sitting position,

then pulled his feet up to examine his skates. "I don't want to be like the bad workman, but I swear these things aren't doing what they should."

Fran laughed. "I know that feeling. Sometimes you're sure you were trying to go left, and suddenly your foot's shooting off to the right."

"Exactly. There's probably a life lesson in that somewhere." He got shakily to his feet. "I knew I should have tried DJing or bought a flashy car."

"Then we never would have met!"

"It's been worth all the bruises for that." Bart rolled his neck, and something *clicked*. "Time for you to stop waiting for me and get your skate on."

"Are you sure?"

"I can see you itching to do it. It's been a long day, and you need to let off steam, not waste your whole evening looking after an old gnome."

"You're not old. You're experienced, venerable, distinguished."

"Funny how they never say those things about young people. Now go, have fun. I'll see you in a little bit."

Fran took off, zipping around the track as fast as her skates would carry her. Instead of being passed by other skaters, she went past them, the world blurring at the edges of her vision. All the burdens of the day, all the responsibilities that came with running a business and containing the Source, fell away. There was no space in her mind for anything except the track, the skates, and what lay ahead. Her mind was her body, her body her mind, the two working perfectly in sync.

The roller skaters weren't the only ones at the skate

park. There were skateboarders too, many of them prac-
ticing tricks on the pipes. Around the edges were people
who'd finished for the day or came along to watch their
friends. As she zipped around the top of the track for the
third time, she noticed a middle-aged man in workman's
clothes, his long dark hair tied back, watching her with
casual interest. It was nice when people admired her
skating.

She shot around the track a couple more times. Bart
had found his feet again and stuck his thumbs up at her as
she passed. He would be okay for a little while yet.

A crow flew into Fran's path, flapping its wings and
cawing for her attention. She ducked and swerved to
avoid running into it, then kept going around the track.
Much as she enjoyed the crows' company, she didn't want
to get so close that they were trying to occupy the same
space.

As she came back around the track, the crow was there
again, flapping its wings and squawking at her. She slowed
down, and the crow fluttered beside her.

"What's gotten into you guys today?" she asked. "Do I
suddenly smell of tasty worms?"

The crow *cawed* and flew in closer to her. Fran swerved
away, and the crow followed her off the track. It then fluttered ahead of her, heading for one of the benches. The guy
with the dark ponytail sat there with two more crows
perched on the back of the bench, flanking him like small
feathered guards. Apparently, there was someone the
crows wanted her to talk to.

Fran rolled over across the packed dirt, raising a hand
in greeting.

"Hi," she said. "I'm Fran. It looks like we have some mutual friends."

"Hi, Fran, I'm Woodrow." He opened his hand, revealing a fistful of birdseed. "I'm not sure that I have friends so much as a pack of mercenaries hovering about to take my pay."

His voice was deep and rumbling, fitting his sturdy build and steady demeanor. Something about him felt familiar, but Fran couldn't work out what.

"Maybe these guys are trying to drop me a hint." She gestured at the crows as they dove for the seeds. "Trying to persuade all humans to carry crow food with them."

"Maybe." Woodrow chuckled. "That seems optimistic of them, but crows are ambitious birds."

"Do you know much about them?" Fran sat on the bench next to him. One of the crows landed on her knee.

"More than most, less than I'd like. I work in nature, and you can't help picking up a sense for the animals and plants you encounter. After a while, even if you've never done anything special with that tree or bird or insect, you can still understand it quicker than most."

"I'm like that with technology. Even if I've not worked with something before, I can look inside, and straight away I'll start to understand what it's for and how it does it. The answers just open themselves up, you know?"

"I do, but not for technology. I've never mastered much more than the ballpoint pen."

"I'm sure that's not true. There's so much technology these days. Lots of people feel overwhelmed by it all, especially if they weren't around when it was created. Not that I'm saying you're old. You don't look old. Except for those few gray hairs, but everyone gets some of those, right? Even my mom, though she dyes them, and now that I think about it, I really shouldn't tell people that."

"It can be our secret."

"Thanks! And I meant it. You don't look all that old."

"Thank you, but I'm older than I look, and I've come to terms with that."

"Better than looking older than you are, right?"

"I suppose so."

One of the crows cawed, drawing their attention back to the track. Bart had skated off the edge and was making his way over to the bench.

"Hey, Bart." Fran waved. "This is Woodrow. I'm meeting strange men at the skate park again."

Bart laughed. "Is that how you describe me?"

"Not often." She grinned. "I guess it is turning into a habit. Hey Woodrow, do you skate?"

"I prefer to interact directly with the world, not put wheels between it and me."

"Are skates all that different from your boots?"

"They look harder to balance on."

"He's right there." Bart maneuvered himself onto the end of the bench and swung his legs underneath. The wheels on his skates spun. "I'd be a lot more stable if I hadn't taken up this hobby."

"I bet your balance is better in other places now," Fran said. "It's, like, a transferable skill."

"You sound like a job application."

"Hopefully never again." Fran waved away the ghastly thought of being judged by recruiters.

"You like your job then?" Woodrow asked.

"Love it." Fran grinned. "I run my own company. Bart's part of the management team." She lowered her voice. "Right now, everyone's part of the management team, but we're gonna get bigger soon, right, Bart?"

"I certainly hope so." Bart peered past her at Woodrow. A crow hopped into Woodrow's lap, spread its wings, and stared at Bart like he was another crow trying to steal its lunch. "What do you do, Woodrow?"

Woodrow rubbed his chin thoughtfully. Fran had the funniest feeling that he ought to be stroking a beard, but it wasn't there. Maybe it was the gesture, or perhaps he reminded her of someone she'd once known.

"I've done a lot of different jobs over the years. But that's not what brings me to Mana Valley. I'm here to meet my daughter."

"That's really cool," Fran said. "Has she just been born?"

"No, but sadly, I've not been there in her life."

"You should get her a present. Does she like books, or Legos, or those toys where you plug the bits of circuit boards together to make a little robot move? You might have to go to Earth for those, but there are people, like, all over the place who can portal you across. They have some of the best gifts for kids over there."

"I'll bear it in mind." There was a look of amusement on Woodrow's face. "What did you like when you were younger?"

"Books. Chemistry sets. And programming on this secondhand laptop my mom gave me. Oh, and those pony toys, you know the brightly colored ones with the cute names? I kept a different one by my bed every night."

"Well, then I'll try to think of something as good as that."

Woodrow took another handful of seed from his pocket and scattered it on the ground. The crows hopped down to feast, and other birds flocked in to join them, pigeons and sparrows and flame birds that had migrated down from the mountains for the summer.

"What brings you to the skate park, Woodrow?" Bart asked. "Does your daughter come here?"

"Well, I saw a bench, and I saw my crow friends, and I thought this seemed as good a place as any to rest. When you're used to being out in the wilds, the city can feel a bit overwhelming, especially a city like this one." Woodrow stretched. "I should get going. I've interrupted your practice for quite long enough."

"We don't mind," Fran said. "Right, Bart?"

"Of course not," Bart said, without conviction.

"Still, I have places to be." Woodrow held out his hand to shake theirs again. "It was a pleasure meeting you, Fran. Meeting both of you."

He got up, brushed seed from his trousers, and walked away, leaving only a scent of pine needles where he'd sat. As he walked across the scattered birdseed, the birds fluttered into the air, getting clear of the imposing man marching through them. Once he'd passed, the birds settled back down to pecking eagerly at the ground. The crows weren't among them.

"That was nice," Fran said. "It's always fun meeting new people."

"Hm." Bart shrugged. "I suppose so."

"I thought you liked meeting new people."

"Oh, I do." There was a long pause while Bart swung his legs and stared at the birds. "I thought that there was something off about him."

"Really? He seemed very nice to me. Friendly, feeding birds, likes nature, in town to meet his kid. What's not to like about that?"

Bart hesitated. If he could've pinned down what was bothering him, he would've said it, but it was only a nagging doubt. He didn't want to plant that too deeply in Fran's mind. Instincts could be wrong, and she listened to him so carefully. He didn't want to turn her against someone for no reason or to make her world more jaded than it needed to be.

"I'm sure you're right. It's probably your crows putting me on edge. Those sorts of birds used to eat bodies on battlefields, and I sometimes feel like they're looking at me as a snack."

Fran laughed. "Oh, Bart, you're a long way off dying yet. Now come on, let's get down there and get skating. The exercise will help to keep you healthy."

She got off the bench and made her way to the track with Bart following.

"Where are the crows, anyway?" she asked. "They're not still eating, are they?"

"I think they followed Woodrow. Maybe they're planning on eating him."

"Gross." Fran shook her head. "Tell you what, let's race."

"Hardly fair. You're four times as fast as me."

"Then we'll race on those terms. I bet I can get around four times before you get around once."

"You're on." Bart rolled out onto the track. "Ready, steady, go!"

Fran laughed and shot out past him as fast as she could. The wind whipped her hair, the world blurred past, and the worries of the world faded away.

CHAPTER EIGHT

"You have such lovely skin," the makeup gnome said as she brushed powder across Elethin's cheeks. "I hardly need to do anything at all."

"Thank you," Elethin replied. "You're so sweet."

She looked at herself in the dressing room mirror. She was proud of her looks, but she had to admit, there was value in having her face tended to by a professional, especially when she was about to get in front of the cameras. The lighting in a TV studio could be unforgiving, and makeup artists understood what was needed to balance that.

On a screen in the corner of the room, the latest episode of *Orchard of Stars* was playing. Working with Mana Wave over the past month, Elethin hadn't had time to watch her usual soaps. She hadn't realized that she missed them until now.

"Are you allowed to watch that in here?" she asked. "Shouldn't you have the Morning Program on so you know when your clients are needed?"

"They always give me plenty of warning," the makeup gnome said. "Once you've watched Don's morning monologue ten days in a row, you really need something else." She glanced up at the screen. "Besides, today is when Nastya comes out of critical care, and we find out if she really has amnesia. I think she's been faking to try to win Jim back."

"I don't think it's Nastya in the hospital," Elethin said. "I think her evil twin Tiffen has replaced her again. Remember when Tiffen took over her florist business? She had a mole on the back of her hand that Nastya doesn't, and Nastya's had her hand bandaged since they brought her in after the crash."

"Oh my gosh, you're right!" The gnome stopped, open-mouthed, and stared at the screen. "Ooh, that's a brilliant twist." She turned her attention back to Elethin's makeup. "I wouldn't have had you down as an *Orchard* fan, a smart business elf like you."

"I got into it when I…" Elethin hesitated. "When I had a lot of time on my hands."

While her time in prison was a matter of public record and a shame that she felt hanging around her at all times, she was starting to accept that not everyone she met knew about it. Not every reference to bars or shared showers was a dig at her, and some people simply had no clue. She liked that they didn't know, and now that she didn't feel she had to explain it away to everyone, she instead tried to avoid letting anyone know.

"That's brilliant, that is," the gnome said. "I'll tell my friend who does makeup there that you like her show. She'll love that."

"Really?"

"Oh yes, she loves watching you business news people. She says it's like a soap opera all of its own."

"Well, I promise, I'm not my evil twin in disguise."

"Exactly what an evil twin would say." The gnome winked and stepped back. "Perfect, but then you always are, aren't you?"

Elethin smiled. Everyone used to say things like that about her. Now... Well, now a producer had appeared around the door, calling her to the studio. She said goodbye to the gnome and followed him.

The lights were low as the producer led Elethin into the studio. He showed her to a seat across a small coffee table from Don Karelsky. The *Morning* Program host wore his usual outfit of pinstripe suit and red tie.

The look struck Elethin as a little too cutthroat for a wizard starting to go soft around the edges with age and who had never had the hardness that the business world itself needed. But he had an audience, and now was her chance to shine in front of them.

The lights went up, and Don smiled his big, fake smile at the cameras.

"Welcome back to the MVTV3 *Morning Program*. I'm Don Karelsky, and today I have a returning guest: Elethin Tannerin, Director of Communications at Mana Wave Industries. Elethin, you look lovely, as always."

Elethin made sure not to show her disdain for his condescending tone.

"You're looking very smart yourself, Don. We don't say that enough to male executives, do we?"

"Sure, I guess." Don shifted uncertainly in his seat, then

found his firm mental ground again. "So, Mana Wave made a big splash a month or two ago, the hot new property on the magitech scene, but since then we've had nothing. No product releases, no pre-publicity, not even a public appearance by your CEO. What's going on, Elethin?"

"As you know, Don, the early days of a business involve a lot of behind-the-scenes work, but we're pleased to announce that our first round of exploratory funding has been a big success..."

The conversation went back and forth for ten minutes. Elethin made two investors and a single contract sound like more than they were, Don dug for secrets so ineptly that he almost got stuck on his questions. If this was the best that the TV station could afford, Elethin pitied the future of journalism. On the other hand, it was exactly what she needed to do her job, keeping Mana Wave in people's minds, making sure they maintained their positive public profile.

"One last question," Don said, as a warning light blinked over one of the cameras and a producer tapped nervously at a clipboard. "I like to finish by asking my interviewees a little about themselves as people, so tell me, are you dating anyone at the moment?"

No one like you, she thought, with a little shudder at the look on his face.

"The only people I meet right now are other executives," she said. "Our business is just too busy."

"You couldn't date someone you met through work?" he asked eagerly.

"I don't like to mix business and pleasure. Except, of

course, for the absolute pleasure of being interviewed by you."

"Ha, ha, ha! Well, I think I'll end it there. Thank you, Elethin Tannerin." Don turned to face the camera. "After the break, we'll be back with the heartwarming story of a panda cub that had magic in its eyes. First, these messages from our sponsors."

The lights dimmed. Elethin hurriedly got out of her seat and got away before Don could speak to her. A rejection, however carefully phrased, could hurt his feelings. A simple absence would leave her on better terms with someone whose questions she would want to answer again once they had a product to sell.

She handed her clip-on microphone and audio pack to a producer, fetched her jacket and handbag from the green room, and followed the signs to the studio's exit. As she approached the door, a witch hurried up, heading for the same exit.

"You're Elethin Tannerin, aren't you?" the witch asked.

She was relatively young, in human terms, somewhere in her late twenties perhaps. She wore a smart suit and had her hair cut in an asymmetric bob that complemented her sharp features.

"That's right." Elethin eyed the witch. "You're not a producer here, are you? They don't dress this well."

The witch laughed.

"No, I don't work here. At least, not in that sense." She held out her hand. "Laurel Anders. I'm a consultant with Karmic Charisma, the PR firm."

"I've heard of you." Elethin shook the offered hand.

"You work with some of the big magitech companies, don't you?"

"We try, but you know what clients are like. Sometimes you have to leave them to make their own mistakes." Laurel rolled her eyes. "That's why I'm out here."

She took her other hand from behind her back, revealing a packet of cigarettes and a lighter. "One of my clients is interviewing for a podcast, and he's not listened to a word I said. The whole thing's a train wreck, and I can't even do damage limitation until afterward. I needed something to steady my nerves." She pushed the door open. "Speaking of which…"

She stepped out into the sunlight. Elethin followed her.

"How did you know my name?" Elethin asked. There were two options, her current work or her old scandal, and she knew which she was hoping for.

Laurel paused to light a cigarette, and Elethin saw the moment of hesitation that the gesture contained.

"Nuada," Elethin said resignedly. "You've read about the old legal case."

"Well, yes, but…" Laurel looked around, then shrugged. "Fuck it. I told the others we should be honest about this. I know about you because meeting you is one of the reasons I'm here today."

"Excuse me?" Elethin frowned. What was going on here? If this turned out to be a journalist raking up the past, there was going to be trouble.

"All that stuff about the client is true, but I was half-watching the *Morning Program* while George went off the rails, waiting to see when you'd be leaving."

"Why?" Elethin let an icy sliver of anger into her voice.

"Oh, nothing bad! I mean, don't get me wrong, I know all about your past. The crimes you were complicit in at Nuada, the things you did to minimize your sentence, the reputation you got while you were in Trevilsom. You've been a very bad elf."

"I'm leaving now." Elethin turned on her heel.

"No, wait! I mean that in a good way." Laurel grabbed Elethin's elbow and turned her back around. "I know this stuff because we want to recruit you. We've done our due diligence, and we think you would make a fantastic addition to Karmic Charisma.

"You're smart, charming, know what to say and what not to say. You've managed difficult situations, not only for clients but for yourself. You have enough edge to keep people listening. And those looks..." Laurel took a step back and whistled as she ran her eyes down and back up Elethin. "Let's just say that they help generate positive attention."

"You want to recruit me?"

"Sure. You're wasted working for some two-bit startup that nobody would've heard of if not for you. Hell, you managed to spin that naked dwarf story into positive attention. That is..." Laurel made a chef's kiss gesture. "That is exactly the sort of talent we want on our side, and not on anyone else's. What do you say?"

"As you pointed out, I have a job already."

Laurel took a drag on her cigarette, waited a moment like she was expecting something more, then blew out a smoke ring.

"That was the point where you were supposed to counter-pitch," she said. "Tell me how you love working for the plucky startup, feel deep loyalty for the people there, see huge potential in its future."

"Why say it myself when you can say it for me?" Elethin asked.

"Because it's pure bullshit. You took that job because you were desperate. Whatever they're paying you, we can offer better. Like, much better. Riverfront apartment better. Red carpet events better. All the money and prestige that the Valley can give to a PR professional, and believe me, both parts pay off big."

She ground out her cigarette on the top of a trash can, then raised an eyebrow at Elethin.

"Well?"

"I'll think about it," Elethin said. "And I'll need a substantial offer to think about."

"Of course. If you decide that you're interested, we'll need to go through the full process, including an interview, to make sure that you're as impressive as you seem to be."

"Oh, I am." Elethin swept a hand down her body. "Remember?"

Laurel laughed.

"Hard to argue with that, but I have to get back inside. By now, George probably thinks he's been a genius, and that's when he says the stupidest things." She opened the door again. "I'll message you with what the offer would be. Then, if you're interested, give me a call."

She headed back inside, and the door slammed shut behind her.

Elethin stood for a long moment, looking at the door. An offer of employment, and with a proper agency. Had she done enough to earn such a position back?

Of course, she had, just by being her. She deserved the money, the black tie galas, the secret conversations with powerful people. She deserved the chance to shape the world and see her work plastered all over the news, not only on Don's shoddy little *Morning Program*.

On the other hand, Laurel had touched on something real when she presented the argument for the other side. There was potential in Mana Wave Industries, which might pay off hugely for Elethin if she stuck around. No, she didn't feel any loyalty to the people there, that sort of feeling was for idiots. But she would miss the chance to make Gruffbar miserable and maybe even some of Fran's ridiculous positivity.

She turned and stalked away from the TV studio. She had a lot to think about.

CHAPTER NINE

"I'm still not convinced by this idea." Smokey sniffed the phone's screen. "A smellophone sounds neat in theory, but why would anyone need it?"

"No one needs filters for their photos, but they're fun," Fran said. "That's what we can sell this one on. Fun."

Smokey wrinkled his nose and took a step back across the workbench. He ran a paw across the fur behind his ear.

"Maybe. What sort of apps would go with it?"

"Smell recognition. Smell creation. Comedy smells. Smells for relaxation. Ooh, how about a perfume app?"

"You know that comedy smells just means a high-tech stink bomb, right?"

"Huh, I guess, maybe." Fran shrugged. "Maybe people will be more imaginative. I know I will."

"What do you think, Sin?"

Singar looked up from the pieces of her sign language teacher, which she was converting into a novel input device for video games.

"I like the technical challenge," she said. "The receptors

are easy, but even using magic, it's going to be hard to make something that releases the right smells because no one does anything like that. It could take years to get it even close to right."

"Years." Smokey shook his head. "We need something that will pay off sooner than that."

"I'm sorry to say it, but there's no profit for us in phones." Bart walked into the workshop, carrying a tray loaded with coffee cups and cookies. "To get into that market, you need to be a far bigger company. The best we could manage would be to develop new technology and find someone to buy us out. That doesn't fit with Fran's dream."

"No way!" she said. "I want to grow a company for me, not for a takeover."

"No phones then." Smokey pushed the device away from him. "What's the next idea?"

Fran crossed "smellophone" off the list on the whiteboard, then took a cup of coffee. She rubbed her eyes.

"My next idea is to take a break and let my brain cells recover. I feel like we've been doing this for weeks."

"We have, remember?" Singar grabbed a coffee too. "We'll stick with it until we get the right idea or get our feedback from the FBI."

A loud knocking sounded through the basement. They looked at each other in confusion.

"Is that from upstairs?" Singar asked.

"Construction in the street?" Bart asked.

"It's our door." Smokey tipped his ears back. "But who would be knocking on our door?"

"Oh my gosh, I totally forgot!" Fran dashed out through

the office and up the stairs. She flung the door open. "Liam, you're here!"

"Hi, Fran." Liam stepped through the doorway and peered down the stairs. He had a large bag under each arm. "So this really is it. I got confused by the carpet shop."

"They let us stay here because of a thing." Fran waved him down the stairs. "Come on. I'll introduce you to everyone."

"Wow, this place is quite something." Liam looked around as he followed her. "Is that a big mirror under that sheet?"

"Yeah, but don't look. There are bad things in there."

"In a mirror?"

"I can explain later." She led him into the workshop. "Liam Wade, this is everyone. Everyone, this is Liam Wade, head of sales for Prestige Craft and our newest collaborator."

Liam put down his bags and took the time to introduce himself to everyone while Fran went to fetch coffee. As she walked past, she noticed that Gruffbar was still at his desk.

"Are you joining us?" she asked.

"It's tempting, but I've got work here. Maybe later."

"And Elethin?"

"TV, remember?"

"Oh, yes! I hope that went well."

Fran returned to the workshop and handed Liam the coffee.

"Thanks, you're a star." He smiled at her, then turned back to the bags he'd been emptying onto the workbench. They were full of electronic and magitech devices, from portable gaming systems to tablets and compact stereos.

"What's all this?" Fran asked.

"One of the options we were talking about the other day was working together on entertainment devices, right?"

"Sure, that could be a lot of fun."

"You don't have an entertainment prototype?"

Fran glanced at the smellophone, sitting discarded at the end of the bench. In the face of Liam, with his sharp suits and corporate experience, it seemed like an absurd, even childish idea.

"Nothing worth talking about."

"Then we should start by looking at what other people are producing." He pulled out a red drone with a yellow stripe down one side. "I think this one's for some sort of immersive game?"

"*Kill Strike*," Bart said. "When you wear the goggles, other people's drones look like attack helicopters hunting you down, and the whole city's a ruined landscape full of NPCs."

The others looked at him in surprise.

"I didn't think you were a gamer," Singar said.

Bart blushed. "It was one of the things I tried before I found skating, and perhaps more importantly before I found this job."

"Ah, part of your late-life crisis."

"Mid-life, maybe, and I'd hardly call it a crisis." Bart had turned a deeper red.

"Are we going to play with these?" Fran tried to turn the conversation back onto safer ground.

"We could, sure," Liam said. "Then we could see what ideas we get for products. Or we could take them apart, do some reverse engineering, see how they work. Maybe we'll find a few bits of tech that we can, well, let's call it aspire to surpass."

"You mean things we can copy," Bart said, folding his arms across his chest.

"That's another way to put it, yes."

"I'm in." Singar already had a screwdriver out and was dismantling the drone. "I've been curious for a while about how these things connect up to the goggles' projections."

"Give me the processor once you find it," Smokey said. "I want to see what software they're running."

"This is going to be so much fun!" Fran opened the back of a new gaming system and started carefully removing components. "Do you think we could add a magical part to one of these?"

"This is fun?" Bart asked, a little bewildered. "All you're doing is taking things apart."

"Makes a change from building things that turn out to be no use," Singar said. "Besides, Liam's right. It's the best way to learn how things work and how we can make better versions."

"I suppose."

A busy few hours followed as the team carefully disassembled devices, sometimes working alone, sometimes together. Fran and Liam talked about their favorite music while they dismantled a stereo, and she was surprised to discover that he liked a lot of the same bands she did. It wasn't often that she found someone else who loved comedy music.

"What's the point of a song without a punchline?" he asked.

"Culture?" Singar asked. "Civilization? To stop us drowning in Weird Al clones?"

"But I love Weird Al!" Fran said, Liam's words echoing hers, and the two of them laughed, while Singar groaned and Smokey purposefully put on some music with no jokes at all.

Soon, the workshop was full of newly extracted components and notes about how they fit together. Colored stickers helped to differentiate which devices they'd come from in case they wanted to reassemble something later.

"I'm surprised you're so practical," Singar said as she passed a drill to Liam. "Don't you work in sales?"

"Sure, and I love the thrill of pitching a product, but there's a reason why I got into tech." Liam lowered the drill to the casing of a device, looking for the weak point he'd intended to crack open. "My Earth degree was in business and electrical engineering so I could understand the practical side."

"Your Earth degree? Since when is that a thing?"

Liam laughed. "It's how people talk about it in the big firms. These days, lots of the top Mana Valley people get a qualification here and one on the other side of the portal. It's how you set yourself up for both sides of the magitech business."

"I hadn't thought of that." Fran looked down at the components in front of her, suddenly feeling inadequate. "I've only got my Earth degree. Does that mean I'll never make it to the top here?"

"Don't be ridiculous!" Liam nudged her with his shoulder. "I've only known you a few days, and I can already tell that you're one of the smartest people in this city. There's a reason I'm here with you guys, and it's not for Bart's cookies." He smiled at the gnome. "Although those are delicious."

"Thanks, Liam." Fran nudged him back. "It's been a frustrating few weeks. I think I needed to hear something good."

"You're Fran Berryman. That should be good enough for anyone."

Bart stood on a stool at the end of the workbench with a cup in his hand, staring at the litter of components.

"Enough, already." Singar waved in front of Bart's face. "You've been brooding for twenty minutes, and it's the least Bart thing I've ever seen. What's bothering you?"

Bart drew a deep breath. "I don't want to spoil the fun, but..."

"No one says that unless they're about to take all the fun away, so get on with it."

"I just... Is this ethical?"

"They're machines. They don't feel any pain."

"I mean taking apart other people's machines, stealing their ways of making things. It feels dubious to me." He looked at Fran, carefully not catching Liam's eye. "What do you think?"

If she was honest about it, Fran had never given the question any thought. She'd been taking machines apart to see how they worked since she was eight years old, and her mom had been mad that the TV no longer worked. At least now she could put them back together and even call it a learning experience. She also knew that she sometimes had a blind spot where tech was concerned, and she didn't want to do anything that could get them into trouble.

"Gruffbar!" she called. "Have you got a minute?"

Gruffbar stomped in, looked around, and climbed onto one of the stools so he could properly survey the workbench. He stroked his beard as he looked at their work.

"Well, that's cheap." He pointed at one of the drone components. "Terrible alloy in the wiring. The first drop of damp will make it corrode."

"I have a legal question," Fran said.

"Uh-huh." Gruffbar picked up a motor and turned it over in his hands, examining the workings with a dwarf's eye for the mechanical. "That's what I'm here for."

"Could we get into trouble for this?"

"For what?"

"Reverse engineering. Taking apart other people's machines and stealing their ideas. Like, should we stop doing it?"

Gruffbar gave her a long, steely stare, then laughed.

"By my beard, you almost got me there." He shook his head. "Stop this. Ha."

"No, I mean it. Is it the wrong thing to do?"

"You're serious?" Gruffbar put the motor down. "Okay, well, I'm a lawyer, not a priest. I'm not here to judge right or wrong. What I can tell you is that everybody does this, and nobody says it publicly. Don't accuse each other, and no one risks a defamation suit from the one company in a hundred that doesn't do it."

"So we can carry on?"

"As your lawyer, my advice to you is don't be obvious and don't get caught. Past that, you're fine." He reached across the table, picked up a screwdriver, and started disassembling the motor. "It's years since I've done this. I'd forgotten how much fun it was."

"I know, right?" Fran grinned. "Thanks, Gruffbar. You're the best."

Still standing at the end of the bench, Bart sighed.

"I never asked if it was legal," he said. "I asked if it was right."

"I get where you're coming from," Liam said. "But sadly, it's a necessity. As soon as you release technology, other people will reverse engineer it. Either you join in, or you lose out. Really, if it means that customers get better products, isn't it for the best in the end?"

"But you're copying other people!"

"No, we're learning from them. And from what we learn, we'll make something different, something better. Doesn't that sound like the right thing to do?"

"Maybe, I guess..." Bart hopped down to the floor and gathered their cups. "I guess I'll go make more coffee."

As he headed out of the workshop, he heard the others laughing behind him, bound together in the fun of deconstructing technology, as provided by Liam Wade.

CHAPTER TEN

The Evermores gathered in the garden of their house. Hidden from view by the trees that sheltered the area and the rising hills at the rear, they formed a circle. Midday sunlight streamed down brightly on them.

"I know that some of you are dissatisfied," Winslow said. "Others have attacked us twice, and we haven't struck back or taken steps to protect ourselves beyond the most basic precautions."

He looked around the circle. This wasn't his chance to talk. It was theirs. It was important to let them feel heard before he moved on to the solution. Important to ensure their cooperation.

"It feels bad," one of them said. "We've lived safe and secure for so long because we were told, if anything hurt us, we would fight back. So why haven't we?"

"It's a fair question. Why do you think?"

"Because of the Source," Enfield said. "Capturing it was more important than protecting the few of us who are chasing it. Now that it's secured, we can deal with other things."

"Very good." Winslow said. "Remember, we are Evermores. We endure. We have patience. We can take the time that others don't."

"What if it wasn't an attack on us?" one of the others said. "What if they were specifically after Enfield? He got hit with the magical attack, and the kidnappers tried to grab him. We should consider the possibility that this is about one person, not the group."

Her comment was logical, and it had a certain appeal. If this was one person's problem, it gave them a different option. Instead of fighting back, they could cut that person loose, sacrificing Enfield for the greater good. Winslow wasn't above such tactics, but unfortunately, he could see the hole in her argument.

"Enfield, can you think of any reason why someone in this world would be after you?" he asked.

"No."

"Can any of the rest of you think of a reason?" They shook their heads. "We haven't been out in the world for long, haven't made the personal connections or animosities that would earn something like this. While it's possible that someone has taken an irrational dislike to Enfield, the effort involved doesn't match that well. So, we must assume, for now, that this is about us as Evermores and proceed on that basis."

"Proceed?" someone asked. "What does that mean?"

"It means that we're going to strike back."

After the tension of the preceding conversation, that

announcement brought relief. Evermores who might've been wary about this fight were now keen because it was better than inaction or continuing to debate between themselves.

Winslow stepped into the middle of the circle and set a disk down in the grass. It was the width of a human hand, made of clear, polished crystal, and as the sunlight fell upon it, a glow appeared in the center of the disk.

"We don't know much about our attackers," Winslow said. "From their attack on Enfield, we gained an image of something dark, nightmarish, the opposite of the order and light we represent. That might explain why it is attacking us.

"As importantly, we glimpsed how it attacked. A strike by sympathetic magic, reaching through the world. A brute force attack, not nuanced, but powerful. In essence, it struck out blindly but managed to hit its target. We can do better."

He drew a deep breath and opened his hand. A small box made of light appeared, then opened, revealing a strand of coiled darkness within.

"I have been holding onto this since the attack," he said. "A fragment of the magic they used against us. We can use it to reverse what was done to us, to channel magic against our opponent. We won't know what we're attacking, but we will know that we're hitting our target, and if we hit it hard enough, perhaps we can put it off targeting us ever again."

"Can't we make an exploratory attack?" Enfield asked. "Then use what we learn to strike it harder, more precisely?"

Winslow shook his head. "This will use up the captured power. We have only one shot. Are you ready to take it?"

The other Evermores looked around at each other. One by one, they turned to Winslow and nodded.

"Good." He stepped back and took his place in the circle. "Let us begin."

Centuries of casting magic together meant that the Evermores were well-tuned to each other, well-practiced in shared spells and the principles behind them. By instinct, they followed Winslow's moves as he began casting to see how their efforts would fit together, what he was doing and how they could contribute.

Their hands wove through the air, catching the strands of sound from their songs, forming a spell from them, one that focused on the fragment of black magic, and through it, the being it came from. While sound was an important part of the Evermores' magic, it wasn't the part they would strike this creature with. It was a channel, a way of shaping the power and directing what came next.

Light poured from them, streamed through the crystal, and became something stronger as the focused sunlight shaped it. It gained in purity and brightness, turning from the light by which they saw the world into the sort of light that would burn away and demolish the cold corners of reality in which evil lay.

The blaze of light intensified. The shape made by the sound closed it in. Winslow made one more gesture over the black magic, and a pathway opened, following its power through the world.

Howard Phillips sat behind his desk, looking over the fragment of prophecy that had led him to the Evermores. There had to be something he'd missed that could tell him more about these magicals—these guardians of Earth's magic, holders of a greater power. He couldn't let anything stand in his way. If they existed to oppose him, he would annihilate them. First, he needed to find them. He needed a clue.

A tentacle crept out through a gap in the skin at his wrist. It touched the point on the parchment where his magic had burned a hole, right through the word Evermore. That had been a foolish, impatient act. He'd learned almost nothing by it, had failed to capture or contain any of them. An act of impatience. He would do better from now on.

He was setting the parchment down when the air began to glow around him. He frowned and looked up at the lights, but they hadn't gone on. Sun streamed in through the window, but it shouldn't have been this dazzling.

Phillips got to his feet. This wasn't only light. It was magic. He was under attack. He raised his hands and started casting, summoning a layer of protection from the darkness in which he normally dwelled.

He wasn't quick enough. The light coalesced around his arm, so bright and pure that it burned. He stifled a screech as his suit and the skin beneath it fell away in flakes of ash, and the light fell blazing on the dark and twitching flesh beneath.

Freed from the confines of the skin suit, the tentacles in that arm swayed and played their part in the casting. Magic streamed from them, as thick and deadly as unrefined oil.

The light burned and his black flesh withered, but the magic soothed it, formed a defensive layer, and absorbed the power of the light.

The focus of the light shifted, gathering with greater intensity around Phillips' head. His eyes hurt, not only those visible through the holes in the skin suit, but the ones underneath that stayed hidden and protected. The skin crumbled and peeled away, exposing them too.

The pain was intense, but Phillips was no stranger to it. He was the Darkness Between Dreams, the stuff of which nightmares were born, and such things were full of pain and confusion. All he had to do was focus and redirect this sensation, turn it into something that he could work with.

He gathered his pain, let it rise through his weeping eyes, and unleashed it. The torment ran back along the channel down which the light had reached him, wherever it came from. At that moment, he recognized the shape and construction of the funnel. They were using his magic against him.

"Evermores." He muttered the word like a curse. Then he spoke it louder, using it to direct the darkness and the pain, to send a torrent of his power down the channel.

The power assaulting him burst apart in a dizzying flash and was gone. There was no more magic in the room. The ordinary sunlight coming in through the windows seemed gloomy by comparison with what had come before.

A light on his intercom blinked.

"Are you all right?" Julia asked. "I felt a wave of power from in there."

"I'm fine," Phillips snapped and hit the button to sever the connection.

Tentacles flailing and his true face exposed, he walked to the back of the room. Still reeling from the attack, he summoned enough coordination to open the hidden wardrobe. He cast off the remains of the damaged suit and the skin that had lain under it, then began putting on a new disguise. He moved with outward calm, but inside he was fuming.

The Evermores had struck back at him. Now he would make them regret it.

In the garden in the foothills, the bright light faded and the Evermores lowered their arms. Several of them sank to the ground to sit or lie exhausted in the grass, drained from the magical struggle they'd undertaken.

"Did we get them?" Enfield's eagerness showed in his tone. As the Evermore on the receiving end of attacks, he had more reason than the rest to want this over with.

"We achieved something." Winslow pressed down the pain he'd felt thrown at them. He didn't want the others to know how badly that could've gone. "Not as much as I hoped. We face something dark and powerful, something that was able to push our power back, even when we worked together."

"Like the Source?"

Winslow shook his head.

"They're powerful, but not that powerful. Familiarity helps us manage the Source, making it seem weaker facing us than it truly is. This opponent seemed stronger because they were new and we didn't know what we were dealing with."

"Do we know any more now?"

Winslow considered that question. In the heat of the magical conflict, there had been little time for him to pay attention to his opponent, to sense the details of what he faced. For the most part, there had been the battle of wills.

One of them struck with a tide of light. The other flung up barriers of darkness, then drove the light back. What he'd sensed had mostly confirmed what he knew already. This was a creature of darkness and nightmare, something repulsive, destructive, and chaotic, a being that made his nerves thrum with a terrible tension.

There had been something else as well. In the first few moments as the Evermores' magic hit and he'd known that they were affecting the enemy, he'd felt something fall away. There had been a sense of a human-like figure, however blurred by distance and magic, which then slid away to reveal something else, the vast and ancient spirit underneath.

Now that he thought about it, the currents of magic around the figure had seemed familiar. So much magic, varied and vibrant, shot through with the strange ripples that its power gained when it combined with magic.

"Whoever they are, they're in disguise," he said. "They're out here somewhere in Mana Valley, pretending to be one of its inhabitants. Just another magical. Under-neath is something far more terrible."

He hesitated. The Evermores had a purpose already: to contain the Source and maintain magic on Earth. That was why his group was here in Mana Valley. They didn't need distractions. Their burden was heavy enough.

If they kept getting attacked, that would undermine the work. Which meant that really, hunting down this darkness was in the interest of the cause. It was part of their mission, at least until they got the Source safely back to Earth and its old prison.

It wasn't only curiosity, although he admitted he felt that too. There was a bigger picture here.

"We're not done with this thing," he said.

CHAPTER ELEVEN

Fran walked across Worn Threads, carrying her backpack over one shoulder and her skates in the other hand. She yawned. It had been another long day in a series of long days as Mana Wave Industries worked up more prototypes. It didn't help that she still had to meet with potential investors, as Bart tried to capitalize on the investment they'd already acquired.

"We have money now," she'd pointed out.

"Money attracts more money," Bart had said. "Especially when people are talking about it."

That meant rushing back and forth between their basement base and a series of meeting rooms, which were starting to look more and more like one another with each hour that Fran spent in them. The water coolers. The wall-mounted screens. The matching chairs and tables. A sea of sameness when she longed for novelty.

"Hold the door!" someone called as she pushed open the carpet shop's door. She looked back to see Liam hurrying after her. He wore the playful smile that always seemed to light up his face.

"I thought you left already," she said.

"Smokey was explaining some code to me. Got distracted and lost track of time, which is particularly annoying because I wanted to talk with you."

"With me? About work stuff?"

"Well, yes, there is some work stuff to talk about. Though honestly, I'd be happy to talk with you about anything."

Fran blushed and looked down at her feet.

"I suppose it's too late now?" Liam asked.

"Not too late." Fran pursed her lips. "I guess we could head back into the office."

"Sure, or we could go grab a coffee somewhere. I'm paying, as long as you take me somewhere decent, and I figure you must know the good places around here."

"There's the Blazing Bean, we used to work there, and we still go hang out when we have time."

"I've seen their takeout cups around the office. Clearly a place worth checking out." Liam's expression changed, and he pressed a hand against his forehead. "Wait, unless this is intruding on your social space. Is this where you go to meet your friends too?"

"What friends?" Fran laughed. "The only people I see outside of work right now are my roommate and my mom. You'll make a nice addition."

"You must have other people you hang out with."

For a moment, Fran thought of Winslow, Enfield, and the rest of the Evermores. They weren't exactly friends, and she wouldn't say they hung out. Besides, Evermores business wasn't something she should be talking about.

"No," she said. "Only the Mana Wave crew."

"Then I'm sorry to take up more of your time with business, but maybe we can talk about other things too. I'm curious about the skating. Are you part of a club or something..."

They wandered down the street, heading for the Blazing Bean. Fran found Liam remarkably easy to talk to. He was so relaxed in himself and seemed genuinely interested in whatever she had to say. When he spoke up, it was to ask more questions or occasionally to share an anecdote about a place he'd visited or something he'd done in his work.

The Blazing Bean was busy when they arrived, thanks to the early evening crowd of people killing time after work or meeting up for their evenings' entertainment. A group of wizards and witches performed tiny illusions in the window. Half a dozen dwarves in suits ate muffins and talked about mining, and a gang of students argued about movies at the tables in the middle of the room.

After a few minutes' wait behind other customers, they reached the counter. Cam smiled from behind the register.

"Hi, Fran. What can I get you this evening?"

"Do you have any new flavored syrups?"

"Sorry, no."

"And I've definitely tried all the coffees?"

"Every style, every size, every strength."

"Guess I'll have a cappuccino then and a latte for Liam."

"Hey, you remembered." Liam smiled and nudged her. "Thanks, and remember, I'm paying."

They fell to talking again while Cam made the drinks.

"Another work meeting?" Cam asked as he presented their drinks.

"Oh, yes." Fran beamed. "This is Liam. We're working with his company. We came here to talk technology."

"Cool." Cam smiled. "One of your old tables is free at the back."

"Brilliant! Come on, Liam."

"Have a nice evening."

Cam watched Fran and Liam head for the corner table, where they settled in next to each other. It was great that her business was growing and other companies were paying attention. Fran was awesome, and she deserved all the success she was getting. The only downside of it was that Cam didn't get to see so much of her since she didn't keep coming into the Blazing Bean for meetings. It was good to see one happening again.

He turned his attention to the next customer and the one after them. Business was good, and he was busy for the next half-hour, constantly shifting back and forth between the register and coffee machine. In the moments between taking orders, he glanced up and saw Fran still having her meeting. It was going well because she was smiling and leaning forward, talking excitedly.

At last, the rush died down a little. Cam took his laptop out from under the counter and opened the folder for his project. Not the thesis he was still supposed to be writing up, but the other project. The one that mattered.

Getting more of the prophecies he'd been working with from the city archive had thrown his whole concept of what he was looking at into chaos. The usual mix of cryptic fragments and disconnected details made it hard to piece together what the prophecies were trying to tell him or how they related to the world he lived in. More information should've made things clearer. Instead, it had left him wandering in a fog of thoughts.

The Evermores were key. He knew that much. Whoever the Evermores were. They were going to bring some sort of disaster to Mana Valley. Shining towers would fall. Darkness would come.

He glanced toward the back of the room. How could he have thought that Fran would have anything to do with this or with these Evermores? She was building a better world, not the sort of person to tear it down.

No, he wasn't supposed to be thinking about Fran. He should be concentrating on the prophecies while he had time. Both time between customers and time before the disaster came. His family had never listened to his warnings, but if he found the real conspiracy, someone would have to. He only needed to put the pieces together.

Darkness, that was a piece that came up over and over again. Darkness and terror threatening the land. It could've sounded generic and vague, but something in the way the writing referred to it made this threat sound more substantial. It was made of shadows, perhaps, but were these literal shadows or metaphorical ones, the shadows in people's minds?

He looked across the room again. Fran was smart. Maybe he could ask her what she thought about all this...

No, that wasn't how it worked. He was only looking for an excuse to spend time with her, and if that was what he wanted, he should be direct. Ask her out. What was the worst that could happen? Nothing worse than was already coming, according to these prophecies.

He turned his attention back to the screen. He'd transcribed all the pages that seemed relevant from the book he'd taken from the archive. He might have missed bits, and he would certainly look again once he finished with these parts, but there was still meaning to squeeze out of what he had. There was a knack to understanding prophecy, to working out what it hid and what it revealed, a knack that he'd developed through years of practice reading strange and obscure texts.

Normally, this was work that got his brain engaged, but today his eyes skimmed over the words without really taking them in. Instead of imagining the scenes the text described or the connections between the words, he imagined taking Fran to a restaurant, the cinema, or out for a drink in one of the local bars. He imagined sitting close to her, like that Liam guy was doing, but talking about something more interesting than work. He imagined holding her hand. He imagined leaning closer and—

Enough. He would ask her out today. Then, perhaps, he would be able to concentrate on other things. Once he stopped bouncing off the ceiling in excitement, of course.

"Are you still serving?" A blond witch in her twenties approached the counter with a smile.

"Sure, yes, what can I get you?" Cam put his computer away under the counter again.

"Cappuccino and coffee cake." She smiled. "Cute glasses, by the way."

"Thanks. I'm kind of stuck with them. Got to be able to see all the beauty the world holds, you know?"

"Oh, totally. Things like movies and art…"

"Exactly. You miss a lot if the world's a big old blur."

"Have you seen the new modernist exhibit at the city gallery yet?"

"No, is it any good?"

"I don't know, haven't seen it either, yet."

"Here you go." Cam handed over her order. "Have a nice evening."

The witch hesitated for a moment.

"Thanks," she said, then headed for a nearby table, glancing back with a smile as she went.

A movement at the back of the room caught Cam's eye. That Liam guy who had been meeting with Fran was getting out of his seat. He said something to her, picked up a briefcase, and headed for the door, leaving her by herself.

Cam swallowed. This was it, his opportunity. His chance to take a chance. He was pretty sure she would say yes, and if she didn't… Well, he would be very disappointed, but at least he might be able to concentrate again.

"Hey, Jo!" he said.

Another member of staff looked around from refilling the cake display.

"What's up?"

"Can you cover the register for ten minutes? I'm going to take a break."

"Sure thing." Jo glanced at the table where the blond witch was sitting. "Gonna seize the moment, huh?"

"That's the idea." Cam took a deep breath, then hurried past the blond witch's table to the back of the room.

"Hey, Cam!"

Fran's huge smile made Cam's heart skip a beat. She looked so happy. That had to be a good sign, right? If she responded to him that way, she was hardly going to say no.

"Hi, Fran. How was the meeting?" He sat next to her, so it would be easier to talk.

"What meeting? Oh, this!" She laughed and blushed. "Yeah, it was totally great. We've come up with some fantastic new ideas to work on, and Liam's going to see what resources his company can provide to help make prototypes."

"That sounds great. I wish you guys were still working here, so I could see what you're making."

"I promise, as soon as there's anything worth seeing, I'll bring it in." She jiggled in her seat. "There's something else as well…"

She leaned in closer, so Cam did too.

"Something else?" He matched her smile.

"Something that's not only about work that I wanted to tell you."

"Funny you should say that because I wanted to ask you something."

"Really?"

"Sure, but you go first."

"Okay, well…" She took a deep breath, then looked at him with her biggest grin yet. "Liam asked me out for dinner."

Cam blinked. He could feel the thoughts failing to connect in his brain.

"Liam asked you…"

"Liam who was in here just now. I haven't been on a date in, like, forever. I'm super excited."

Cam swallowed. Of all the directions he'd thought this conversation might go, he hadn't considered this option. The sinking feeling in his stomach told him it wasn't one he wanted to think about.

"What do you think?" Fran asked. "He's cute, right? He seems like a nice guy. It turns out he likes loads of the things I do, and that hardly ever happens."

"Hardly ever," Cam said quietly.

Fran sighed. "You're no use. I guess I should go talk to one of my girlfriends." She laughed. "By which I mean Josie."

"Sure, yes." Cam finally managed to pull his thoughts together. Even he could tell how false his smile must look, but Fran didn't seem to notice, too caught up in her excitement. "Good for you, Fran."

"Thanks! Oh, hey, what did you want to ask me about?"

"Huh?"

"You were going to ask me something?"

He hesitated. He could still ask her. It wasn't like she was in a relationship with Liam. He wasn't trying to steal her away. Still, she seemed so happy about this date. She was clearly really into this Liam guy. How could he compete with that? He didn't want to make things difficult for her.

"Flavored syrup," he said. "For the coffee. Is there anything we don't have that you'd like us to get in? As our main customer for novelty coffees, you seemed like the woman to ask."

"Ooh, how about fiery ginger? I know it's not autumn yet, but that warming flavor is great all year round."

"Fiery ginger. Got it." Cam stood up. "Well, I'd better get back to work. You have your date."

Fran laughed, and Cam's spirits sank a little further.

"Not this evening I haven't, but I should head home and tell Josie all about it." She jumped up. "Thanks, Cam. You're the best."

She headed out the door while Cam went back to the counter. He didn't even notice the blond witch smiling at him as he walked past her table.

CHAPTER TWELVE

Handar and Julia followed the uniformed gnome down the stairs into one of the city archive basements. It was a room the size of a warehouse with its vaulted stone ceiling lit by glowing magical crystals. Long rows of wooden shelves stretched out ahead of them, pressed tight together, each row marked with letters and numbers indicating the books it contained.

"That's tightly packed," Julia said.

"Ah, we have an ingenious system to fit them all in, while making the books available." The gnome beamed with pride. "You see these boxes? Well, they—"

"I've been before," Handar growled. "I'll show her."

"There's no need to be rude." The gnome looked up at the scowling Kilomea and did a double-take. "I mean, of course, sir. I'll leave you to it. If you need anything, wave at the cameras."

He pointed at a security camera mounted in the corner of the room. Others were placed elsewhere along the walls.

"Those are new," Handar said.

"We had an incident. We've tightened up security as a result."

"I approve." Working in security as he did, Handar liked to see people put in more effort. If only the cameras had been there during his previous visit, it would've been easier to do what he was doing now.

"Thank you." The gnome gave a relieved smile. "Enjoy your research."

The gnome hurried away, leaving Handar and Julia alone with the books.

"I'll show you how these work." Handar pointed at the box attached to the end of one stack of shelves.

"What, you think I've never been in a professional archive before?"

Julia reached the box before him and tapped on the lid. A tiny yellow imp poked its head out of a hole in the front and looked up at her.

"Left," Julia said. "Now."

"Can't." The imp pointed at the shelves next to it. "Need to move the others first."

"Then I suggest that you tell them all to move." Julia leaned close to the imp. "Or else I'll…"

Her voice dropped to a whisper. Handar didn't hear whatever she said, but when she straightened, the imp was shaking. It dashed off along the row, jumping from one box to the next, tapping frantically on the lids and shouting "Left!"

"Thought you was the nice one." Handar rubbed one of his tusks as he reappraised his colleague.

"Some magicals respond best to kind treatment, others… Well, worlds don't get conquered by nice."

There was a rattling of chains in the recessed tracks beneath the ends of the shelving units. The chains tightened, then the units moved, crossing the floor. A fresh set of shelves stood revealed.

"Was this the one?" Julia asked.

"Think so."

"You think so?"

"I don't do libraries. These all look the same to me." Handar pulled a piece of paper from his pocket and compared it with the sign on the end of the shelf. "Yeah, this is the one."

The two of them walked down the length of the shelves until they were facing a row of hardbound books, their matching spines marked with silver lettering. Julia took one off the shelf, opened it, and breathed deeply.

"I love the smell of old books." She turned to the title page. "Nearly two hundred years old, and it'll last better than anything printed on all that cheap acidic paper from twentieth-century Earth." She put the book back on the shelf. "You're sure that the one you were looking for is gone?"

Handar scanned the shelf, just in case, then pointed at an empty spot.

"Yeah, it's missing, and those short dimwits upstairs couldn't even tell me if it had gone recently. But it ain't coincidence that the shelves came in on me as I was looking for it."

"Agreed. So..."

Julia pulled out her wand and a piece of chalk. She scribbled some runes on the floor, then chanted over them. A scatter of silver dust filled the air around her, tiny motes of magic looking for the room's memories. Handar walked up the room a little way, so he could watch out for any new arrivals while viewing what she found.

The points of magic came together, hazily at first. They formed the shape of a gnome looking up at the shelf, picking out a book, then putting it back.

"Too far back," Julia muttered and waved through the image. The magic rearranged itself, became an elf, a dwarf, an elf again. "Getting closer…"

A blurry image formed. Its shape was like a witch or wizard, or a shifter in their non-animal form, but the outline was blurry. While the previous figures had shifted between vague and distinct with facial features flickering in and out of the image, this one remained unclear the whole time. The face was blank, the body hazy enough that Handar couldn't guess at their gender.

The figure leaned forward and took a book from the exact place where Handar's book should've been, the book that Mr. Phillips had sent him to find. They flicked back and forth through the book, pausing several times to read particular pages. Then they looked up, as if startled by something.

There was a second's pause. They glanced back at the book, then hastily rearranged the shelf where it had been and hurried off. The magical motes turned back into an unformed cloud. A few seconds later, the cloud reformed into an image of Handar himself, walking up to the shelf.

The real, current Handar growled and stepped closer.

Julia waved. The image froze, then wound backward, until the blurry figure stood in front of the shelf again.

"Make it clearer," Handar said, his voice low.

"I can't." Julia frowned. "They were disguising themselves with some sort of spell. Unless..." She ran her fingers through the image. "Unless they're a mundane human, and the building's memory is less clear because of their lack of magic."

"A mundane, here?" Handar snorted. "My money's on the disguise. No mundane human's gonna mess with the boss."

"I tend to agree." Julia waved, and the image disappeared. "Still, best to consider all the options."

She scuffed out the chalk marks on the floor, and the two of them walked past the shelves, back to the edge of the room. Imps peered fearfully out of their boxes at Julia.

"You can't get anything from around here?" Handar asked.

Julia shook her head. "Memory susceptibility is a complex matter, but it comes down to intensities. Events in the stacks made it matter enough to leave a trace. We won't find anything relevant here."

Handar walked over to the wall and looked up at one of the security cameras. It wasn't a new model, and the flaked paint around the screws on its bracket indicated that the gnomes had moved it from a mounting somewhere else.

"Maybe we can find something elsewhere," he said. "Like, if they filmed people coming in and out of the building..."

"Excuse me, Howard?" Julia stood in the door to Phillips' office. "Do you have a minute?"

"Sure." Phillips leaned back in his chair. "Come on in."

Julia walked into the office, followed by Handar, who shut the door behind him. They took seats across the desk from their boss.

"We didn't have anything scheduled, did we?" Phillips asked.

"No, but we've been working on something." Julia exchanged a look with Handar, then nodded at him to talk.

"It's about that book you sent me to find," the Kilomea said. "The one you thought might have all them prophecies."

"I thought someone thwarted you in that matter?"

"Yeah, it didn't go well." Handar scowled and cracked his knuckles. "Here's the thing, though, sir. I didn't want to let it lie. I let you down, and I don't leave things like that. So we've done some investigating.

"Someone got to that book before me, and now we know a bit about who they were. We saw a memory in the archive, and it was blurry, but it's a start. Someone human-shaped, using magic to cover their tracks."

"Or possibly a mundane," Julia added. "Although that seems unlikely in this context. Even with the humans moving in from Earth at the moment, it seems unlikely that they would be involved with something like this."

"Yeah, so not that." Handar shook his head. "Wizard, witch, or shifter, probably. They got into the archive before me, took the book before I could, then caused all that trouble."

He ground his teeth at the memory of the shelves closing in on him, the frustration of chasing a target he couldn't catch, the chaos of the escaping imps, and the gnomes rushing around trying to restore order. He didn't like to think of himself as someone vulnerable to embarrassment, but it was the only way to describe his feelings.

"Is there a point to all this?" Phillips asked.

"Absolutely, Howard," Julia said. "We now know something about who took that book and have the opportunity to learn more. Handar persuaded the archive's security staff to share their surveillance footage from that day with us. We don't know yet who we're looking for, and there are a lot of people going in and out, but we could start identifying likely suspects, running up profiles, doing some research. If they're getting in the way of your plans, then—"

"No." Phillips shook his head.

The other two looked at him, then at each other, confused.

"I thought this was important," Handar said.

"And given the progress that we've made already..." Julia's voice trailed off uncertainly.

"I appreciate your dedication," Phillips said. "This is related to something larger, and I'm pursuing other paths toward it now. Less direct ones."

"This guy's out there, though," Handar said. "With your book. The little shit that trapped me between them shelves." He clenched his fist.

"I said that I'm pursuing other paths." Phillips' voice became steely. His hand pressed against the desk and the tip of a tentacle crept out of the sleeve. "Do I have to repeat myself?"

Handar stiffened in his seat. He wasn't going to disobey a command from a superior, however much he wanted to. If the order was to drop this, that was what he would do.

"Yes, sir," he said.

"Julia?"

She nodded. "Of course, Howard. It's your business, your choice."

"Good." Phillips got out of his seat and walked over to the window. His skin was a little lighter than it had been earlier in the week. Handar wondered if he was wearing a new skin suit, one that needed to get more sun. If that was the case, why the change?

"Anything else?" Phillips asked.

"I don't think so," Julia said. "Handar?"

Handar shook his head. "All good, sir."

"Then I won't keep you any longer."

They got up and left the room, closing the door behind them.

Usually, after leaving a meeting with the boss, Julia would sit straight down behind her desk outside his office, ready to get back to work. Today, she stood with her arms folded and a small frown wrinkling her forehead.

"Is it me, or is something wrong?" she asked.

"Different skin suit," Handar said quietly, glad of a chance to let out some of what was jamming up his head. "What does that mean?"

Julia rubbed her eyes. "I don't know, but I put a lot of magic and effort into that spell at the archive. I'm loath to let it go to waste."

"What you saying?"

"I'm saying that perhaps we should pursue this ourselves, quietly, to see where it leads."

Handar frowned. He wanted to do as she said, but he knew he shouldn't. Sure, he wasn't a soldier anymore, but orders were still orders.

"Why?" he asked at last, looking for a way out of his mental contradictions.

"In case this is something that could still threaten him. In case it's something that could come back to bite us. Simple curiosity." Julia shrugged. "Instinct, I suppose. Do you need more than that?"

"Yeah, I do." Handar shook his head. He knew what was right, and he should stick to it. "Orders is orders, and we've got ours."

"And those video recordings the archive sent you?"

He shrugged. "If we need them in future, we've got them. Until then, it's time to get back to work."

He walked away from her and the office, hoping against reality that he could also walk away from the thought still wriggling in the back of his mind—the desire to get back at whoever had been in those archive stacks.

CHAPTER THIRTEEN

Josie led her team into the testing room. It still felt weird to think of them as her team, but there was no denying it. As team manager, she was now responsible for the work and well-being of half a dozen other people, not only herself. She smiled at them all as they came in, and made sure everybody was sitting comfortably before she closed the door and got a box out of a locked cupboard.

"How's everybody doing?" she asked.

They nodded and smiled and made the sort of noncommittal noises most people made when asked a question by their boss.

Gathering now, Josie realized how little she knew about her immediate colleagues. When Simon had managed the team, he hadn't exactly been big on team bonding or collaborative work, preferring to keep them all in their niches. Josie liked a more cooperative approach. Aside from anything else, it made life more fun.

"Hands up if you've been working on the Manaphone already," she said.

Debby, a chatty witch of around the same age as Josie, raised her hand. So did a dwarf with a plaited beard. The rest of the team shook their heads.

"We were doing quality assurance on samples from the computer lab," said Ted, a gnome with pale skin and wavy black hair. He gestured at the elf next to him. "Consoles and controllers."

"I was on apps," said the next tester around.

Last was a recruit brought in to fill the gap left from Josie's promotion. She shrugged. "Whatever you tell me to do, that's why I'm here."

"Cool." Josie smiled. "Well, we're setting other work aside for now while we focus on the Manaphone. It has the most urgent deadlines, and dealing with one product at a time should give us more focus."

Ted looked at the elf, who shrugged.

"We know about the consoles," Ted said. "We've been doing it for years. It's what we're good at."

"Soon you'll be good at this." Josie opened the box. "I believe in you guys."

They sat on stools around a long workbench, with power points down the middle to plug in products and testing tools. She went around the outside of the bench, handing each tester a Manaphone from her box.

"This is the latest model," she explained. "The design folks are happy with it, or they wouldn't have sent it down for testing. Up until now, we've focused on how well it does the things it's designed for and whether they work. Obviously, that's important, but I think that we can do more."

"More?" Ted frowned. "Are you saying that you want us

to do extra work?"

"No, only to think a bit more imaginatively while you're working. Look out for the things that the phone doesn't do, especially the ones you wish it did."

"Like, things that other phones do?" Debby asked.

"Sure, if you think they're worth doing. Not only that. Think about what you'd like to see in a phone. It doesn't have to be realistic. We're thinking about ideas here."

"This sounds a lot like design work," Ted said.

Several of the others nodded. The new woman seemed happy with that idea, but the people on either side of Ted didn't.

"Don't worry, nobody's going to ask you to make these things function," Josie said. "It's about sharing ideas. Think of it as your opportunity to make the phone a bit more like what you'd want."

"This isn't what we do," Ted said.

"Maybe it wasn't before, but it is now." Josie held up one of the phones. "Hopefully by working together, we'll notice things that we might've missed alone. So, first thing, we're going to look at navigating the main menu…"

They worked through a series of exercises that Josie had planned to see how easy it was to navigate the phone. She made a note to herself to repeat these exercises with more outsiders. People in the company were too familiar with its technology to give an objective perspective.

Josie was pleased to see how quickly the team got to grips with the task at hand. Most of them worked enthusiastically and rapidly from one step to the next. Debby and the recruit were the first to come up with new ideas, which

Josie wrote on a board at the end of the room for everyone to see.

Once they got the ball rolling, the others joined in. Within an hour, it felt like a race to the wackiest idea, with people throwing out possibilities as they sprang to mind, playing off one another.

"This is amazing," someone said as they fiddled with the calendar app. "My first phone could barely even send me a reminder to pick the kids up from soccer."

"Ooh, idea!" the recruit said. "A phone that picks up the kids from soccer for you!"

They laughed.

"Even better." Debby grinned. "How about if the phone could play soccer for the kids? It does everything else, right?"

They laughed again, all except Ted, who glared at his handset in stony silence. The elf sitting next to him stopped laughing when he saw Ted's expression.

"They might sound dumb, but they all go on the board," Josie said, wielding her pen like a wand. "We'll work out later which ones are worth reporting to the design team."

Ted snorted and muttered something. Josie glanced at him. She'd been trying to let his negative attitude slide, not to draw attention to it or make a big fuss, but this was starting to get to her. Perhaps worse, it was affecting the attitude of the others sitting near him. She couldn't have one grumpy person sour the mood of the whole team. It was time to deal with it.

"What was that, Ted?" She held her pen up as if waiting to write something on the board.

"Nothing." He didn't look up from his Manaphone.

"I'm sure you said something."

"Nope." He shook his head.

The others looked from Josie to Ted and back again. Nervousness replaced their smiles. Debby sat with her back rigidly straight as her eyes darted back and forth.

Josie drew a deep breath. She'd never had to deal with discipline issues before, but that was what she had here. The joys of promotion...

"Ted, can I talk to you outside, please?" she said.

Ted finally looked up. If she'd been expecting a hint of apology, or any acknowledgment that he might be in the wrong, she was going to be disappointed. He looked back at her defiantly.

"Sure."

He waited until she opened the door, then followed her from the room.

There wasn't a lot of privacy in the corridors, where people might walk past at any moment on their way from one appointment to the next. Josie led the way down the hall until she found an empty meeting room. She led Ted in, then shut the door calmly and firmly behind her. She was in charge, and she mustn't let her nerves show, or she would lose control of the situation.

"Do you have a problem with this work, Ted?" she asked.

"It's not my work," he said, arms folded, glaring at her.

"You're a product tester, aren't you?"

"That's right."

"And we're testing a product?"

"Not the sort of product I test."

"I'm sorry, is there something in your contract that says you only work on consoles?"

"It's what I've done for years."

"Now it isn't."

His lip curled in a sneer. "Those consoles need testing. When they're not ready on time, I'm going to tell them whose fault it was."

"If we're not ready on time, I'll tell them myself. But that's not going to happen."

Ted's only response was another snort.

"Are you not interested in working on the Manaphone?" Josie asked. "Most people are excited about it."

"I liked what I did before."

"I'm glad to hear that, but you can't keep doing the same thing forever."

"Simon let me."

There it was. She'd thought there might be something more behind this.

"You're not working for Simon anymore. I'm in charge now."

"Yeah, well, you shouldn't be."

Josie was momentarily unable to respond, taken aback by how direct he was in his complaints.

"What do you mean by that?" she asked.

"I've worked on this team for a decade. I've put in the hours. I got on with the job. That manager position should've been mine. Then you turn up, and a few weeks later you get promoted? That's bullshit!"

Josie took a step back, stunned at the level of anger in his voice. Ted had shocked himself as well. The defiance in his expression turned to uncertainty, then into fear in the space of a few seconds. He knew that he'd crossed a line, and he feared what might follow.

Josie drew a deep breath and braced herself. She was in charge. She had to remind herself of that so she could remind other people too.

"I earned this job. I turned up here, I applied myself, I worked hard, and I used initiative. I solved problems that people hadn't spotted. I made an effort.

"From everything I can see, that's exactly what you haven't been doing. You've been sitting on your ass for a decade, doing the same thing with the same product line, never learning, never growing, never challenging yourself.

"I gave you a chance to try something new today, and you sneered at it. With an attitude like that, who do you think is ever going to give you more responsibility? If you regularly turn up for team exercises like you did today, with a toddler's bad-tempered attitude, snorting and scowling and dragging down team morale, I'm amazed you still have the job you have, never mind any dreams of promotion."

Ted couldn't hold her gaze any longer. He looked down at the floor, and his lower lip wobbled. He didn't say anything, but his silence didn't feel defiant any longer. It felt pitiful.

That was better, at least. Josie felt as though she'd asserted her authority. She still didn't feel great about the situation. The problem wasn't that she'd upset him. That was something he'd brought upon himself. It was the impact this might have on his work and the people around him. She had to give him at least one more chance to adjust to the new status quo, and that meant offering an olive branch.

"I'm sorry that you find this frustrating," she said. "It can't be easy seeing someone new come in and take over, or having your work suddenly change after so long. If you're struggling with the adjustment, you can come and talk to me about it. But you don't get to take your frustration out on me or anyone else in the team. Is that clear?"

Ted nodded.

"I'm sorry," he mumbled.

"I'm glad to hear that. If you're still here, you clearly have some talent. It's time to make better use of it." She opened the door. "I'm going back to the testing room. When you're ready, come and join us."

She headed back down the corridor, her pulse racing. She'd never done anything like this before. Had she done right, both in tearing him down like that and in inviting him to come back to work? She had no idea. All she could do was follow her instincts.

When she got back to the room, she was relieved to find that the others were still hard at work. They'd got through most of the testing exercises the design department had sent, providing ratings far quicker than expected. They'd also added some more ideas to the list on the board.

"All right, everyone." Josie hid her tension behind a smile. "Another half-hour of the tests, then we'll go through our ideas and decide which ones to feed back. I'll need a volunteer to write that up."

Pleasingly, several hands went up.

"I'll pick someone later," she said. "For now, we—"

The door opened, and Ted walked in. That was quicker

than Josie had expected. She tensed as she saw his frown. Was he going to cause a scene?

"I have another idea for the board." He closed the door behind him.

"Okay." Josie picked up the pen.

"Can we get an app that warns you when you're behaving like an asshole? I think I need it."

He smiled uncertainly. Someone laughed, and Ted joined in. The laughter spread around the room as he sat and got back to work.

Josie smiled. She didn't add that idea to the list. She didn't think they needed it anymore.

CHAPTER FOURTEEN

"It's quite a mess you have here." Elethin looked around the workshop. "Add some takeaway wrappers, and you could get a license to become the new municipal dump."

Fran looked around. There was a lot of mess, heaps of components spread across the workbench, the floor, spilling out of boxes over to one side. Half-completed ideas for devices occupied chairs or hung from hooks on the wall.

When they'd first set the place up, Singar had taken so much care to make it orderly and neat, with everything in its place. Over the past few days, as they'd frantically worked through prototypes on their way to whatever came next, the clutter and debris had piled up. It wasn't exactly an ideal working environment anymore.

"Maybe we should do some tidying," she said. "What do you think, guys?"

Smokey looked around his computer and shrugged.

"It's not so bad." He waved his paw and accidentally

knocked a packet of cat treats into the litter around his desk. "Although maybe I should clear up a bit…"

Singar blinked. Her eyes were bloodshot, and her shirt wrinkled. Too many long nights and early mornings of development were taking their toll.

"Dung and droppings," she muttered. "The elf's right. How did we let it get to this state?"

She jumped down off her stool and gathered tools to return to their places on the shadow board on one wall.

"I like it," Liam said. "It feels like a place where real creativity is happening."

Fran smiled as he caught her eye. It was good to have him here, supporting her, helping them develop new ideas. They should've teamed up with another company sooner.

"Creativity or a workplace accident," Elethin said. "You choose."

"This company can't afford to be liable for an accident," Gruffbar shouted over the partition. "Tidy up your mess."

"Later," Elethin said. "For now, I need to talk to you about brand management."

"I'd rather tidy up." Smokey jumped down from his seat. "And I hate tidying up."

He picked up an empty packet between his teeth and carried it over to the trash can while Singar roamed back and forth, rolling up cables and putting materials into boxes.

"I know that, as technicians, you don't like to be bothered by little things like our image," Elethin said. "But it matters, and it affects your work. If we're going to sell products, we need a strong brand, which means coming up with devices that fit the brand identity. Since you're still flailing around looking for something to make, now seems like a good time to think about it."

"Substance first, image later," Singar said as she gathered screws scattered across the floor. "This isn't the place for PR."

Instinctively, Fran wanted to agree with her. Still, she'd seen how powerful brand identity could be for a company like Philgard, and she knew how great Elethin was at her job.

"What do you think, Liam?" She looked for someone to provide a way through her conflicting opinions and her team's.

"Coming from sales, I've seen how important image is to attracting customers," he said. "More than that, I've seen how a concept or an image can inspire designers. It doesn't do any harm to think about it."

"Let's do that, then." Fran turned to give Elethin her full attention. "Do you know what our brand is?"

"In a word, quirky." Elethin placed a laptop on the workbench and started a slide show playing. The first images that popped up were of members of their team. "In as far as we have a public image, you designers shape it. Fran's TV appearance and her vibrant clothes. Smokey getting arrested naked in the street. Singar's success created unusual machines for maker contests."

"You know about those?" Singar stopped what she was doing to look at a picture of her holding a trophy.

"It's all over your social media, which is most of what people know about you." Elethin shook her head. "Honestly, did any of you read the briefing I sent to you on media relations?"

There was a general shaking of heads. Elethin scowled and crossed her arms.

"As I suspected. Well, here's the deal. We are perceived as an odd company staffed by lovable eccentrics and people like that, the few people who have heard about us, at least.

"Remember the investor meeting where you made them play video games? That's odd, it's funny, and it's attention-grabbing. We need to build on that foundation, and the best way we can do that is to lean into fun and quirky, to build a product line and public image around our sequin-wearing, roller skating, game-playing CEO."

"But our core technology is a battery," Singar said, setting aside her tidying to take a seat again. "Don't battery buyers want things like reliability?"

"For customers, the battery is a means to an end. No point focusing on that."

"Well then, our other product is a containment unit to capture escaped magicals and monsters. That hardly screams fun."

"Our product that we can't tell anyone about because of the non-disclosure part of our contract?" Elethin raised an eyebrow. "Please, tell me how you'd build a public image around that, in the alternate reality where we were allowed."

Singar stiffened, looked as if she was about to say some-thing snarky, then let out a breath. "All right. Fair point. Still seems weird that we're doing that while trying to become a company of wacky fun times."

"Hardly the weirdest thing around here," Elethin pointed out. Her slide show had moved on to images of the fun and quirky, from cartoon characters to unusual clothing to eccentric people and places. "I made a mood board, which I assume you're all going to ignore. So why don't you tell me, what ideas do you have for fun, quirky devices?"

The team looked at each other uncertainly.

"I wrote an app once that comes up with insults for politicians, based on their names," Smokey said.

"Politics isn't fun," Elethin said. "It's the anti-fun. It makes people feel bored or bad, and neither of those will work for us."

"I could adapt it to come up with insults for your friends and family."

"Which is mean-spirited. Let's try for something better, shall we?"

"My flying carpet was fun to ride," Fran said.

"Good, that's a start." Elethin dug a sheet of paper from under the creative debris and wrote down "flying carpet." "Although there is the risk of accidents to consider there since broken necks won't exactly make us popular. What else do you have?"

"I built these clockwork monkeys that climb over each other. They're fun."

"Clockwork monkeys..." Elethin wrote again. "Keep going..."

"A water bomb projector," Singar said. "I built it when I was younger. Instead of throwing or launching water bombs, it uses a small enchantment to teleport them so they appear above your target's head."

"Definitely silly, keep going."

"There was my smellophone," Fran said.

"Smellophone?" Elethin managed to look both confused and disgusted.

"It's like a normal phone, except it can send smells. I didn't think of it as silly, but you could maybe use it that way. We'd kind of given up on the idea as impractical though."

"You gave up on a smell telephone?" Liam laughed. "I can't believe you weren't going to use it! It's such a cool idea."

Fran blushed. "Thanks, but the tech is expensive, and we didn't think it would be popular enough."

"I'd definitely buy one."

"Could you make other devices with the same technology?" Elethin asked.

"Maybe, but I have another idea…"

For the next two hours, they kept adding ideas to the list. When they started running out of energy, Gruffbar fetched coffee and cake from the Blazing Bean before returning to his desk. Somewhere along the line, Singar started tidying again for something to do with her hands. The others joined in, except for Elethin, who kept writing down the ideas they threw into the air as they put tools and components back into their boxes.

"A joke projector."

"A random punning machine."

"A game where you chase illusions of penguins through the street."

"The penguin thing, except that it's motivating you to exercise."

"Zombie penguin running app."

"Clockwork zombie penguins!"

As the ideas ran out, they gathered around the work-bench again. Together, they looked over the list.

"Some of these are truly terrible ideas," Singar said. "Stupid, impractical things no sane person would buy."

"You thought of half of them," Smokey pointed out.

"I'm an inventor. I don't need to be practical."

Fran looked at the list. She found lots of things funny, but they weren't items she felt they could build a business around. They needed something substantial that would demonstrate the power of her battery design. That would prove its value while creating this fun, quirky image they were heading for. It was a tough combination.

"Do the devices themselves have to be fun?" she asked. "Or can they be things that deliver fun?"

"What do you mean?" Elethin asked.

Fran scratched her head. She wasn't sure what she meant.

"Think about a bicycle," she said. "It's not particularly fun, right? People made it as a way to get from place to place. Other people made it fun by learning to do tricks, having races, decorating their bikes in cool ways. The bicycle isn't fun. It's a fun delivery system."

"Hm." Elethin tapped her pen against the paper. "I think I see what you mean, in principle, but does it work in the modern tech sector?"

"Of course it does." Liam smiled at Fran. "We use computers as fun delivery systems all the time. Phones too. Sure, they have a load of other uses, but that's not why we love them. We love them because they let us play our favorite songs and watch videos of cats."

"True fact." Smokey swished his tail back and forth. "We're the stars you all aspire to be."

"Making computers or phones isn't exactly a unique selling point," Elethin said, "and we can't compete against the big names on their terms."

"So we refine it," Fran said. She wasn't sure if it was the caffeine and sugar talking, but she suddenly felt excited. "A pure, purpose-built fun delivery system. Something that delivers games and shows and music and everything people love. Something that fires fun straight into your life."

"That's a console," Singar pointed out. "Someone already invented it."

"Oh." Fran sagged. "How about a magical one?"

"Philgard makes those."

She sighed. "So much for that."

"I don't know…" Singar had a thoughtful look on her face. "There's something in this, I can feel it, like a tingle in the back of my skull. If I can just work out what…"

Elethin sighed. "So after two hours, we have a tingling in your skull? I'd hoped for more."

"We'll come up with more," Fran said. "We've been coming up with ideas for new devices for weeks. We'll keep doing that, but now we'll be thinking about fun and quirky, about how they fit into that. We're bound to come up with something. If all else fails, we go back to the magical breakfast devices, only this time they tell jokes."

"No!" Singar and Smokey said together. "No more breakfast."

Fran grinned. "Then that should motivate you."

"Well, thank you for your time." Elethin picked up her laptop and headed back past the partition to the office.

Fran hurried after her.

"Elethin, do you think this is going to be okay?" she asked. "Like, can we make a brand that sells with everything we do?"

For a moment, Elethin didn't speak. Then a bright smile filled her face. "Of course, Fran. You get back to your inventing. Sooner or later, I'm sure that you'll come up with something."

"Thanks, Elethin."

Fran went back into the workshop. Liam was helping Singar and Smokey with the last of the clearing up.

"Everything okay?" he asked.

Fran hesitated. Elethin seemed fine on the surface, but something about her reaction had made Fran feel tense. She shook it off. It was probably the caffeine talking again.

"New idea," she said. "Bear with me on this one because it's going to sound like I'm totally targeting kids, but I think there's a big market among grown-ups. What if we made an enchanted bouncy castle?"

CHAPTER FIFTEEN

Elethin walked out of Worn Threads and over to the bus stop on the far side of the street. Simply standing there made her tense, muscles tightening in her shoulders and belly. Once, she'd been the sort of person who rode every-where in hire cars or her employer's private limousine. Now she had to use public transport, with all the dirty, smelly people who occupied it, the boisterous masses of the ignorant and unrefined. Some days, she wanted to weep at how appalling it all was.

A Kilomea walked out of one of the nearby buildings and joined her at the bus stop. He was wearing dirty jeans, a tattered t-shirt, and a ring through one of his tusks. She suppressed a shudder as he came to stand too close, smelling of sweat and brick dust.

"Busy day?" he asked with casual familiarity.

"It's been fine." She didn't look at him, only folded her arms across her chest and kept her gaze on the road, looking for any sign of an approaching bus.

"Mine's been busy. Turning that place into shops. Can you believe it?"

Elethin didn't answer. She spent her whole working day forcing herself to be pleasant to people. She didn't have to keep up the effort now.

"Nice suit," the Kilomea said. "You one of them tech executives?"

"No. Well, yes. Oh look, the bus is coming."

A covered wagon trundled down the street toward them, pulled by a pair of fast-running lizards. Elethin occasionally wondered whether Oriceran would ever abandon these forms of transport, as Earth had, and embrace the civilized elegance of the motor car. Still, if they hadn't done it while she'd been in prison, they probably weren't going to do it now.

The bus pulled up, and Elethin got on board, paying with an app on her phone. The app saved her a few cents on each journey, and every little bit counted right now.

Most of the seats were full. She found one next to an elderly Arpak with her wings tucked in under a shawl and perched carefully on the edge. The less of the seat she touched, the less likely it was to leave stains on her suit, one of the few nice possessions she still had. Until she could afford others, she couldn't risk damaging the one thing that marked her as a real professional.

The bus jolted away from the curb, and Elethin grimaced as she was flung back against the seat. She swayed with the vehicle's movement through the streets of Mana Valley, past shops and offices, apartment blocks, and leisure complexes. Someday soon, she would eat out again, not only at the chain restaurants in those complexes but at the elegant sorts of establishments she'd once known. Places where they made the food, not just heated it. Places with refinement.

The question was, could she achieve that while working for Mana Wave Industries?

She thought about Laurel Anders, standing outside the TV studio with a cigarette in her hand, offering Elethin a job. Right now, Mana Wave was paying out just enough to pay her bills, and even that had taken some negotiation with Bart.

Karmic Charisma would pay her a proper wage, one that matched her skills, one that could restore her to her old social standing. The sort of money that paid for nice suits and shoes, for dinners in fancy restaurants. Not that she would need to pay for many of those dinners: they could so often go on expenses if you were meeting with the right people. She wasn't meeting with the right people now, by any definition of that phrase.

"Careful with your feet," the elderly Arpak said.

Something sticky was oozing down the floor from farther back in the bus. Elethin shifted her feet in time to avoid staining her high-heeled shoes and tried not to think about what the fluid was.

"Those can't be good to walk in." The Arpak squinted at Elethin's heels. "How do you stay upright?"

"Poise and practice."

The bus rolled on, stopping every two minutes to let people on and off. Elethin fended off shopping bags and briefcases as people pushed clumsily past. This could've been productive time, responding to messages on the company's social media accounts, but she couldn't quite bring herself to do it. She was away from Mana Wave for the day. She didn't want to think about them.

The bus got emptier as they emerged from the heart of the city and headed out into the cheaper housing zones along one edge. At last, Elethin pressed the button for the next stop and got out of her seat.

"Take care, high heels," the old Arpak said.

"Thanks." Elethin forced a smile. At least the woman had been good enough to keep quiet most of the way.

The lizards skittered to a halt, the doors opened, and Elethin stepped down onto the sidewalk. Litter lay scattered across the dirty street, and people had piled up garbage bags next to the apartment building's steps. Was it garbage day, or had they run out of space in the building again? Elethin wished she didn't have to think about these things.

Someone had broken the building's front door lock. She didn't understand how that ever happened. It wasn't like anyone was going to break in. No one in the place had anything worth stealing. Was it local kids, bored and looking for something to break? Was it the result of one of the fights she kept hearing from neighboring apartments?

At least the elevator was working, although one look inside put her off using it. The mold that had been living in one corner since she moved in was now expanding across the floor, and it almost seemed to twitch. She'd told the building manager about it twice, but nothing ever seemed to happen. Rather than tread in that mess, she headed up the stairs. They weren't much better, but at least she didn't have to stand on the same spot for more than a second.

This was how she felt working at Mana Wave too—like

she had to keep moving so she didn't notice what she was standing in. Sure, the company had potential, the same spark of creativity that Fran brought as CEO. But the company, like its leader, lacked focus, and no matter what Elethin did, they kept getting distracted.

They'd been talking for weeks about what to make next. She understood the value of this creative time, but they needed to focus, make a choice, and start making a real impact. She'd hoped that talking to them about the brand would do that, but they still had nothing. Without something to pitch, her talents were going to waste. That meant any chance she had of progressing her career was withering too.

She heard the argument in her hallway before she even emerged from the stairs. It was the shifter from apartment 403 rowing with her boyfriend again. Elethin had no idea why the woman hadn't ditched him. All he seemed to do was stress her out and drink her beer, as she shouted any time they fell out. Now here he was again, standing in the hallway with his shirt unbuttoned, yelling at the top of his lungs.

"You've been going out and shifting with Robby again, ain't you? Don't deny it! I can smell him."

"What if I have?" The woman appeared in the doorway. "Robby's my pal. We've got a right to hang out."

"On the full moon, when you're both hot and bothered? I ain't standing for that. You need to stop seeing him."

Elethin stopped and stood, waiting impatiently. The guy was blocking the way to her apartment, and she didn't want to have to ask him to move, or worse yet to push past him. Give it two more minutes and either he'd storm off, or these two would be noisily making up in the bedroom. She could wait for that. She shouldn't have to.

"You want me to stop seeing my friends?" the female shifter asked indignantly.

"He ain't your friend. He's some loser hanging around, waiting to bone you."

"Robby's gay, you asshole."

"Yeah, right. That's what they all say, these nice guy losers."

"There's only one loser in my life, and I'm looking at him."

"Why you..." The guy pulled his hand back, ready to deliver a slap. His fingertips had turned into claws.

Elethin didn't like to get involved in her neighbors' business. She didn't even want to know about it. Still, that hand ready for a blow made something lurch inside her. Without thinking, she brought her hand up and cast a spell. The guy's shirt twisted up around his head, threads unraveling and restitching. He struggled as the cloth wrapped across his face and tied his arms together.

As the woman looked at her boyfriend in confusion, Elethin stepped in, facing him.

"I saw you," she hissed. "Raise a hand to her again, and I'll stitch up more than your clothes. Understand?"

"What the hell?" There was a tearing sound as the man struggled to free himself. He flailed a free hand at Elethin. "I'm gonna mess you up, you crazy—"

Elethin brought her knee up sharply. The shifter let out a pained gasp, then bent double.

"Words are usually my weapon of choice," Elethin said.

"If I ever see you again, I'll use them to call the authorities. Are we clear?"

The guy groaned and staggered off down the hallway, peering out through a rip in his tangled shirt.

The female shifter looked uncertainly from her departing boyfriend to Elethin.

"I don't know anything about you," Elethin said. "You could be a crime scene cleaner or a war criminal for all I care, but whoever you are, you're better than that guy."

"Thank you," the woman said quietly. "What happens if he comes back?"

"Then you send him away."

"I don't know if I can."

Elethin snorted in exasperation and strode off. Some people were no use at all.

The lock on her apartment door was stiff, but at least it worked. The lightbulb flickered when she turned it on, but at least it was working, unlike the hot tap in the bathroom, which duct tape still covered. The maintenance guy had promised to fix that a week ago and a week before that.

She flung herself down on the sofa bed that occupied a sizable part of the single space that served as bedroom, living room, and kitchen. If you could even call it a kitchen when it was only a microwave, a kettle, and a hotplate. The sofa was as lumpy now as it would be when she folded it out to sleep on. A giant spider scuttled across the cracked ceiling.

She took out her phone and looked at her messages again. There it was, Laurel Anders' message with her proposed pay at Karmic Charisma. That was only a starting point. If they were actively approaching Elethin, surely she could ask for more.

She closed her eyes and imagined a different life. An apartment in the center of the Valley with a real kitchen, a working hot water tap, and two properly stuffed sofas. No, make that three. A bedroom with a wardrobe full of suits, instead of hanging the two she had from a nail driven into the wall. New shoes, cocktails, restaurants, takeout meals, and nights out with the better sort of people.

Except that when she imagined the night out, somehow Fran was there. Not only her, but Singar, Bart, and Smokey, even Gruffbar sitting at the bar with a whiskey in his hand. They weren't glamorous. They weren't sophisticated. They weren't the power players like Elethin wanted to spend time with. Yet somehow, there they were, wedged into her imagination.

She looked at the message again. There were reasons to stay with Mana Wave if she wanted to take the risk. Nothing idiotic like loyalty to the people who'd taken the first chance on her after she got out of jail. Real reasons, like Fran's technology and the possibility that it would all pay off. Getting in on the ground floor of a tech innovator was the stuff that made fortunes.

No. She had to be realistic. Most tech startups failed. If she was starting to feel attached to this one, that was a reason to leave, not to stay. She had to get out before it was too late.

What Karmic Charisma was offering was a dream come true. Why not take it?

She hesitated, thumbs an inch away from replying to

the message. They'd offered her six figures worth of reasons to say yes, so what was stopping her?

Through the paper-thin wall, she heard the sound of her idiot neighbor making up with her terrible boyfriend. A chunk of plaster fell from the ceiling, bringing a spider down with it. Elethin gritted her teeth. If she screamed in frustration, one of her neighbors might take an interest, and she couldn't face that.

Her thumbs darted across the phone, typing out a message.

How soon can you arrange an interview?

CHAPTER SIXTEEN

Birds soared over the foothills above Mana Valley, singing sweetly to one another. On the slopes below, brightly colored flowers filled the air with their delightful scent while rabbits and deer dashed between the trees. Together, they basked in the sort of golden sunshine that famous painters dreamed of ever capturing on canvas. It was as close to perfect as a morning could get.

"Maybe I should be back in the office," Fran said as she walked up the hillside, along a trail beside a babbling stream. One of her crows flew beside her, croaking back to the other birds' songs. "I mean, this is time I could be working on the prototypes."

"Francesca Berryman," Irene said sharply. "You cannot spend every waking hour working. Start down that path, and you'll end up alone, with nothing to your life but work."

"I like my work."

"Still, there's more to life."

"Can't the other parts wait?"

"What happens if you push yourself too hard and burn out? How are you going to work then?"

"Slowly?"

Irene stopped and turned to face her daughter with her hands planted on her hips. Wearing walking boots and sturdy clothes, with her hair tied neatly back, she looked like she could've been a tour guide or an instructor on an Outward Bound program instead of a tourist out seeing the sights.

"What did Bart say to you yesterday?"

Fran kept her eyes on the ground as she walked past, mumbling.

"I'm sorry." Irene raised her voice as she strode after her daughter. "What was that? I couldn't hear it."

"He said that he was really worried and that I should take a day off."

"What did Gruffbar say when you told him you were planning to work today?"

Fran mumbled something.

"I'm sorry, I couldn't hear you again. I know you can speak clearly because you spent your whole childhood doing it. So, remind me, what did Gruffbar say?"

Fran sighed. "He said that if he saw me in the office today, he'd break my kneecaps, and I could take a day off in the ER because that would be healthier than carrying on like this."

"Why did they say those things?"

A smile disturbed Fran's sulky expression. "Because they're my friends, and they're worried about me."

"So, should you be in the office today?"

For a long time, the only reply was the *thud* of their boots against the trail and the flapping of the crow's wings.

"No," Fran said at last. "And it is kind of amazing out here."

They reached the top of a ridge, and a valley opened in front of them. Firebirds darted back and forth between the trees, leaving flaming trails through the air. Fran's crow fluttered up to fly with them. Blue and purple squirrels jumped from tree to tree, using skin flaps between their legs to glide across the wider gaps.

As Fran and Irene watched, the leaves fell from one part of a tall tree, and others burst from the next set of branches around, like spring appearing right next to fall.

"What is that?" Irene asked.

"A clock tree," Fran said. "The leaves grow and die in the same pattern every day, so you can use them to tell the time. The rumor is that they were created by accident in a magical pocket watch factory a couple of centuries ago. They only grow around Mana Valley and in a couple of specialist gardens at magical colleges because they need the dense magical atmosphere to survive."

"This place is amazing." Irene smiled and looked around. "Truly breathtaking. Why didn't you tell me about it before?"

"I guess I don't get out of the city much. Although I'm pretty sure I did tell you after that camping trip when I first moved out here."

"Well then, why haven't I visited before?"

"Because you don't like to be away from home?" Fran started walking again, and Irene followed her. The crow circled overhead. "Honestly, Mom, I'm kind of surprised by this whole move out here to Oriceran. It's not like you."

Irene made a face. "Perhaps I wanted a change."

"This is about the Evermores, isn't it?"

"Well, yes. I have to make sure you're all right."

"I can look after myself, Mom."

"You're wearing mismatched socks, dear. Sometimes you need a little help."

Fran looked down, past her pink flamingo t-shirt and cutoff jeans. One thick green sock and one short yellow one poked out of her walking boots.

"Maybe I wore odd socks on purpose," she said.

"Did you?"

"Look, a flying raccoon!"

The creature hovered at the side of the trail. It was like an ordinary raccoon, but with large butterfly wings sticking out of its back, and those wings beat frantically to keep it in the air.

"Aren't you amazing!" Irene took out her phone and snapped a photograph. "So fearless, watching us like that."

"I guess they don't see many people up here. We are off the beaten track."

"Just the way I like it." Irene took some more snaps of the surrounding trees. "This place is so wonderfully unspoiled."

As they carried on along the trail, the raccoon flew beside them, just out of reach, alternately looking ahead and shooting them anxious glances.

"Do you think he's trying to tell us something?" Fran asked. "Like the pets in movies that are trying to tell their owners about a lost kid or an accident or how the person next door really loves them?"

The trail turned sharply left.

"I think he might be telling us about that."

Only a few feet from them, a tangle of branches hung low across the path, weighed down by a nest of dirt and woven twigs. In the nest sat three baby raccoons, their delicate wings not yet strong enough to carry them into the air. The other parent hovered in front of them, looking at Fran and Irene with a mixture of anger and fear.

"It's okay." Fran held up her hands. "We don't want to hurt your babies. We only want to get past."

She moved to the edge of the track and kept walking. As she got closer, one of the adult raccoons, the one she had decided was the father, flew in front of her with its teeth bared.

"No need for that! We'll be gone soon, I promise."

Fran hoped that her tone and frantically waving arms might get the message across, but the raccoon was unimpressed. It flew at her, claws waving.

"Argh, help!"

Fran staggered back, desperately windmilling her arms in front of her face, trying to stop the raccoon from attacking her. Its claws were surprisingly sharp and left deep scratches across her skin. Her crow flew in to defend her, but the raccoon knocked the bird away with a swipe of its paw.

"I've got it, dear." Irene grabbed the raccoon from behind and pulled it away. Then the mother raccoon landed on her head, plunged its paws into her hair, and pulled.

Irene yelped and stumbled back, letting go of the father raccoon, which flew at Fran again.

"Please, stop," Fran called as it pushed her back in among the trees. Her heel hit a root, and she fell, sprawling in the dirt and leaf mulch. "We don't want to hurt you."

That seemed like an irrelevant point right then. She stood no chance of hurting the raccoon while it was giving her quite a beating, biting and scratching and pounding with its feet. Its wings beat frenziedly, filled with the furious energy of a creature protecting its young.

"Enough!" Fran closed her eyes, held a hand up in front of her face, and cast a blinding flash of light. The raccoon squealed and lurched back through the air, rubbing its paws against its face.

Fran got to her feet and unfastened the hoodie tied around her waist. She slowly stalked up to the raccoon, which was spinning in circles in the air, blinking and flailing blindly. It caught sight of her a moment before she reached it, but that wasn't fast enough. Fran brought the hoodie down over the raccoon, wrapping it in folds of thick, fleecy fabric. She hastily tied the arms around the opening, then pulled the string of the hood tight so the raccoon could only poke its nose out as it struggled against its soft prison.

With the captive raccoon under her arm, Fran strode out onto the trail again. Irene was staggering in circles, the mother raccoon still clutching her hair, dodging the flashes of light she shot at it. The babies had crawled out of the nest and were moving around with them, trying to bite Irene's ankles. They were so tiny and fragile, Fran was more worried that one of them might get crushed than that they might do her mom any harm.

As she approached, one of the babies turned to face her. It made a shrill impression of a growl, then leaped onto her boot and tried to chew through the toe.

"It'll all be okay." Fran ignored the little creature's efforts.

She raised her hand and fired a carefully focused beam of high-pitched noise at the raccoon on her mom's head. The creature shrieked in shock and clapped its paws to its ears. It fell away from Irene's head and fluttered back a few feet. When it realized that the noise was over, it raised its paws again, ready to fight.

At that moment, Irene had seized an advantage, picking up the two babies still at her feet, one in each hand. The little creatures squirmed, but she kept a tight hold. The mother froze in the air, only her wings beating, waiting in dread to see what would happen next.

"We really don't mean any harm." Fran peeled the other baby off her boot, walked over to the nest, and set it in among the woven twigs. With the father still wrapped up under her arm, she twisted her hand around to pull a dried mango bar from the side pocket of her backpack. She unwrapped it and dropped pieces into the nest. The baby sniffed at them, then picked up one between its tiny, adorable paws and chewed on it, making happy little sounds. The crow landed on the edge of the nest and watched, its head tipped to one side.

Irene carefully placed the other two baby raccoons in the nest. They immediately joined their sibling in feasting on the unexpected and tasty treat. The mother hovered over them, then tentatively settled on the side of the nest, looking from her babies to the women in something like approval.

At last, Fran unfastened her hoodie and let the father raccoon out. He burst into the air and hovered above them, snarling and hissing. Then his partner made a sound, and he looked down. Seeing the contentment on the faces of his offspring, he calmed down a little, though he still stayed well out of reach, ready to charge in and attack if anything went wrong.

"We should go," Irene whispered.

"I suppose." Fran took out her phone, snapped a photo of the baby raccoons, then stepped away from the nest.

She and Irene walked down the trail a short way to give the raccoons their space. The crow settled on Fran's shoulder.

"I should have a look at those scratches, dear," Irene said.

"Oh, yeah." The moment had caught Fran so thoroughly that she'd forgotten about her wounds. Now that she remembered, the sharp pain of them rushed back.

She sat on the trunk of a fallen tree. Irene took a first aid kit from her backpack and a bottle of water. Using the corner of a soft scarf as a cloth, she cleaned Fran's wounds. Back where they'd come from, the father raccoon still hovered, watching them with suspicion.

"He was very protective," Fran said.

"Fathers can be like that."

"Was my dad?"

Irene tensed. For a moment, her gaze went from Fran's scratches to the crow on her shoulder.

"Your father was complicated."

Irene took out some antiseptic and applied it to Fran's scratches. The stinging sensation would normally have been a distraction, but her mom's reaction made Fran want to ask about her father even more.

"Why don't you talk about my dad?" Fran asked in a small voice. She suddenly felt very vulnerable, in a way that a frenzied raccoon attack could never achieve.

Irene's hand went to her mouth, and she chewed for a moment on the edge of her thumbnail. Then she looked directly at the crow.

"This is private," she said. "Between my daughter and me. You go away."

The crow tipped its head to one side and cawed.

"I said shoo!" Irene lashed out at the crow with her hand. The bird took to the air, flying away with a harsh croak.

"Did you need to do that?" Fran asked. "The crows are friendly, and it's not like he's going to understand any of it, never mind tell anyone."

Irene dabbed Fran's scratches with the cloth. Her other hand was still at her mouth, her teeth worrying a nail. "I wanted us to be alone. That's all."

"Mom, are you okay?" Fran took Irene's hand. Her mother was trembling.

Irene drew a deep breath, lowered the hand from her mouth, and looked Fran in the eye. "I'm sorry that I didn't tell you about your father. I should've asked if that was something you wanted, but it never occurred to me. Or perhaps it did, but I was too worried to face it."

"Why worried? Was he a bad man?"

"Your father wasn't available for you."

"Other people's dads were there."

"Well, quite." Irene half-raised her hand to her mouth, then stopped herself. "There didn't seem much point in telling you about your father if he wasn't going to be part of your life. Maybe that was the wrong choice. I don't know. I was trying to do the right thing for you."

"Oh, Mom." Fran flung her arms around her mother. "You're here for me. That's all that matters."

CHAPTER SEVENTEEN

Howard Phillips knelt in the middle of his office. He'd sketched a ritual circle on the carpet in chalk dust, and candles flickered around its edges. The rotten scent of incense that would've made any real human sick filled the air.

He reached up, placed his hands on the back of his neck, and peeled open the top of his skin suit. It fell away from around his head, revealing the nightmare shape beneath. Eyes bulged on the ends of stalks. Tentacles crept out around the edges of his collar.

On the floor in front of him was a lead tablet, into which he'd scratched the word "EVERMORES." It was an old magic, crude magic, but one that could still work if the caster knew what they were doing. It was a way to vent his anger that magicals had been using for thousands of years. A way to strike a blow.

He ran fingers over the tablet, its cold, smooth surface, the sharp raised edges of the letters. Yes, this would work.

He'd told his lieutenants to be patient, and he'd meant

it. It would be smart to work slowly, carefully, to build up information on his opponents, to prepare before he faced them. Still, he felt the absence of the burned away eye as his eyes swayed on their stalks. He felt the injury they'd done him. No one had hurt him in centuries, and the anger it raised in his belly wasn't something he could refuse. He shouldn't do this, but he would.

He waved, and the flames of the candles turned to black. Then he picked up a stylus, an ancient pointed iron rod, and drove it through the lead. As the tablet bubbled and let out a cloud of oily smoke, he started to chant.

Enfield stood in the kitchen of the Evermores' shared house, with the door and windows wide open. Three small pans were bubbling on the stove, and another sat cooling to one side. He dropped a handful of herbs into a mortar, added several crystals, and pounded them with a pestle, grinding them to dust.

"Couldn't you do this somewhere else?" one of the other Evermores asked as she passed through. "This is where we cook, you know."

"I'll clean up afterward," Enfield said. "Where else am I supposed to make potions?"

"Your room, the garage, anywhere but here."

"If we had a proper alchemical lab, I'd use it. I need somewhere with water, heat, and suitable surfaces to work on. For now, that means the kitchen."

The other Evermore shook her head as she headed out the door and into the back garden.

A chime rang on Enfield's phone. In response, he switched the heat off under one of the pans and added a sprinkling of silver dust. The liquid in the pan shimmered, then went still.

Winslow walked in with a book in his hand and looked around. "Stocking up for a sale?"

"Getting ready, just in case," Enfield said. "If we have an enemy out there, we should be prepared."

"We always have enemies out there. That's what happens when you help to define the world."

"We have an enemy that's attacking us. Some precautions seem sensible."

"Very good." Winslow drummed his fingers against the book's cover, which showed a black and white photograph of a man posing in the street. "Enfield, how are you feeling? I imagine that the attacks could have disconcerted you. You're younger than most of us with only a few decades of experience. It would be understandable if you needed to go home and take some time to settle yourself."

"I'm fine." There was a *crunch* as Enfield ground the herbs and crystals in his mortar. "I want to do what we came here for."

"You think you're still up to that task?"

"I do."

"Very well. If you say so."

Enfield looked up at his superior.

"That wasn't agreement."

"Well observed. I have concerns. You seem unsettled."

Enfield hesitated. What was he supposed to say? Admitting that one of his concerns was Winslow's behavior—about the things he wasn't saying, the small discrepancies between the elder's words and the reality Enfield saw—seemed like the surest way to get sent home and never have a chance to resolve his doubts.

"I'm worried that you might send me home." It was close enough to the truth to be convincing. "How many more chances will I get to spend time out in the world?"

"Not many, if we do our job right." Winslow looked at Enfield for a moment, then nodded. "I understand. I was young once. Just try to keep your emotions steady. I don't want to unsettle the others."

"Of course, master."

Enfield bowed his head and went back to work. Seemingly contented, Winslow headed outside with his book.

Enfield ground the contents of his mortar a little longer. While he worked, he looked through the doorway from the kitchen into the dining room. There, the Source stood trapped, caught in the magical net of the containment unit. It glowed brightly, and from time to time the magic trembled as the Source made another attempt to escape.

The whole situation unsettled Enfield, this tension between the power of the thing they'd captured and of the technology holding it, between the immense forces they dealt with and the uncertain circumstances they found themselves in. The need to keep the Source secure and the other need, sooner rather than later, to move it.

"Pay attention, Enfield," one of the other Evermores said as he walked in. "Your potion's burning."

Enfield sniffed, then shook his head. "No, it isn't." He would've known. He'd had plenty of workshop accidents in his younger days.

"Then what's with the black smoke?"

Enfield looked around. Black smoke was drifting past the kitchen window, thick and oily, but it didn't come from inside.

He set the pestle and mortar down and stepped outside. Above the kitchen window, crude letters five feet tall had appeared across the house's brickwork as if carved by a giant chisel. "EVERMORES." The smoke was streaming from those letters.

"It's them again," Enfield said, dread clutching him. "We're under attack."

The smoke billowed out around him, then changed form. It took on the shapes of nightmarish hounds, their fur black, their eyes glowing red, and their teeth pale as bleached bones—creatures made of smoke and nightmares, growling from deep in twisted throats.

"Winslow!" Enfield shouted. "Evermores! We're under attack!"

Two of the creatures leaped at him, and there was no more time to give warnings. He flung a blast of light at one, and it howled in pain. The other hound slammed into him, knocking him to the ground. Its paws pressed against his chest, claws digging into his flesh. Its breath was hot against his face as its head closed in, teeth going for his throat.

Enfield pressed his hands against the hound's face, pushing it back, trying to keep those teeth away. He hooked a finger into the corner of its mouth, tugging, trying to twist it aside. Drool ran from its chin and burned as it touched his skin.

In desperation, Enfield pulled one hand back, and in

the second before the hound could bite him, fired a blast of light into its eyes. The creature shrieked, and its claws dug deeper into his chest, but its grip on him was less sure, its body less stable. One leg slipped off him, scratching him on the way. He took the opportunity, grabbed its leg, and leaned into the movement.

The hound fell off him, falling to one side, and Enfield leaped onto it. The two of them rolled across the garden in a cloud of dark smoke, grabbing and tearing at each other, both of them growling and fighting for all they were worth.

Around them, others were fighting too, the Evermores battling for their lives against the hounds. There were flashes of light in a hundred different colors, and strange sounds. Smoke filled the air, clawed at Enfield's throat, and made him gasp for breath. His arms trembled, and he became weaker.

The creature got on the top again, pressing him into the lawn. This time he was ready, despite the weakness of his muscles and the dizziness threatening to overwhelm him. He pressed both hands against its chest and let rip with all his power.

The blaze of light was intense, and the hound screamed in pain as it leaped off him. The smoke from the hole in its chest was different, not dark and thick but gray and dusty, falling like ashes.

"Get away from me!" He fired another blast of light. This one hit the hound full in the face. Fur burned away, and skin peeled back, revealing black bones.

Enfield rose to one knee. The hound was bracing itself,

about to charge him again. He'd spent almost all of his power. He gathered everything he had left.

The creature charged. Enfield fired all his magic in a single bright beam of light. There was a *hiss*, a *screech*, and pounding paws on the lawn. The hound slid to a halt at Enfield's feet, lifeless and unmoving. White smoke ran from the pencil-thin hole his light had burned through its head.

He got to his feet and looked around. The others were fighting hounds across the garden, but that wasn't what worried him. The real worry was the light flashing from the house.

Enfield ran through the fight, through the door, through the kitchen, into the room where the Source was held. A hound lay on the floor, its head hanging limp, and Winslow stood over it. The elder Evermore didn't look triumphant. His face was strained, his power streaming from him into the containment unit.

"Quick, Enfield," he shouted. "Bolster me. We have to stop the Source getting out."

Beside the hound, torn wires trailed from the base of the containment unit.

"If the containment unit is broken, how can we ever hold it?" Enfield asked.

"It's still working but damaged, and it needs our help. Now quick, bolster me before the Source gets out."

Enfield held up his hands and started to chant, but only the faintest flicker of power emerged. He'd used too much fighting the hound in the garden.

"Quickly!" Winslow said.

"I can't. No, wait, I can."

Enfield dashed back into the kitchen and grabbed one of the pans. The potion hadn't quite finished processing, but it should be good enough. At least, he hoped it would. He raised the pan to his lips and gulped it down. The liquid was still so hot, it burned on the way down, but he couldn't worry about that. This was the best hope he had.

The pan *clanged* empty on the floor. Clutching his roiling stomach, Enfield stumbled back into the dining room. The world was spinning around him and his guts hurt like hell, but he felt his power returning, boosted by the potion. He opened his mouth, fought back the urge to vomit, and chanted.

Light flowed from his hands, wrapped in the sounds of the spell. Strands of power ran from him to Winslow, who grabbed those threads of magic out of the air and fed them into his spell. The binding tightened around the Source, and it finally became still again.

Other Evermores ran in, battered and bleeding, light glowing from their hands.

"You two, reinforce the binding," Winslow snapped. "You, call Fran Berryman. We need Mana Wave's help right now." He looked at Enfield, and now he wore a triumphant smile. "I'm very glad you didn't go home. You've saved us from disaster today."

"Thanks," Enfield mumbled. Then he dashed out of the room as his stomach finally revolted.

Howard Phillips peered at the smoke drifting from the last melted remains of the lead tablet. The smoke had shown him brief flashes of the fight, images of the hounds he'd summoned, and the way the Evermores had fought back.

His enemies were strong. That was no surprise. They'd fought off the creatures. Still, these were only an imitation of the beasts he would release into the world once he opened the way to the nightmare realm—a weaker version. The real thing would surely overcome these Evermores.

He smiled, blew out the black flames of the candles, and pulled the skin suit back up over his head. As he pressed his face back into place, he glimpsed the carpet and how the molten lead had burned it. He would have to get that replaced. It was a small price to pay for this sense of satisfaction.

CHAPTER EIGHTEEN

Fran stepped out of her mirror portal and into the Evermores' garden. She was so used to seeing the place neat that it came as a shock to see it like this, with smoke in the air and the bodies of strange hounds scattered across the ground.

"In here," one of them called to her from the kitchen door.

Fran closed the portal and pocketed the mirror, then followed the Evermore into the house. Inside was equally bad. Smoke drifted around the ceiling, pans were boiling over on the stove, and another pan lay on the floor. Light flared in the doorway from the dining room, and when she stepped through, Fran saw why.

The Source was straining against the boundaries of its containment unit. Winslow and two of the other Evermores were using their magic to hold it in, but it was clear that this situation couldn't last.

"What happened?" she asked.

"That did." Winslow pointed at a dead hound like the

ones outside, lying next to the containment unit. Its teeth had scratched the mirror base, and there were torn wires next to it.

"Was it trying to steal the Source?" Fran knelt to examine the damage.

"I don't think so. If that was the plan, the rest would have followed it inside. I think it saw a power source and thought it could weaken me by attacking it." He grimaced as the Source made another bid for freedom, its bright body battering at the containment field. "In a sense, it was right."

Enfield walked in, wiping his mouth with the back of his hand. He looked pale, and his skin was damp with sweat. There were red stains on the front of his shirt.

"Are you okay?" Fran asked.

"I'll live," he croaked. "How's the containment unit?"

"Fixable, as soon as Singar gets here. She's bringing parts and tools."

"How soon will she be here?"

The roar of a motorcycle engine answered that question. A black Harley-Davidson pulled into the driveway in front of the house and skidded to a halt by the front door, with Gruffbar clinging tight to the handlebars. Singar leaped down from behind him. The two of them untied a set of boxes strapped to the back of the bike, then hurried into the house.

"Wriggling dung." Singar looked at the damage the hound had done to the containment unit. "You're lucky the whole thing didn't explode."

She set her toolbox down, opened the lid, and took out a screwdriver. Then she crouched beside the unit and started unfastening parts. "Fran, find some cables to reroute the field while we fix the base. Enfield, you know what the spare battery packs look like, right? There should be some in the red crate. Bring them here."

While the technicians set to work, Gruffbar took off his helmet and looked around. This was the first time he'd seen where and how the Evermores lived. The fight might've trashed it, but there was money under all of this, and he was quickly reevaluating how much work Mana Wave did for them for free. He was in favor of saving the world, but there was no reason why it couldn't pay.

Singar attached the new batteries, then pulled a wire out. The magical field flared. The Source flung itself against its cage, and the field buckled.

"One more minute." Singar looked up at Winslow. "You can manage that, right, old man?"

"Of course," Winslow said while the other Evermores raised a chant. Magic flowed between them and around the field.

"Chisel." Singar held out a hand. Fran handed her the tool, and she slid it under the edge of the magical field. "That thing's teeth managed to scratch one of the runes. I need to reinforce it, and…"

She scratched on the mirror's surface for several seconds, then drew back her hand. The Source writhed and twisted. The magic around it strained.

"Your turn, Fran," Singar said.

Fran took the Willen's place. She set a pair of battery boxes down next to the containment unit, ran wires to the closest clusters of crystals, and flipped a switch. The runes glowed brighter, and the field grew rigid. The Source flung itself futilely against the barrier one more time, then subsided.

Singar wiped the sweat from her brow.

"Is that it?" Winslow said. "The unit is fixed, the Source secure?"

Singar laughed bitterly.

"Dribbling dung, if it was that easy you could do this yourselves." She shook her head. "That's the temporary fix. It'll hold it while we do repairs and add some reinforcement. Importantly, it means that you lot can drop your spell and get out of our way." She jerked a thumb toward the door. "Anyone who's not working on this, get out. I need peace and quiet to do my job."

"As you wish." Winslow headed for the door, taking the Evermores with him.

"While we're out there, we should talk business," Gruffbar said.

"Enfield," Singar called. "You stay. We'll want the extra pair of hands."

"If I can help, I will." He sat back down on the floor beside her and Fran while the others left. "What would you like me to do?"

"Start by fetching the thaumic monitor. I want to get some proper readings on what's going on here."

Using a variety of tools from Singar's kit, they assessed the condition of the containment unit, measuring the flows of magic and electrical energy, the magnetic fields surrounding the prison, the types of powers at play. Enfield prodded the shield with a screwdriver and Fran poked at it with her magic, all while Singar took readings.

"This damage wasn't only about that hound," she said. "Take a look."

The others gathered around the tablet that she'd been using to collect and display their data.

"Oh," Fran said. "That's interesting."

"It is?" Enfield asked. "What am I supposed to see?"

On the screen was a complex graphic that used colors and textures to show the strengths and interactions of various magical forces woven together into the containment field. To Enfield, it looked like a bunch of rainbow-colored smudges, but the others were looking at it like they were reading an incredibly informative book.

"This is the break that came from the hound ripping things out," Fran said. "This next to it, it's a bigger tear. Not unrelated, but, like, not the same thing."

"Someone saw a weak spot and tried to make use of it," Singar said. "To make it bigger."

They all looked at the Source, glowing in its prison of magical energy.

"Could the Source do that?" Fran asked. "Is it smart enough?"

"Must be," Enfield replied.

"I thought it was all about instincts, not planning."

"Attacking the weak spot seems like a pretty instinctive move to me." Enfield didn't sound completely convinced.

"Whatever." Singar shrugged. "We need to rebuild the wiring, add some backups in case this happens again, and strengthen the field in case there's damage we didn't spot. Good thing we've got parts left over from building the FBI's copy."

"Have you heard any more from them?" Enfield asked

as he helped unload components from their boxes. "About how the field tests are going?"

"Nothing yet," Fran replied. "Agent Baldwin said that we might not hear anything until they've finished. So either everything's going so well that they don't need our help with the equipment, or it's going so badly that they're never going to work with us again, and they have to warn all the other government departments about us first." She smiled to convince herself as much as anyone else. "I'm joking on that last part. At least, mostly joking."

"Well, you tried." Singar handed her a bundle of wires. "Fran, you show Enfield how to align an extra set of crystals. I'll be doing the fine work around the mirror attachments. Don't disturb me until I finish."

She took a pair of earplugs from among her wrinkled folds of skin, stuffed them into her ears, and set to work.

It took all the rest of the afternoon and well into the evening to get the field stabilized and strengthened. Somewhere along the line, Winslow sent pizza in for them, and they took a break. Enfield ate more slowly and carefully than usual.

"Half-finished potions aren't good for anyone," he said. "They're even worse boiling hot."

"You should have a potion to fix that," Singar said.

"There is one. I hadn't made it."

"Not as smart as you thought, huh?"

"In the same way that you weren't smart enough to make your technology proof against monstrous hounds."

"Can't plan for everything."

"Exactly." Enfield glanced at Fran, who was rearranging

her pizza toppings into a smiley face. "What happened to your arms?"

"Huh?" She blinked at him, then looked at her scratched forearms and laughed. "Flying raccoons. It was sort of cute and sort of terrible. I can tell you about it once I've digested and my brain is, like, properly back in the room, you know?"

"I do. Low blood sugar's a real killer. Gets even worse when you use too much magical power."

"Was that why you looked so bad when we turned up?"

"Among other things." He looked down at his food with a frown.

When they got back to work, they weren't only doing repairs anymore.

"I talked to Winslow," Fran explained. "He wants us to start preparations to move the Source. After today, he's even more worried that it's not secure enough here."

"What sort of preparations did he have in mind?" Singar asked. "Buy it a train ticket to Evermore town?"

"I thought maybe we could add some extra stabilization to the field, then try summoning small portals around it. If we measure the interactions, we'll have a better idea of how to avoid—"

"Okay, okay, I get it." Singar tapped a screwdriver against her claws. "You're right. It makes sense to do that while we've got all this kit up here and we have Enfield to do the Evermore portal thing."

"Are you up to doing that?" Fran looked at Enfield with concern. His fingers had been shaking before dinner, and though that had stopped after the pizza, he still looked pale.

"I'll be fine," he said. "It's only small portals, right?"

They added more circuits and crystals, some attached to the base of the containment unit, others spread around the room, connected by wire and strings decorated with small cards showing magical runes. With every adjustment, they checked the containment field just in case, but it was holding strong. From outside, they could hear Gruffbar, Winslow, and the other Evermores drinking beer and chatting.

"Aren't you worried that you're missing the fun?" Singar asked.

"There's always more fun to have somewhere," Fran replied brightly. "I'm enjoying spending time with you guys. What could be better than an evening of invention?"

"I guess it's more fun than being him." Singar pointed at the Source. The Source nodded. "Yeah, you understand."

"Not him, it," Enfield said. "The Source is a force, not a person, however it looks. I know that its shape can be misleading, but it—"

"Like dung is that not a person," Singar said. "He heard what I said, he understood, and he nodded, didn't you?"

The Source nodded again.

"See?"

Fran frowned. She'd been accepting Winslow's word this whole time, but what if he was wrong? Worse, what if he was lying?

She picked up a card with a rune drawn on it, a spare leftover from the strings. She held it up so the Source could see.

"Can you make this shape?" she asked.

On the other side of the magical field, the Source raised

a hand. Fran half-expected it to do nothing relevant. Instead, its hand transformed into the shape of the rune.

"What about this one?" She held up another card. Again, it imitated the shape. "And this one?"

For a third time, the Source made a runic shape. Then it stepped back and stood with its arms folded, its featureless, glowing face seeming to watch her.

"It might be nothing," Enfield said. "Maybe instincts and forces of nature become complex in how they react to magic."

"Or maybe Winslow's been lying," Singar said. "Maybe this thing has more smarts and feelings than he's willing to admit."

Fran looked at Enfield, whose brow creased with worry.

"What do you think?" she asked quietly. "How much do you trust Winslow?"

"I don't know anymore," Enfield whispered.

CHAPTER NINETEEN

"If you could have any magical power in the world, what would it be?"

Cam, who hadn't been expecting any questions, never mind that one looked up in confusion.

"What was that, Jo?" He looked down the counter at his colleague, who was refilling the cake display.

"I said if you could have any magical power, what would it be?" Jo waved the tongs he'd been using to move brownies around. "No, wait, let me guess…"

Cam sighed and shut the lid of his laptop. He wasn't getting as much research done as he wanted anyway, not because of any great flood of customers, but because of his distractibility. His mind wasn't settling as it should.

"You'd want to read super fast," Jo said. "You spend so much time with your nose in a book that I bet you'd love to get through more of them." Jo picked up a supplier's catalog that they kept under the counter and riffled through the pages, the whole lot flying past in a matter of seconds. "Ah yes, another fine read, on to the next one."

"I do have things in my life apart from reading and this place." Cam prickled at the implication.

"Really? Like what?"

"Like… Well, all right, like not much else right now, but once I've finished my thesis, I'll get back to having a life."

Except that wasn't true, was it? Partly because with all the time he spent on other research, he was never going to finish the thesis. Partly because even once he finished that, the other research had to continue. Although no one else knew it, the world was relying on him.

"Sure, pal." Jo chuckled and started stacking cakes again. "You want to know what I'd have?"

"Fire magic."

"How'd you work that out?"

"You told me last month when you were planning that barbecue."

"Huh, yeah. Tell you what though, that was a good barbecue. You should've come."

"Maybe next time."

"Yeah, right."

Feeling that he'd probably fended off the need for conversation, for a little while at least, Cam opened his laptop again and got back to reading through broken fragments of prophecy and speculation, trying to piece it all together. The darkness, the destruction, the Evermores, the uncertainty about where the future of the world was heading…

"I'm going to fetch more donuts from the back," Jo said. "Try to keep your eyes on the counter."

"I always do."

Cam sat behind the register, where he would be sure to notice any approaching customers. If he didn't do that, someone would stop him reading on his shift, and that would be a colossal waste of time. He wished he was in the same position as Fran, able to spend his time following his passions, working on the things that mattered to him. Maybe one day, if he could ever convince his family that he was really onto something, and not a crackpot with no gift for magic.

A blonde witch in her twenties walked up to the counter with a thick book under her arm. She smiled at Cam. "Hi, there. How are you doing?"

"I'm great. And you?"

"Pretty good. Figured this was a good place to sit and read." She tapped the book, then glanced at Cam's laptop. "You usually have a book on the go, don't you?"

He laughed. "Yeah, a lot of the time. Today, I'm going over my notes." He reached for the coffee grinder. "Cappuccino, right?"

"You remembered!" Her smile widened.

"All part of the service. Coffee cake again, or something different this time?"

She licked her lips. "I'll have the blondie, please."

"Coming right up."

While Cam foamed milk and fetched cake, the witch talked about what she'd been reading, an art book covering some of the same modernists as an exhibit at the city gallery.

"I heard that the exhibit's really good," she said. "Thought I might go someday soon, but art's always more interesting when you have someone to talk about it with, to get different perspectives, you know?"

"Yeah, I get that." Cam put her coffee and cake on the tray. "Can't you talk one of your friends into going?"

"Most of them aren't really into art."

"That's a shame. Hopefully, you'll find someone." Cam turned his attention to a dwarf waiting behind her. "What can I get you?"

A small line of customers had formed, and new arrivals kept Cam busy for the next twenty minutes. Every time someone else came in, he looked up to see if it was Fran or any of the Mana Wave crew, but it never was. Admittedly, if she came in she might've been with that Liam guy, which wasn't what Cam wanted to see, but he could've tolerated it to see Fran. He missed having her around.

"I don't think this is what I ordered," an elf said as he handed over her drink.

Cam looked down at the cup of frothy vanilla-flavored coffee with silver sprinkles on the top. "Sorry. My mind must have drifted. I was thinking about another customer."

He set that cup aside and made a fresh one, making sure to pay attention this time. Once finished, he called to Jo.

"Can you take over here? I want to take my break."

Needed to take a break, more like, to get his brain back into gear. Twenty minutes out from behind the register, solidly focusing on his research, should help shift his thoughts away from Fran.

"Sure, no problem." Jo walked over and took Cam's place. "Hey, is this yours?"

He held out the accidental coffee with the silver

sparkles. Cam looked back, his laptop and a book already under his arm.

"I guess so." He took the cup.

He went to one of the tables at the back of the room, like he usually did if they were free. Convenient, out-of-the-way tables, good for concentration. The tables where Mana Wave used to sit when they worked in the coffee shop. The blonde witch was sitting at one of those tables, and she waved at Cam as he walked past. His hands full of books and coffee, he smiled and gave her a brief nod in return.

He sat with his back against the wall, opened the laptop, and opened the book to a page he'd bookmarked with a sticky note. It was the start of a chapter on the interpretation of prophecy by a scholar from the Eternal Towers College, which had one of Oriceran's leading departments for the study of prophecy and scrying.

Cam had never had the chance to study the subject at college, had barely even realized that there were whole teams of people thinking and writing about how prophecies could be unpacked. He hoped this one could help him understand the pieces he'd found.

He read a couple of pages and took a sip of his vanilla coffee. He didn't normally go for such sweet drinks, but he could maybe get a taste for it. The shiny silver sprinkles made him smile, reminding him of Fran's sparkling tops and sequined shoes. He wondered if she'd ever studied prophecy. It seemed unlikely, given her work, but some science grads took courses in the arts. Maybe he should ask her, just in case.

Except that would mean telling her about what he was

doing, and he still wasn't sure what connection, if any, there was between her and the Evermores. He trusted Fran, but what if the Evermores were close to her and she let something slip? Or what if telling her about the prophecy led to her getting the same treatment he'd received from his family, mocked for believing in truths that the rest of the world considered crazy?

He shook his head and forced his attention back to the page. He needed to start taking some of this stuff in.

"Back to the books, huh?" the blonde witch said, leaning over from her table. "Are you studying something?"

"Research," Cam said. "For my, uh, thesis."

"Oh wow." The witch smiled at him across her coffee. "A proper academic, huh? What are you studying?"

"History."

"History is so fascinating." She cupped her head in her hand. "What period are you looking at?"

"Seventeenth-century Earth. The unseen influence of magical factions on the conflicts in Europe during that period. Things like the English Civil Wars and the Thirty Years' War. You know much about them?"

"Not really. Wasn't there something to do with religion?"

"Something to do with religion? Yeah, you could say that." Cam grinned. There was a reason why he'd gotten into history in the first place and why he'd decided to research this topic.

"Religion is the lens through which we understand so much of that period. The conflicts, the cultural and social transformations, the terrible wars. Sure, there's a lot of work that considers the religious upheavals as symptoms of other trends, maybe a bit too much of that, in fact. But one of the potential underlying trends that nobody's properly looked at is the influence of magicals because no one at the time knew that there were shifters and wizards and people like that dealing with their own struggles. Of course, until a generation ago, almost no one on Earth knew about that or talked openly about it, so there's no scholarly tradition, which makes it completely new territory for..."

Suddenly realizing how much he'd been talking, he halted. The witch had been looking at him the whole time, her only reaction a small smile. "Sorry, I'm boring you, aren't I?"

"Not at all. I love hearing people talk about the things that enthuse them. You can make anything interesting if you're insightful and passionate about it. Passion is so important, don't you think?"

"It really is."

He thought about Fran again and her passion for magical technology. She'd managed to turn that passion into focus, into commitment, into getting the job done, while he kept getting distracted.

"Sorry, I should get back to this." He smiled sheepishly and gestured at his book. "I only get so many breaks, and if I don't make myself focus on the work, I'm never going to get it done."

"Sure, of course." The witch blushed. "Sorry for distracting you."

"No need to apologize! It's always good to talk."

"Well, maybe we could talk again sometime when you're a bit less busy with your studies?"

"Absolutely. Next time you're in, I promise at least thirty seconds of undistracted conversation."

"A whole thirty seconds? I am lucky!" She laughed. "Be careful. I might hold you to that."

She winked and turned back to her coffee while Cam got back to reading his book, occasionally adding a note from it to the huge file full of research on his laptop, almost none of it relating to seventeenth-century Europe. Fran came from Earth, didn't she? He wondered if her family had originally been European, how they had been affected by the conflicts of that period.

He rubbed his hands across his face. This was getting ridiculous. As if he didn't have enough distractions already, between fending off his thesis supervisor, doing his shifts in the shop, and dealing with day-to-day reality, now he had this terrible case of Fran on the brain. He was letting himself get distracted from the most important work he'd ever done. Maybe if he'd gotten around to asking her out, he might've been able to focus.

No, a more realistic part of his brain told him. Then he would have been even more distracted. Maybe it would've been a good sort of distracted. It was important to have a life outside of work, right?

"Hey, Cam!" Jo called from the counter. "You coming back soon?"

Cam looked up. A line of customers had formed, and Jo, never as fast with the coffee machine or the register as Cam, struggled to serve them. Cam glanced at the time on his computer. His break was nearly over anyway.

He downed the last of his coffee, complete with vanilla

syrup and silver sprinkles, and smiled at the thought of someone else sprinkled with sparkling colors.

"See you around." He grabbed his laptop and book.

"See you." The blonde witch smiled and waved as he walked past. "Enjoy your research."

"I'll try."

First, he had coffees to serve.

CHAPTER TWENTY

Singar walked into the Blazing Bean with a bag over her shoulder and a reusable coffee cup in her hand. Cam and one of his colleagues had just got a queue of customers under control, and she didn't have to wait long to get served. That was good. After wasting a whole day dealing with the Evermores and their containment unit, she needed to get back to her work.

She rubbed her eyes and yawned, baring her pointed teeth. The whiskers wobbled around her rodent nose.

"Hi, Singar." Cam leaned over the counter to take her cup. "Black Americano?"

"Extra strong, plenty of sugar," she said. "I need the wake-up call."

"Long night working on new ideas at Mana Wave?"

"Yep." The lie emerged instinctively. Everyone at the company understood that they shouldn't talk about the Evermores to outsiders, so they usually described anything relating to them as company business. It wasn't untrue. It just wasn't the sort of work that was going to build their business.

"Have you worked out what your new product is going to be yet?"

"Why do you think I look like this?" She pointed at the extra bags under her eyes. "Day after day, brainstorming ideas and improvising prototypes." She shook her head. "See, I even used the word brainstorming like I meant it. That's how bad this has got."

She accepted the coffee and waved her card across the payment machine, then slipped the card back into the pocket of her shirt.

"This is why I need this." She held up the coffee like a banner she would follow into war. "To give me a bit of mental energy, shake some ideas loose."

"A world of inspiration cupped in the palm of your hand."

"Something like that." She waved and headed for the door. "Later, coffee boy."

Outside, the sun was shining brightly. Singar unhooked a pair of shades from her bag and covered her beady eyes, then walked on down the street. As she walked, she looked around her, trying to get inspiration from everything she saw. Sometimes that was what was needed, random things in the world providing the grit around which a pearl of an idea would form.

A bus stop. What could they make for that? One that talked to you about what bus was coming? No, too practical. They were supposed to be delivering fun.

A billboard where the ads emerged into three dimensions,

using illusion magic to sing and dance and sell the products to passersby? No, far too obnoxious. Singar didn't want to live in a world where the adverts were even more in her face.

A wizard walked past, pushing an infant in a stroller. The tiny child was waving a stick like it was his very first wand. Was there something in that, making wands for kids that only cast fun, harmless spells? No, too cute, and the market was too limited. Plus she could imagine the look on Gruffbar's face when she told him she wanted to empower tiny children magically. The mayhem that would cause was a lawsuit waiting to happen.

Still lacking inspiration, Singar reached Worn Threads. The doors were open, and she strolled in, taking off her dark glasses as she entered the welcome shade. Gail, one-half of the couple who owned the store, was behind the counter, doing crochet.

"Another one turning up late." She looked out from behind her curtains of long blue hair. "You lot must have really been burning the midnight oil."

"Unfortunately, yes."

Singar thought back to the Evermores' house and the hours they'd spent running tests on the containment unit while Enfield summoned small portals around it to see how they affected the magical field. The guy wasn't as completely useless as she'd first assumed. Shame he was stuck with the rest of those over-aged idiots.

The work had been interesting, which was something in its favor at least, and Singar felt she had learned some things about magical fields from what they'd done. An hour spent toying with magical technology, testing the limits of what a device could do and how you could improve it was never an hour wasted. What they'd learned might even be useful when they went over to mass production for the FBI contract, if that came through. Right now, it would've been better if they'd focused on potential new products, the ones that might earn them money soon.

Down the stairs at the store's back, she reached Mana Wave HQ. Elethin, Bart, and Gruffbar were at their desks, the dwarf wearing dark glasses and holding his cup of steaming coffee. He'd still been drinking beer with Winslow when they'd stopped working last night, and he seemed to be suffering the consequences now.

"Did you get my email?" Elethin asked, more loudly than usual. Gruffbar winced, and the elf smiled.

"Which email?" he muttered.

"The one I just sent."

"I'll read it later."

"Okay, you do that." Elethin turned back to her keyboard and started typing as noisily as a living being could.

Past the office space, Singar reached the workshop. Smokey was at his computer and Fran was at the central workbench, yawning as she soldered circuits together.

"Morning," Fran said brightly, despite the yawn.

Smokey looked up. "Actually, it's already—"

"Don't care," Singar snapped as she slung her bag of parts onto the bench. "We were working late last night. Where were you?"

"Paws and Claws meeting. I have other things going on outside this place."

"Good for you." Singar's voice was heavy with sarcasm.

A crow landed on the workbench and peered curiously into Singar's bag. It croaked and pecked at a wire.

"No, it's not a worm." Singar shooed the bird away. "If you do that again, I'll pull all your mangy feathers out one by one."

She set her coffee down, climbed onto a stool, and carefully emptied the bag's contents.

"Hey, it's your image projector!" Fran looked with interest at the largest item Singar had taken out, a device with the common magitech combination of wires and circuitry, crystals and runes. "Have you been making some changes?"

"Trying to."

Singar forced herself to slide the device into the middle of the workbench. Her instinct was to hold her work close, to stop others interfering with or imitating what she did. However, one of the great advantages of working with Fran was that she came up with ideas Singar wouldn't have thought of, whether the inspiration for an entire device or a surprising solution to a technical challenge.

Some of those ideas were garbage, but some of them were brilliant, and Fran didn't seem to mind her pointing out which were which. It wasn't a feeling that Singar was comfortable with, but she had to admit, they worked well together.

"After Elethin's brand talk, this was an obvious one to go back to," Singar said. "Theoretically, it could project images on any topic. Educational videos, warning signs, whatever. But the original thought was entertainment, and that seems to be where we're heading."

"It's a fun delivery system!" Fran said brightly.

"I hate that phrase."

"What's to hate? It's a lovely idea, and Elethin said it could be useful for branding."

"Two more reasons to hate it."

Singar set her phone down on the workbench and brought up a photo of complex, intertwined magical circuits.

"What's that?" Fran asked.

"It's the magically grown tech we saw around that kemana crystal under San Jose." Singar tapped the screen, zooming in on part of the circuitry. "The place where we captured the Source."

"Ooh, I forgot about that."

"You forgot about capturing the Source?"

"No, that would be silly, even by my standards. I forgot about the circuits. Do you think they could be useful?"

"There are some interesting ideas in there, things I've not seen before. I've been trying to use some of them on the projector to see if I can make it better."

"That's so cool! Can I help?"

They set to work rebuilding the projector. At Fran's suggestion, Smokey also started working on it, looking into the software behind entertainment systems, considering what might be involved. As he made notes and filled research documents with chunks of other people's code, the other two built their new version of the device.

"Hi, guys." Liam walked in, carrying a holder of cardboard cups and a Blazing Beans bag. "I brought coffee and cake."

"I do like cake." Fran took the bag and looked inside,

temporarily distracted from technology by the desire for sugar.

"You two look exhausted," Liam said. "Late night out on the town?"

"No, we were—" Fran stopped herself in time. The Evermores were still supposed to be a secret, something they only shared among themselves, and much as she liked Liam, he didn't count as an insider yet. Soon, once they'd established the working relationship between their companies, and once Winslow had a chance to meet and approve of him, then she could tell him about that side of their work. Until then... "We were working on new ideas."

"You really know how to live." Liam laughed. "I guess this makes you great business partners if you're so committed to the cause. What are you working on today?"

Singar flicked a switch, and the projector hummed into life. After a moment, a hazy image appeared above it: a well-known Willen rock singer, her guitar around her neck, raising a middle finger to the world.

"Got to show you all a positive role model," Singar said. "Delivering fun, right?"

She changed a couple of wires and flicked another switch. The image shifted. It was still the same Willen in the same pose, but the picture quality was better, the light that formed it adding clarity and sharpness that hadn't been there before.

"This is with the new circuitry," Singar said. "Already an improvement."

She tapped the screen of her phone, which connected to the projector with a wire. The image rotated in the air.

"Did this turn a two-dimensional picture into three

dimensions?" Liam looked at it like a dwarf who'd stumbled into his private gold mine.

"No, this was a 3D render off the web." Singar tapped the screen, and the image stopped moving again. "That's not a bad idea if we can work out how to do it."

She reached out to run a finger through the image to see how it disrupted the light. As she touched it, she felt something beneath her fingertip.

"Is that solid somehow?" She kept pressing. Her hand went in, disrupting the image, but there was more resistance than light alone should have given. She pulled her paw out and looked down at the circuitry. This was unexpected and full of potential.

"Wow." Fran prodded the image and giggled as it resisted her touch. "I wonder what happens if I shine light through it."

She was about to summon light, then remembered just in time that she was keeping her Evermore powers secret from Liam still. She pulled out her dummy wand, waved it, chanted the word of a spell, and let her light flow.

The light shone through the image, which went a little grainy, then started to move as if animated. The hand with the raised finger waved back and forth as the Willen's face curled into a punk rock snarl.

"Uh, Fran." Singar tapped the projector. "Look."

The new circuitry that Singar had added, the part inspired by the kemana, was glowing, light shining brightly from small crystals that had previously been mute and even glowing from the wires.

"Wow, how did that happen?" Fran asked.

Singar looked from the circuits to the light shining

from Fran's hand. Everything had changed once Evermore magic had entered the equation. The kemana that the Source had been so intent on disrupting inspired the circuits. There was a connection there. This magical technology was related to Evermore magic, or something like it, and could tap into that power.

If they could tap into it, this could give them a huge edge over their competitors, a way to make use of more of the same magic that Fran had been putting into her batteries. Maybe even a way to tap into that magic without the limited resource that was Fran Berryman touching every single thing they made.

This raised questions too, about that kemana, maybe about other kemanas, and about how they related to the Evermores. Questions that made Singar suspicious.

"Does this have something to do with my E—" Fran stopped herself just in time again. "With how I cast magic?"

"Probably only something in the new circuits," Singar said. The less they shared in front of Liam the better. She didn't want to give him even a hint of something that might make Fran and her secrets vulnerable. "Let's take them apart, have a proper look at what's happening, and see what we can do. If this can improve the images we project, we could end up delivering a whole truckload of fun."

CHAPTER TWENTY-ONE

Josie sat at her computer, typing up the notes from the latest round of Manaphone tests. Today had specifically been about the sensors, checking for sensitivity and problems with interference. It wasn't as exciting as their initial free-wheeling test session, but Philgard Technologies took a very thorough approach to its work. That was part of how the company had become such a dominant force in magitech.

She reached for a carrot stick from the tub sitting on her desk. She should've stopped work two hours ago, like everyone else on the team, and headed home for a proper meal. Still, they were so close to finishing this round of tests, and she wanted to show management how well her team could beat their targets.

Footsteps approached, sounding loud through the empty office.

"You're still here?" Julia Lacy approached Josie's desk. "No wonder you're making such a good impression."

"I try."

"No, you succeed." Julia glanced at the carrot sticks. "Healthy eating, huh? I was thinking of going for some sushi. You want to join me?"

"One second…" Josie wasn't going to turn down a chance to hang out with the boss's PA, especially when Julia had been friendly and supportive so far. Still, she'd done so much work on this already. She wanted to make sure there was something for other people to see tomorrow. She typed a last couple of sentences, including a promise of more to come, then hit "Send." "All right, let's do it."

She switched off her computer, put on the jacket hanging over the back of her chair, and grabbed her handbag. On the way down the office, she put her remaining carrot sticks into a fridge in the communal kitchen.

"Where are we going?" she asked as they waited for the elevator.

"There's a place on the corner that does great sushi and cocktails. The manager always keeps me a table when I ask."

"On the corner… You mean Sorceress Sushi?"

"That's the one."

"I've never been there. It looks very elegant." By elegant, Josie mostly meant expensive, but she didn't want to admit that out loud. She didn't want to say anything that might offend or annoy her new friend.

"You're on the management track now," Julia said. "You can afford to treat yourself sometimes. In fact, you practically have to. It's part of how you build the right image."

The doors of the elevator opened and they stepped inside. Julia hit the button for the first floor.

"The right image?"

"Sad to say, promotion around here is as much about who you know as what you know, and presentation is part of how you manage that. Don't worry too much. The first round of martinis is on me."

It was only a few minutes' walk from the lobby of Philgard Technologies to Sorceress Sushi. As Julia had said, the manager, a red-headed elf with a tiny piercing through her nose, had reserved a table. She welcomed them both warmly and led them to their seats.

"The usual to drink?" she asked.

"Absolutely," Julia replied. "Martini for you too?"

"Why not?" Josie grinned. "I've earned it today."

"We earn it every day."

As the manager headed off, Josie looked around their table, trying to spot a menu. Julia laughed.

"No need to order your food here. The place has an enchantment that lets them identify the perfect sushi for you."

"That seems like awfully specific magic."

"It's what makes it so good. You always get the meal you wanted."

"But they had to ask about the cocktails?"

"Apparently the chef's magic only works when there's rice involved. Don't worry though. They have some of the best cocktail waiters in the city, so that part's great as well."

Josie relaxed a little and looked around her. The restaurant had the right level of background sound, a little minimalist music, and a quiet bubbling of conversation. On the walls were abstract paintings that looked like they'd been inspired by mountains and waves, with smooth gray and blue curves that were soothing to see. The furniture was as elegant as the staff, all neatly turned out in matching vests, and the customers were the sort of suited magicals she saw in the pages of business magazines.

"You didn't abandon some plan for this, did you?" Julia asked. "I should've checked first. Don't want you giving up on a date simply because the boss' PA came calling."

"No date." Josie shook her head. "I was seeing a guy for a little while, but nothing serious, and he started getting jealous when I got promoted. Once it stopped being fun, it wasn't worth it."

"Ha!" Julia shook her head. "I've seen that before. Half the divorces in Philgard come from when women get promoted, and the other half can't cope with playing second fiddle."

"That happens a lot?"

"More than in some of the other firms. Magitech's better than a generation ago, but it still has an excess of testosterone at the top. I'm lucky. When I got to Philgard, there was an informal network of women in place, supporting each other's careers. As others moved on, I've tried to maintain that tradition."

"So I'm part of a crusade?"

Julia laughed. "You could put it that way. But I only recruit witches I like to help fight the good fight."

Their cocktails arrived, followed a moment later by two platters of sushi. While the manager stood by, smiling, Josie picked up a pair of chopsticks and took her first bite.

"Oh my!" she exclaimed. "That is so good!"

"Exactly what you wanted?" the manager asked.

"And I didn't even know it!"

"Just checking." The manager winked. "Bon appetit." Then she walked away.

"You know, you're making quite a splash at the firm," Julia said. "Your feedback on the new Manaphone was far better than what we'd been getting before. Howard was very impressed."

"Howard Phillips?"

"Of course. Who else would I mean?"

"I…" Josie took a sip of her martini to cover her moment of bewilderment. It didn't seem right for anyone to refer to Howard Phillips, this giant of magitech, so casually as "Howard," but she supposed it was his name. For the second time, she was being told that he had seen her work —not only seen it but liked it. "So they're going to use it to refine the phone?"

"Oh yes!" Julia chewed thoughtfully on a piece of sushi before she continued. "It's caused quite a disturbance, actually. Howard didn't only send it to the implementation and manufacturing teams for refinement. He's sent the phone right back up to the original design group, along with a copy of your feedback and a demand that they get more ambitious."

Josie looked at her sushi to keep herself from staring at Julia. She was trying hard not to feel overwhelmed. After all, this was what she'd joined the company for, wasn't it? In the hope of making a real difference, bringing innovation and refinement to their products, being part of how the very best magitech was made. It was happening so suddenly, so quickly, she hadn't prepared herself. She'd seen how her team had responded to her sudden rise…

"Isn't this going to piss some people off?" she asked.

"Of course it is."

Josie groaned. "It all seemed to be going so well."

"It is!" Julia pointed at Josie with her chopsticks. "You need to learn not to be afraid of treading on people's toes. Anyone who makes a real difference will make some people mad, some of them for good reasons, some for bad ones, some for no reason at all. You can't make a difference without making a disturbance, and you're here to make a difference, right?"

"Absolutely."

"Great. Then don't let their hurt feelings get in your way. You've done something valuable. The ones smart enough to see that will get over it all once the dust settles. The others are the ones you'll have to fight the whole way up, so there's no point in appeasing them."

Josie took a long drink from her cocktail. What Julia said made sense, but it was a lot to take in.

"So I need to be more ruthless?" she asked.

"When people call a woman ruthless, they're usually only trying to put her back into her box. Don't accept that label. All you're doing is your job, and you're doing it damn well."

Josie ate some more of her sushi. That and the cocktail were helping to settle her nervous tension. Julia was right. There was no reason why she should feel bad. In fact, she should feel excited right now. She was rising through one of the most powerful companies on Oriceran. She had the personal attention of Howard Phillips. She'd made friends with his PA.

"Go on." Julia looked at Josie's face. "Whatever the

thought is that you're not quite letting yourself say, now's the time to bring it out."

Josie ate another piece of sushi, then drew a deep breath. She would encourage her friends to think some things about themselves but felt she couldn't say them about herself. In Julia's presence, she felt like it might be all right.

"I'm really good at what I do," she said. "I'm a goddamn god of magitech."

"Damn right you are!" Julia laughed and raised her glass. "Here's to that."

They *clinked* glasses, then polished off their martinis. At a wave of Julia's glass, fresh cocktails appeared.

"You know your impact goes beyond the Manaphone, right?" Julia asked.

"There's more?"

While they ate the rest of the sushi, Julia explained the other changes Phillips was considering based on Josie's feedback. He was looking at reforms to the company's whole design and quality assurance process, ways to get more high-quality feedback, to get it sooner, to build better products from the start. Conversations were going on across the highest levels of the business, thanks to what she'd done.

"Don't get too confident about it," Julia said as they polished off the last of the food. "I've seen this before. Sometimes innovation takes hold. Sometimes it suffers a suffocating death by committee. Whatever happens, people will remember your name."

An elf got up from one of the nearby tables and came

over to them. He had striking features, piercing blue eyes, and dark hair.

"Julia." He smiled widely. "Haven't seen you in a while."

"Far too long." Julia smiled at him.

"Who's your friend?"

"Talthin Crane, this is Josie Bullworth, one of the brightest new lights at Philgard. Josie, this is Talthin Crane, CEO of Telespell."

"Uh-huh." Josie fought to keep her cool, faced with another of the biggest names in Mana Valley. "It's great to meet you."

"That's a face that says you've heard of me, but this is the first I've heard of you. If Julia's bringing you here, you must be really something."

"I try, I mean, uh…" All Josie's confidence of a moment before scattered before his dazzling smile and honeyed voice.

"Oh, quit it, Talthin." Julia tapped the executive on the arm. "Get back to your meal, your wife's waiting."

Talthin winked, and the magical charm around him fell away. He was still a handsome and well-dressed man, but Josie at least found that she could think straight again.

"I hope to see you again, Josie." He headed back to his table.

"Wow, he's…" she began once he was out of earshot.

"A total sleaze." Julia leaned forward and lowered her voice to a conspiratorial whisper. "And not worth the effort."

"You mean you…"

"A couple of times. He's fun, but he's still using the same moves most boys learn when they're seventeen. Unless you really want a job at Telespell, you can do better around here."

"I didn't mean to..."

"I know." Julia laughed. "It's a terrible idea anyway, the surest way to lose people's respect. This whole valley is a quagmire of gossip. That doesn't mean you can't have some fun." She spun her glass between her fingers. "One more before we call it a night?"

"Sure." Josie laughed. "Thanks for bringing me here. Tonight has been a revelation."

"Maybe next time we could do this on a Friday so we don't have to consider a curfew? We could hit the bars where the real Mana Valley stars go."

"That would be amazing."

"I'm so glad. It's great to have someone I can do this with again."

Josie grinned. It was fantastic, having someone like Julia she could talk with. Someone who knew how their industry worked and knew the people and places to make progress. A friend who could advise her and also encourage her. Someone good who she could trust.

CHAPTER TWENTY-TWO

Elethin got off the bus a stop ahead of the one outside Karmic Charisma's office. She didn't want them to see how she'd traveled, and she didn't want them to see her before she could tidy herself up from the journey.

Of course, there was a coffee shop on one of the corners along the way, like there was a coffee shop or a bar at almost every free corner in this part of Mana Valley. She went inside and straight to the bathroom to fix her makeup and hair. She also checked that nothing ghastly had gotten stuck to her skirt or shoes while she sat on the bus. With lips touched up, stray hairs tucked back, and her jacket straightened, she confidently headed back out onto the street.

There was another reason why she got off a stop early, and now she looked around carefully before heading for her meeting. She didn't want anyone she knew to see her, especially not anyone connected to Mana Wave. Her colleagues were unlikely to come here, but there were the investors, suppliers, and other contacts to consider.

She didn't want any risk that news of her interview would get back to the others. Not until this was a done deal. She couldn't bear the thought of Fran trying to haggle, debasing herself by pleading with Elethin to stay. It wasn't dignified, and Elethin valued dignity, even in a silly little witch like Fran Berryman.

Karmic Charisma had offices in a modern office block. The place had been built with magic, melting glass panels together to become a single sheet filling the whole front of the building. It was wildly impractical, but she assumed that the owners had the spellcraft to repair the glass if it developed a crack. If not, it would be incredibly expensive to replace. The contrast with Mana Wave's no-rent basement headquarters couldn't have been stronger.

Seventeen different companies occupied different floors of the building, all filling different niches in the complex ecosystem that was Mana Valley business. There were three venture capital firms, two management consultancies, and even an organization that specialized in providing niche magical services. Karmic Charisma was the only public relations firm there. Their logo was among the others in a floating display in the lobby, the engraved stone symbols rotating on some sort of invisible magical disk.

Elethin walked past that particular ostentation and introduced herself to the building's receptionist, who provided her with a temporary security pass and directions to Karmic Charisma. Elethin could've worked the latter part out for herself. "Take the elevator to the twelfth floor" wasn't a difficult concept to master. Still, it often paid to be nice to the little people, so she thanked the receptionist enthusiastically before heading through the security gate and pressing the up button.

The elevator was an imp-powered one, and the designer had thought it would be clever and interesting to show the occupants how their journey was powered. Elethin wasn't so convinced. She found the sight of the imps in their glass cages, hauling on chains to drag the elevator up, more than a little disconcerting.

She smiled and looked at them as if they were something of interest anyway, putting on a show of being the sort of person who was fascinated by architecture and design. Even when you were with strangers in an elevator, it paid to put out the right impression, especially in a building like this, a building she hoped to return to very soon.

When she stepped out of the elevator, Laurel Anders waited for her. The witch held out her hand for a handshake that had the sort of firmness Elethin normally associated with men. Was Laurel trying to assert her dominance, or had she become habituated by too many meetings with senior executives? It didn't matter. They could jostle for position in the hierarchy later, once Elethin was working here.

"So good to see you, Elethin."

"You too, Laurel."

"Some of the others weren't sure you'd take the interview, that the sort of person who works at Mana Wave would be interested in coming here. I told them that you were far too smart to let an opportunity like this go by."

"Good to hear that you have such faith in me. But then, that's why you headhunted me, isn't it?"

"Absolutely." Laurel smiled. "Let me show you around."

The office was everything that Elethin had dreamed of: bright, clean, airy, lit by floor-length windows instead of the electric strip lights that hung from the ceiling at Mana Wave. Not only was there air conditioning, but it worked full time, creating a gentle, refreshing breeze and ensuring that the smells of her colleagues didn't surround her. Of course, there was no smell of solder and experimental magic. Nothing so crude as a workshop here. It was all office space.

She had feared that Karmic Charisma would be an open plan place, but they'd clearly bought into the turn against that trend. Half of the staff had individual offices, teams had individual rooms, and there were plenty of meeting spaces. Glass partitions let light through but could turn opaque at the touch of a wand to provide privacy for meetings and important conversations.

"This is one of the break rooms." Laurel indicated a space with spacious sofas, a breakfast bar, and a tall refrigerator. "Not that we use it all that much. We go out for lunch a lot."

Everything about this made it seem more like what Elethin was looking for. All she had to do was get through an interview, and that wasn't something she'd ever struggled with.

"Here we are." Laurel led her into a room where two more magicals were waiting. One was an elf with flowers sprouting from her hair and the other a broad-shouldered yellow-eyed shifter who moved with feline grace. "Heather, Felix, this is Elethin Tannerin. Elethin, we'll be your interview panel."

Laurel closed the door and sat next to Heather. A padded chair sat across the table from the interviewers, and Elethin sat there. There were no lumps and bumps like in the secondhand furniture they were using at Mana Wave. Even this interview was more comfortable than her usual working conditions.

"It's great to meet you, Elethin. We've heard so much about you." Heather glanced at the table in front of her. Elethin knew from experience on the other side of the desk that the questions wouldn't all come from the list, but it was a good idea to have something you could fall back on. "Let's get this show on the road. What interests you about working for Karmic Charisma?"

"Well, Heather, as you'll have seen from my resume, I've been working in public relations for my whole career. It's more than just a job for me. It's a passion…"

Of course, Heather and Felix would know that from more than her resume. They must've done their research, read the lurid profile piece, the court records, and the neat, journalistic summaries of the whole Nuada business. Involvement in a murderous corporate conspiracy wasn't a shadow that anyone could ever entirely slide out from under. Elethin hoped that if they'd come this far, these people didn't care about that and trusted Elethin to handle herself when questions came up about it. Otherwise, she wouldn't be here.

Still, the issue rattled around in the back of her mind as she answered their first few questions. Why had they brought her here, despite her past? Could she really be good enough to make it worthwhile?

Of course, she could, and she was proving that right now.

"Tell us a bit about your current work," Felix said. "You're employed by a startup called..." He read down his tablet. "Mana Wave Industries. Is that right?"

"That's correct. I'm the director of communications, although you know how it is at a startup. Sometimes the director is also the whole department."

There was no point trying to bluff through that one since they were bound to ask how many people she supervised. Something about the way Felix had asked the question got her attention. Was it her imagination, or was his show of not knowing Mana Wave's name forced?

"Tell us a little about your work there," Heather said. "What sort of challenges do you face?"

Elethin laughed. "Telling you the challenges would be telling you the whole job, in a place like that."

"Well, start by telling us the bits that have been most memorable for you."

They all leaned forward, listening intently.

Elethin had always had good instincts for people, but time in prison had sharpened them to a particularly fine edge. She could tell the difference between people eying up a potential member for their gang and those who'd spotted fresh meat. This was the latter.

What was going on? What response would best help her work it out?

"Director of Legal Affairs Gruffbar Steelstrike recruited me. I report directly to Fran Berryman, the CEO. Everything to do with the company's public image, from content for our website to Fran's public appearances, is managed by me."

"You have a good working relationship with Fran?"

"Absolutely."

"What have the biggest PR challenges been in terms of working with her? Don't worry. You can say whatever you want. Nothing shared here will leave this room."

So that was what this was all about. They wanted information on Fran.

Elethin wasn't above sharing Fran's secrets, but she needed time to work out her strategy here. She filled that time by talking about managing Fran's TV appearance, making sure to cast her involvement in the best possible light and to emphasize what a success it had been. Since they were interested in Fran, she threw in a few small details about her leader's personality to keep their attention.

"It must be challenging to prepare PR materials when you don't have any products to work with yet," Laurel said. "Have you been given advance insights into what your colleagues are developing? How have you made use of those?"

The question was so blatant that it caught Elethin by surprise. They were practically inviting her to share confidential information about her current company. She managed a convincing smile and the beginnings of a suitably vague answer, talking on autopilot while she thought through the situation.

It wasn't only Fran. They were looking for information on both her and Mana Wave. Why?

From the looks they were giving each other, the interviewers weren't content with the answers she was giving them. Felix waved to cut her off.

"Elethin, we value candid information sharing in this company." He fixed her with a predator's gaze. "It's important to know that, if you come here, you will be open in sharing relevant insights with your colleagues. Do you understand what I'm saying?"

She understood all too well. They weren't after her. They were after what she knew about Mana Wave. This was the price she would pay for her new job—dishing the dirt on the old one, sharing all of her current colleagues' secrets.

Why not? She didn't care about them. Those sorts of feelings would only slow her down. Everything she did was for herself, and this was the best option for her.

Still, it wouldn't do to give too much away too quickly, would it?

"Absolutely, Felix," she said. "I think openness like that is so important between colleagues. But as a communications professional, discretion is vitally important, as long as I'm dealing with outsiders."

There it was, her counterpoint, as open a declaration as she could make that she would only tell them what they wanted once they hired her. No juicy secrets until the ink was dry and she was safely inside one of these wonderful offices.

The interviewers sat back and exchanged glances. They understood, all right. Now they had to decide if, given how little they'd learned from her so far, it was worth the price of hiring her to see what else there was to learn. She felt confident that they would pay, but they needed time to discuss that first.

"I think that will do for today," Heather said. "So lovely to meet you, Elethin. Laurel, could you show her out?"

Elethin followed Laurel to the elevator.

"Thank you for this." Elethin turned to give Laurel a happy smile. As she did so, she glanced back across the office. Heather was walking into a meeting room where a man was waiting, and as she went in, she turned the glass wall opaque. Before the glass stopped being clear, Elethin saw the man's face. It was Liam Wade.

So that was who was gathering information on them.

The elevator arrived, and Elethin stepped in. As the doors closed between her and Karmic Charisma, she puzzled over a whole new question. Why was Mana Wave's supposed collaborator spying on them?

CHAPTER TWENTY-THREE

It was a busy Saturday morning in the Blazing Bean. A sales convention in the city's center meant that the coffee shops were full of visitors from all over Oriceran and some from Earth. That had driven some of the locals farther out, making a place like the Bean even busier than usual.

Fran frowned at the sight. She hoped that she could find a table. After all, this had been her idea.

"Hi, Fran." Cam smiled as she approached the counter. He looked a little strained, which wasn't surprising, given how much business was happening. "No to-go cup today?"

"I've come to sit in and relax," she said. "At least, that was the plan…"

"If you're looking for your mom, she's at that table." Cam pointed at a place near the window. "You can't see her because she's in that high-backed chair."

"Oh, thank goodness." Fran grinned. "I know I sometimes lose things, but misplacing my whole mom would be embarrassing."

Cam laughed. "What would you like to drink? Your mom already bought cake for both of you."

"Aw, that's nice of her." Fran looked up at the board. "I'll have a large mocha, extra foam, with the multi-colored sprinkles."

"I think you're the only adult who ever goes for those."

"I'm special like that."

"Unique."

"One of a kind."

"Irreplaceable."

"I hope so. Wouldn't want Elethin to get rid of me and put a clone in charge."

"You think it would be Elethin? My bet's on Gruffbar. He's the one with an ax and an attitude to match."

"No, Gruffbar's a sweetie." Fran considered what she'd said, then nodded. "Yes, a sweetie. Just don't ever let him know I said that."

"How was your date with Liam?"

"Hasn't happened yet. We've been too busy." Fran laughed. "I was so excited at the time, and now it's starting to wear off. So much for building anticipation, right?"

"Sure." Cam handed her the coffee. There was something in his expression that she couldn't quite read, but she didn't have time to ask more. Her mom was waiting.

Fran hurried over to the table where Irene sat, hidden in the depths of a high-backed armchair.

"There you are, Francesca." Irene set aside a book. "I was wondering how long you would be."

"Sorry, am I late? I tried to get here on time, but Josie told me I had to switch off the alarm clock and get a proper night's sleep, then Hoovernator got loose this morning, and—"

"It's fine, dear. You're not late. I'm early. Anyway, it's a Saturday. We have time to spare, don't we?"

"That's not what you used to say."

"Yes, well… Maybe I could've been a little more relaxed when you were young."

"Aw, it wasn't that bad." Fran sat in another padded chair and eyed the plates on the table. "Ooh, cake!"

At that moment, a familiar figure walked past the window.

"Hey, Winslow!" Fran tapped on the glass. "Hey, yoo-hoo!"

Winslow stopped and waved, then turned and headed for the door into the shop.

"This is cool, right?" Fran said. "A chance for you guys to catch up. You've both been so busy since coming to the Valley, I've barely seen you together at all, even though you're the most important you-know-whats in my life." She leaned forward and whispered, "I mean Evermores."

"Yes, Francesca, I understood that." Irene had straightened in her seat. She picked up her cup, took a small sip, then held it in her lap.

"Hello, Fran," Winslow said. "Are you here on your… Oh."

He noticed Irene in her chair. The two of them looked at each other, both wearing stiff smiles.

"Winslow." Irene nodded in greeting. "How are you?"

"I'm very well, thank you. And you?"

"I'm well. How are you enjoying the outside world?"

"I'm enjoying it very much. As you know, I consider it a place worth visiting for short periods."

"Is this still short? I'm sure I remember you saying that anything more than a day carried unnecessary risks."

"Sadly, those risks have become necessary. While I'm here, it would be churlish not to enjoy what Oriceran has to offer."

"I couldn't agree with you more."

Fran clutched her cup and glanced back and forth between the two of them. Their strained voices, rigid bodies, and fixed expressions indicated she'd made a mistake in thinking they might want to catch up.

"It was super cool to see you, Winslow," she said, "but do you maybe have somewhere you need to be?"

"Absolutely. A meeting with a contact from Earth about an errand that might take us there. Another case of balancing the risks and rewards." He looked at Irene. "Properly balancing them."

"I believe I got the balance just right." Irene looked at Fran, then pointedly back at the older Evermore. "Goodbye, Winslow."

"Goodbye, Irene." His face shifted into a smile. "Goodbye, Fran."

Then he left.

Irene sat rigid until he'd passed outside the window and disappeared from view. Then she sank into her padded seat and let out a long-held breath.

"Mom, can I ask a question?" Fran said.

"Can I stop you?" Irene shook her head. "No, sorry, that's not a helpful thing to say. Of course, you can ask, dear. Please."

She didn't sound happy about the prospect, but she hadn't said no, so Fran plowed on.

"What was that all about? You and Winslow being all, you know…" She waved her hands like the arms of a robot. "All stiff and mechanical."

Irene chewed on a fingernail and swirled the last of the coffee around the inside of her cup. Fran sat as patiently as she could, waiting for a response, trying to stop her leg from jiggling up and down. At last, Irene looked across the table at her. Although the coffee shop was full of people, that all seemed to fade away, leaving just the two of them.

"For as long as I can remember, Winslow has been one of the leaders of the Evermores," she said. "Arguably the leader, although that opens a jar of pickles I don't want to taste. His views, his voice, dominated the way we lived for a long time. It was partly about age, partly about power, partly about experience, and partly about the authority that keeps building when you're in a position like that. Do you understand?"

"Sure. He was in charge."

"Yes, but there were tensions around that, and I was at the center of those tensions. I started having doubts about how we lived, what we were doing, and why. I questioned whether certain choices had the positive effects that we claimed they did."

"You mean you started to think that you were the bad guys?" Fran stared at her, shocked.

"Nothing so dramatic, dear. More that good people can do bad things, from time to time, even if they don't mean to. Talking back about topics like that wasn't really done, for all sorts of reasons, some more valid than others.

Stability, security, authority, tradition, the comfort of others… Well, in the end, I decided that I wasn't going to stand for any of them."

"You had a big row with Winslow."

"I decided to leave and live elsewhere. That, arguably, was the most dangerous and offensive argument that anyone could ever make, in the mind of someone like Winslow."

"You make him sound really stubborn and inflexible."

"You probably haven't noticed that side of him. With lives as long as ours, he can afford to be patient. But yes, there's a stubbornness there that you'll have to face in the end if you keep on spending time with him."

For Fran, that had never been an "if." She wanted to spend more time with her mom's people, to learn more about them. She hoped that this conversation didn't make that difficult.

"So Winslow's mad at you for leaving, and you're mad for the things he did before?"

"There's more to it than that. I did and said some things on my way out, things that could've been calculated to upset and anger him. Perhaps, on some level, that's exactly what I was doing. Even when you're thousands of years old, you can still find yourself lashing out when you feel hurt.

"I did feel hurt. The way things went, how Winslow made them go, it stopped my departure being the joyful moment that I'd hoped for. Something that should've been beautiful instead became painful."

Irene drained the last of her coffee and put the cup down on the table. Her hand headed for her mouth, but she stopped it halfway, then reached for the plates of cake.

"Which one would you like, Francesca? I got chocolate salted caramel and a slice of banana loaf with that lovely pistachio topping."

"I'd like more details about what happened between you and Winslow." Fran eyed the cakes. "I'll settle for chocolate salted caramel."

"Then I chose well." Irene handed her the plate and a fork. "I was hoping for the banana loaf."

Fran took a mouthful of her cake. It was sweet and delicious, and for a brief moment, it lifted her spirits. On its own, it wasn't going to be enough. Chocolate was amazing, but even its magic couldn't chase that whole conversation away.

"Okay, it turns out I can't settle for cake." Fran set the plate down, half of the chocolaty slice still intact. "Mom, can you please tell me more? Like, what did Winslow do wrong? What did you do about it? What sorts of things did you say and do? How did the others react? Was Enfield there for all of this? What does it mean for me if I ever want to visit where the Evermores came from? Why are you…"

She stopped to catch a breath. So many questions, she wasn't even sure which one to start with. On some level, she wasn't sure that she wanted the answers, but she had to ask.

There was a pained look on her mother's face. Her cake sat in front of her, barely touched, while she chewed on a fingernail.

"I'm sorry, Mom," Fran said. "Sorry if this is all painful

for you. But it's about me too now, and I think I should know about where I came from."

"You're right. You should." Irene sighed. "That's something else I wanted to talk about with you."

She rubbed her eyes, then looked down at the cake like she saw it for the first time. She pushed the plate away from her.

"What is, Mom?" Fran asked. "What's so important that it could be worth interrupting the rest of this conversation for?"

"Your father got in contact with me."

Fran sat, stunned. Her mother had never said those words before or anything remotely like them. For the first time in forever, her father loomed like a real presence in her life.

"Like, today?" Fran asked.

"Recently," Irene said.

"How recently?"

"In the last few weeks."

Fran didn't know what to say. It could have been worse. It could've turned out that her parents had been in secret contact for years and that she, like a fool, hadn't known. But even a few weeks of Irene knowing without telling her hurt.

"When… What…"

"It's not for me to try to make sense of your father, dear. If I could do that, he might've been in your life all along."

"Did he ask about me?" Fran felt very small all of a sudden, a lost child in a big, scary world. At least she could count on her mom to be there for her. Except that her mom was now where the scary things came from. "Wait, maybe I don't want an answer."

"Of course, he asked about you." Irene leaned across the table to take her daughter's hand. "He asked a lot about you. What sort of person you are, what things you like, all sorts of questions about what you do. And he asked something else. He asked if you might like to meet him." The two women looked into each other's eyes. "It's totally up to you, Francesca, but if you want, I can arrange for that to happen."

Fran looked out the window of the coffee shop. It had started raining outside, big wet drops making dark stains on the paving stones. A crow stood in the rain, looking in at her, its head tilted on one side.

Did she want to meet her dad?

CHAPTER TWENTY-FOUR

A small bell tinkled on Julia Lacy's desk. She smiled to herself, a small, satisfied expression. It paid to put extra enchantments on the building. Some working witches wouldn't have put in the effort, but that was how she had gotten to where she was—by not being like the other working witches.

She pressed a switch on the intercom.

"Howard, Liam Wade has entered the building. He should be with you in a few minutes."

"Thank you, Julia," Phillips replied, then closed the connection.

Julia got back to compiling the reports from design leads on how they were implementing changes to the Manaphone and what proposals they'd come up with for further improvements. Some had taken the hint provided by Josie's stirring of the pot and were getting more imaginative, letting their minds run riot. Others were doing what they always did, putting more effort into justifying themselves than making a better product. Those would be sitting a lot less comfortably in a few months.

The elevator *pinged*. Handar stepped out, followed by Liam Wade. Wade was smiling while Handar wore his usual scowl.

"Hi, Julia," Wade said. "Good to see you again."

"And you, Liam. How was your journey?"

"It's always a little awkward sneaking in through the back entrance, but I made it work."

"I'm sure that a parking garage isn't complex enough to cause you any problems. Unless your business has become a lot simpler lately?"

"I wouldn't know. I'm spending most of my time at Mana Wave, as your boss asked."

"My boss, Liam, or our boss? After all, he's the one pulling your financial strings."

That drew a smile from Handar, his lips peeling back to reveal his fearsome teeth. There were differences in the shade and texture of some, which made her suspect that they might be fakes. She'd thought for a while that she should ask him what had happened to the originals, whether they'd been lost in a combat zone or fell victim to a barroom brawl. Today wasn't the day for that.

Julia knocked on the office door.

"Enter!" Phillips called.

The three of them walked in.

Phillips was standing by the window, looking out across the city. It was his power pose, the one he used to remind people who was in charge. It was a touch that Julia admired.

Some executives saw the desk as their place of power,

putting a barrier between them and the world, reminding everyone of their work and how busy they were. Phillips understood that it was often better to show the results of that work, the power he had over the city, its industries, and more. That it was better to be open and show how little he had to fear from anyone.

"How are things progressing at Mana Wave?" he asked.

"Slowly." Liam flung himself down in a seat. "No sign of your running man, and if anyone is talking about Evermores, they're not doing it around me. Fran almost said something the other day, but then she stopped, and I couldn't dig further without giving the game away."

Phillips turned away from the window and nodded at Handar and Julia.

"Take a seat."

As she sat, Julia stole a glance at Wade. If he understood the sign of Phillips' displeasure at him there, the implication that he should've waited before sitting, he didn't show it. He wore the same smug smile he usually did, one that said he belonged in charge of everything he saw.

"In what context did Ms. Berryman almost say something?" Phillips asked.

"They were working on a new prototype, and it had an odd reaction to a spell. They all treated it oddly like there was something else going on. I don't know why yet."

"This technology, what is it?"

"A new entertainment system. Frankly, it's not half as imaginative as I'd hoped they would be."

"The technology behind it, tell me more."

"I don't know much more. Like I said, progress is slow."

"Too slow." Phillips stood behind his desk, hands

clasped on the back of his seat, glaring at Liam. "I sent you on an important task, and you're letting me down. I don't think you want that."

"You can't rush corporate espionage." Wade clapped a hand over his mouth in what he clearly thought was a comical effect. "Oops, was I not supposed to say that part out loud?"

"This is so much more than corporate espionage." Phillips leaned forward, staring straight at Wade. His eyes became pools of darkness, and when Julia looked into them, a chill ran down her spine. She dreaded to think what Wade saw there that made him press himself back in his seat.

"I'm working on it," Wade whispered. "Honestly, Howard, I'm going to get this done. I just need time to earn their trust and dig around some more."

"You've had weeks."

"I know, but we're hitting a crucial point. They're starting to trust me, to let down their guard. I've talked Fran Berryman into going on a date with me."

"A date?" It would've been hard for Phillips to sound any more scornful.

"A chance for her to let down her guard. She's not had a boyfriend in forever, too busy with her work to find anyone who'll pay her attention. A few nice words, a couple of glasses of wine, a night or two of reminding her what she's been missing, and she'll be putty in my hands."

Julia almost laughed out loud. She didn't know what was worse, the fact that Wade thought his advances would magically make a woman betray all her secrets or the possibility that Fran Berryman might be that pathetic.

"You had better be right," Phillips said. "I didn't send you there to get laid." He drummed his fingers against the seat. "Is there anything we can supply to help you in your work?"

"You mean like something to slip into her drink? I don't need that."

Julia shuddered at how readily Wade's mind had gone there.

"I mean anything. Cameras, microphones, surveillance spells…"

"Oh, you want me to do it that way?" Liam stroked his chin. "Let me think about it. With all the tech and magic in that basement, there's a real risk that it would cross signals with something and give us away."

"Very well. If you think of anything, contact Handar and Julia. They know what we can supply. And Liam?"

"Yes?"

"Get. The. Job. Done."

Phillips strode back over to the window and stood with his back to them.

Julia got up and opened the door. Handar walked out past her. A moment later, the penny dropped for Wade, and he followed, scowling as he went. Julia followed them out and closed the door behind her.

Wade snorted. "Your boss is quite something, huh?"

"He knows what he wants, and he gets it." Julia sat behind her desk. "Do you want anything from us now, Liam? It might look better if you take him up on his offer."

"No, I'm all good. Unlike Handar, I can rely on my charm."

Handar growled, a low, rumbling sound.

"Aw, did I hurt the guard dog's feelings?" Wade looked up at the burly Kilomea. Even faced with the muscles and menace packed tight under Handar's suit, he still looked smug. "Are you going to bite me, or are you going to be a good doggo?"

Handar's fist shot out, straight toward Liam's stomach. To Julia's shock, Liam caught it. The two men strained and stared at each other, both trying to twist the other's arm.

"You want a fight?" Wade said coldly. "I'll give you a fight."

His other hand came around, palm first, slamming into Handar's chest. There was a flash as magic triggered and Handar smashed back into the wall.

"What, you think I don't walk around ready for trouble?" Wade pulled a wand from his pocket. "I always have a few spells up in case I run into a thug like you."

Julia hesitated. Part of her wanted to step in and help Handar. Years of working together had created a certain sense of loyalty, despite everything. Still, she didn't want to cross Wade in case he came out on top, and besides, Handar might not appreciate someone stepping in. This wasn't her fight.

Handar charged at Wade, fist swinging.

"Contego," Wade snapped, and a shield appeared on his arm. Handar's fist slammed into it and slid off.

Wade brought his knee up into Handar's stomach, and both men grunted. Handar was tougher than even the hardiest human being, and though that had hurt him, it hurt Liam's leg as well.

Handar grabbed the edge of the magical shield and used

it to swing Wade around. Wade let the spell go, but the force of the swing sent him staggering into the wall.

"Refrigero." Wade waved his wand, and a bolt of icy magic shot out. Handar ducked, bringing an arm up as he did so, and the spell deflected off something hidden beneath the sleeve of his jacket. The magic hit the ceiling, where it became a sparkling patch of ice around a light fitting.

Handar leaped across the room and into Wade, who was a moment too slow getting his next spell off. A mass of magical glue missed the Kilomea and hit the wall instead, while Handar slammed into Wade, knocking him to the ground. Handar got a couple of good kicks in, but even while he was down, Wade got a spell off. Magic shone along his arm as he formed a fist and slammed it into the side of Handar's knee.

With a growl of pain, Handar sank to the floor. Wade tried to get up, but Handar grabbed hold of him and dragged him down. The two of them rolled across the floor, kicking and punching, thrashing around, magic flying from between them.

The office door flew open, and Howard Phillips strode out. "Enough!" he bellowed.

It was like the moment when a teacher walked into a classroom of misbehaving kids. Everybody froze, Handar and Wade still gripping onto each other, Julia behind her desk, wand in her hand, ready to fend them off if trouble came her way.

"To your feet, both of you," Phillips ordered.

Handar shot upright with his arms straight by his sides, as rigid as if he was back on an army parade ground. His clothes were disheveled, and the altercation had torn a button from his jacket, but nothing on the outside could change who he was inside.

Wade rose more slowly, wiping blood from his lip with the back of his hand.

"He started it." Wade's words only added to the impression of a child caught doing wrong.

"You think I care?" Phillips glared at them both." If you want to hurt each other, by all means, hurt each other. There are few things I relish more among magicals. But don't do it in my office. I have a business to run." He turned to Julia. "Show Mr. Wade out. The back way again."

"Yes, Howard."

She opened the elevator, waved Wade in, and went to stand beside him. Handar glared at Wade as the doors closed between them.

"As I said, he's quite something, your boss." Wade put on a tone of bravado, but his hand was shaking.

"You're the one who's planning on sleeping with a woman to steal her secrets."

"Only reason I'd touch that crazy mess of smiles and sparkles. I prefer my women classy." He ran his eyes deliberately up and down her. "Maybe we could get a drink sometime? I hear you have a taste for executives."

"I have taste, Liam. I pick and choose carefully. I don't think a man who rolls around on the office floor is going to meet my standards."

"Not even after I finish this big job for your boss? I'm going to need a palate cleanser, and you seem like the sort of woman who likes to dine out on success."

The elevator bell chimed, and the doors opened. At a

gesture from Julia, Wade stepped out into the underground parking lot.

"Here you are," she said. "Down at the very bottom."

He grinned at her, that smug, self-confident grin that said he was sure he would win in the end.

"Come on, Julia, what do you say?"

"I say not until hell freezes over."

His fist clenched, and magic crackled around it. She was suddenly very aware that he was powerful enough to hold his own against Handar and that there was no one around to back her up. Slowly, she reached around to the back of her waistband, where she'd stashed her wand.

"Until another day." Wade opened his fist and gave her a small wave. "They all change their minds in the end."

The doors closed, and to Julia's relief, the elevator carried her away.

CHAPTER TWENTY-FIVE

Fran hadn't realized that she missed things about being on Earth until she looked up into the sky. There, the moon hung almost full with its distinctive pattern of light and shade, planes and craters, like a round and smiling face. It was so familiar, that glowing disk amid the sea of stars, a reminder of past nights from stargazing as a little girl to sitting on a college roof as a student, drinking wine at three in the morning. It wasn't that anything was missing from the Oriceran sky or that it didn't provide a beautiful view. It simply wasn't this. It wasn't the home she'd grown up with.

Wolves were howling out among the redwoods. Not only wolves. Shifters. The moon called to them, and so did the kemana. It was a dip in the land, its central crystal cupped in a bowl in the ground, hidden from mundane eyes by the woods and the powerful magics woven around it.

Fran had no idea whether she would've been able to

find it on her own, but she was glad to be there now as the moonlight fell across the ground and made the crystal visible. It had been invisible an hour before.

"Thank you for bringing me here," she said. "It's lovely. Why did you bring me?"

"Who better to help me with repairs than our very own craftswoman?" Winslow answered. "If you can fix a computer or build that containment unit, surely you can do this."

"I've never fixed a kemana before. I've never even tried!"

"Then this will be a useful learning experience for you."

"I don't know anything about how they work. I mean, beyond the obvious, that they give off power that magicals can use. And what I've observed, of course, in terms of magical flows and the alignment of crystals and a few small things about how the normal setup of the surrounding areas. But none of that is repairing knowledge, not really, and—"

"Fran?"

"Yes, Winslow?"

"You'll be fine. You're an extremely capable young woman."

"I am, aren't I?" She smiled. "Thanks."

A crow fluttered out of the darkness to land on her shoulder.

"Did you follow us through the portal?" she asked. "Or are you a local who's taken a shine to me?"

The crow *cawed*.

"I don't know which answer that is, but either way, it's good to see you."

The moon was rising higher, the shadows of the trees shortening, exposing the area around the kemana. Shifters prowled around the base of the crystal in wolf form, an improvised pack coming together for this night to share in the crystal's power. From her position higher on the hillside, Fran enjoyed seeing them greet each other, jumping and darting, barking and howling, a playful gathering. It was all so exciting.

Then she noticed something else. Around the crystal's base, some wolves stopped and shook as if they were having fits. Others stood watchful, tense and expectant, and dragged their comrades away when they fell like this. The twitching wolves lay for a while on the ground until they became still, then dragged themselves to the forest's edge to rest.

It should've put the shifters off going so close to the crystal, but however many fell like that, nothing seemed to change. Others kept closing in, basking for moments in the crystal's bright glow before falling twitching amid the half-rotted leaves on the ground.

There were other magicals present too, witches, wizards, gnomes, and elves. They stood around the edges, out of the roaming mass of shifters. Occasionally, one of these magicals would approach the crystal and reach out a hand to touch it. A smile would spread across their face as the magically transformed moonlight fell across them. Then they too fell twitching and spasming, only to be dragged clear by the guardian wolves.

"What's happening to them?" Fran asked. "Why do people keep doing that?"

"This is a powerful kemana," Winslow said. "It has great

potential to restore magical energy, and many magicals who live in this area rely upon it. They can only access the crystal at the right time of the moon, so when that time comes, a lot of people come here. You should've seen what the crowds were like when it was working properly."

"What happened to it?"

"The Source. This was one of the places it came to during its rampage across North America. We chased it off before it could do too much damage, but as you can see, we weren't fast enough to entirely prevent harm. Look on the south side, close to the base."

It took Fran a moment to work out which side was the south. Once she did, she soon saw what Winslow was talking about.

"Those cracks. They're not supposed to be there, are they?"

"Absolutely not."

"They're changing the patterns of light falling through there."

"Not only light."

"Oh yes, I see! If I squint right, the flow of magic becomes clearer, you know? It's as if, like, I was looking with someone else's eyes."

"Not someone else's. Your eyes, doing more of what they should."

"Cool, well, my eyes are telling me that the flow of magic is getting twisted close to the base." Realization dawned. "That's what's hurting those people!"

"Exactly."

"So why don't they stay back? They could soak up the magic slowly there and stay safe."

"The magic farther away is less powerful. And, as you'll find when we get closer, this power is hard to resist."

As Winslow spoke, another shifter approached the crystal. Sure enough, after a few moments, she fell to the ground, twitching violently. When one of the others tried to drag her away, the shifter dug her claws into the ground, trying to stay close to the very power that was hurting her. In the end, it took three other magicals to drag her out to the edge of the clearing, where she lay under a tree, dejectedly twitching.

"We should totally fix it," Fran said.

"That's why we're here." Winslow walked down the slope through the shadows of the trees. "Come."

Fran followed him through the woods with the crow on her shoulder, toward the shining crystal and the exciting challenge of fixing it. She appreciated the distraction from the thoughts that had been chasing each other around her head for the past few days, all of which related to one question. Should she meet her father?

In some ways, the answer seemed obvious. Everybody wanted to know their dad, right? Except that she hadn't known him for so long, a whole flood of uncertainties came with the question.

What if she didn't like him? Worse, what if he didn't appreciate her? What if the whole thing was weird and awkward? What if she liked him, and he left again, and she never got to know him better? It should've been an amazing opportunity. Instead, it had become a burden in her brain.

Watching Winslow's back as she followed him through the stripes of moonlight and shadow, she wondered if she should ask his advice. He was the oldest person she knew, so he had lots of experience in difficult situations. If anyone could advise her, then surely it was him.

Except that this related to her mom's departure from the Evermores, which was a sore spot. Better to ask somebody else instead. Maybe Enfield, next time she saw him. He might not have millennia of experience, but he at least had more than her.

There she was again, caught up in her thoughts. That was why she'd been so glad when Winslow had come to her, asking if she could help with some Evermore business.

The two of them stepped out into the moonlight. No one paid them much attention. They were merely one more pair of magicals amid the crowd.

Winslow paced toward the crystal, and Fran walked alongside him. Only when she saw a shifter fall over a few feet ahead did she grab Winslow's arm, bringing them both to a halt.

"Wait!" she said. "Isn't it dangerous for us to get closer? We'll end up like these guys, and we can't repair anything if we're twitching on the ground."

"Very good, Fran." Winslow gave a small smile. He seemed weirdly pleased at her working out something he didn't seem to have considered, despite his years. "So, what can we do about it?"

"Some sort of protective field." Fran pulled her dummy wand from the back of her jeans. "If the magic has ties to the light, and the fractured light is causing the problems, maybe a light filter around us?"

"An excellent plan. Please, go ahead."

Fran waved her wand, making it look as if that was how

she directed the magic. A bubble of light formed around her and Winslow, the field shimmering and shifting in response to the erratic light emerging from the cracked base of the crystal. The crow leaped off her shoulder and flew away.

Now they had people's attention. Several of the nearest shifters watched them, some curiously, others warily.

"Isn't this risky?" Fran whispered. "Drawing attention to ourselves?"

"We'll be fine," Winslow replied. "This is a kemana. Weird things happen here all the time."

Fran braced herself as they walked closer, half-expecting her field to fail and the magical light to set them both shaking. However, her magic had done its work. She proudly watched as Winslow ran a hand over it, observing her handiwork. Then they were at the base of the crystal, and his attention turned there, examining the cracks and the discordant power emanating around them. His face resembled a ghost, pale and glowing, sunken eyes dark.

"What now?" she asked.

"What do you think?" he asked.

Fran leaned in and ran her fingers across the cracks. She felt the light and magic almost as strongly as she saw them. It was unsettling the way her senses ran together but also exciting. She took hold of a tendril of magic and let it run across the palm of her hand.

"I think we need to redirect the light. That will alter the flow of magic back to what it should be."

"I think you're right." Winslow had that smile again. "Go ahead."

"Don't you want to do it?"

"You're an Evermore, Fran. Power over light and sound is your birthright. You can do this."

"Okay." She rolled up her sleeves, then drew a deep breath. This was a huge responsibility, trying to make a kemana work. Was she really up to it?

Of course, she was. She'd founded her own business. She'd trapped the Source. She was Fran Berryman, and she could do anything if she set her mind to it.

She waved her wand and started singing. The song started as something familiar, a silly song about Santa Claus going crazy. As she saw how the light responded, she altered her tune. Words gave way to the abstract sounds she'd heard the Evermores use. The melody transformed and the light changed with it.

Around the kemana, a shifter approached the crystal. He gazed up into its light, softly howling to the moon. Others braced themselves, ready to drag him away when he fell, but it never happened. He stood proud and strong in front of the stone, basking in the magical light.

Seeing what had happened, other shifters came closer, then the other magicals. They smiled as they bathed in the crystal's light and it renewed them.

Fran grinned with pride and excitement. She had done this, let people get the magic they wanted again. It was such an interesting challenge, not a problem she'd ever tackled before.

She let her song fade. The light was flowing right now, and she could keep it that way as long as she was there. What would happen when she stepped away? These people would suddenly become sick as the light fractured and the magic twisted again.

"Winslow, what do I do now?" she whispered, trying to keep the panic out of her voice.

"What do you think?" He watched her.

"We have to make it permanent somehow."

"How could you do that?"

"Me?"

"You've done this much. Show me whether you can do the rest."

"What if it goes wrong?"

"Then I'll deal with that. Do you think it's going to go wrong, Fran?"

"Yes. No. Maybe. I don't know!"

"Then focus on what you do know. What needs to happen to make the fix permanent?"

Fran looked from him to the other magicals, the power flowing over them, the crystal, and the cracks in its base. She did this all the time, diagnosing problems and finding fixes. She could do it again. It was like refining prototypes.

"We have to fix the cracks," she said.

"How could you do that?"

"Light power won't do it. The cracks will only bend it again, so something with sound... Oh, yes!"

She waved her wand for form's sake, in case anyone was watching her, then started singing again. It was a different song, deeper and less striking but full of power. Magic flowed with the tune. It penetrated the crystal and shook it down to its very atoms. Broken edges dissolved as the magic touched them, then joined together, the breaks between them healed. One by one, the cracks faded away.

As the crystal healed, the moonlight magic grew in power. The shifters howled, a chorus of wild voices soaring into the night sky. Even the other magicals joined in, caught up in the excitement of their bestial companions.

When all of the cracks were gone, Fran lowered her wand and voice, then stepped back from the crystal. She gave it one last appraising glance, checking for any damage she'd missed, then lowered the protective bubble around her and Winslow and let her magic go.

"Well done," Winslow said. "Now we should go before people decide to ask us questions."

They worked back through the crowd to the edge of the woods. Once they were in the shadows, Fran pulled out her mirror, ready to summon a portal home. Winslow was still watching her, wearing that same small smile that kept appearing before.

"I hadn't tried some of those things before," she said. "I was testing the limits of my powers."

"How did that feel?" Winslow asked.

"It felt good." She looked at him, a creeping realization finally crystallizing in her mind. "You did this on purpose, didn't you? I wasn't only testing myself. You were testing me, seeing what I could do with my powers."

"Why do you say that?"

"Because if this was only about fixing the crystal, you would've brought other Evermores to make sure it got done right. Not having them forced me to do it."

"Well observed, Fran. I hope that you'll forgive my curiosity. I wanted to see what you are capable of. I would like to say that the results impressed me very much."

"Thanks." Fran beamed. "Okay, time for me to do one more thing. Open a portal and take us home."

She looked up at the moon, visible through the branches of the trees. It had been lovely to see the sights of the world where she grew up, but Mana Valley was where her friends lived. That was home now.

CHAPTER TWENTY-SIX

The light in the Mana Wave office the next morning was very different from the woodland night. Beneath the neon of strip lamps, the team gathered around a workbench, examining the latest ideas everyone had been working on.

"Is it some sort of crab?" Fran leaned over to look at the creation Smokey had brought.

"Why would I make a crab?" Smokey's tail swished back and forth.

"I don't know. That's why I asked."

"Well, it's not a crab." He nudged the object with one paw. "Try putting it on your head."

"On my head?"

Watched by Singar and Liam, Fran picked the object up. It was about the size of her hand, a flat plastic disk with a dozen mismatched legs sticking out of the sides. Hardware wasn't Smokey's specialty, so rather than make his device from scratch, he had assembled it from discarded components and leftovers from other prototypes. Those legs had once been levers, fingers, even a piece of battery casing.

"Go on." His eyes were bright as he watched her.

Uncertainly, Fran placed the object on her head.

"Now tell it to start," Smokey said. "There's a charm on it that should recognize the command."

"Okay, sure. Weird thing, please start whatever you're going to do."

Though she tried not to, Fran couldn't help tensing as she waited for the thing to respond. What was it about to do to her?

The legs started moving, tentatively at first, then more confidently. It was like receiving a scalp massage from someone with twice as many fingers as normal who could sense where she wanted those fingers to go.

"Oh, wow!" Fran exclaimed. "That's surprisingly soothing."

"Now imagine that you're a magical with fur," Smokey said. "You turn into a cat or a dog or whatever, but people won't pat you or scratch you because you're not a household pet and they get freaked out when they hear you talk. With this device, you can get all the stroking and scratching you want, and you're in control."

"Doesn't that defeat the point a bit?" Liam asked. "Being in control, I mean? Surely the point of someone else patting you is that you don't know exactly what's coming."

"If you think we like surprise scritches, then you've clearly never met a cat." Smokey shook his head, the seriousness of his observation only slightly undermined by the swaying of his whiskers. "Why doesn't someone else try it?"

"No thanks," Singar said. "I don't want a strange robot groping my head. Besides, there's no fur or hair to put it on."

"Here." Fran smiled and held the device out to Liam. "It's great, honest."

"I don't know…"

"Come on. It'll be fun! Besides, aren't you supposed to be helping us develop our new products?"

"You must have other people who could do this. Consultants you work with, or friends who help with testing."

"We can't afford consultants, and our other friends aren't here."

"Well, we should get some of them in, see what they think of all the ideas you've come up with. It will be a good chance for me to get a better idea of the context that you're working in and the people who are influencing your design choices."

"You seem very interested in other people all of a sudden," Smokey said.

"I'm trying to make sure we're thorough."

"Or you're trying to avoid that thing messing up your hair," Singar suggested.

"No, I…" Liam hesitated, then nodded. "All right, you've got me. That's all this is, an excuse not to mess with style." He ran a hand over his carefully styled hair.

"I'm sure your hair will still look great when we finish," Fran said. "It always does."

"When you put it like that, how can I keep saying no?" Liam lowered himself enough for Fran to place the device on top of his head. "Now I tell it to start, right?"

At the word "start," the device began moving, its legs running through Liam's hair. Within seconds, all sense of style was gone, replaced by a wild mess sticking out in every direction. For all his protests, now that he was wearing the device, Liam had a big smile on his face.

"Say, that's really relaxing. I didn't know how much tension I was carrying up there, but it's... Ow!" He frowned. "I swear, it pinched me. There it goes again, ouch!"

He reached for the device, but it scuttled back across his head, then down his neck and under his suit collar.

"It's still doing it!" he exclaimed in alarm. "Stop! Stop! I said stop!"

He twisted on the spot, one arm over his shoulder, the other reaching up his back as he tried to grab the wriggling machine.

"I'll get it." Fran pulled up the edge of his jacket and grabbed hold of the device. "There, I'll pull it off."

"Ow!" Liam yelped. "What are you doing?"

"Um, I think it's holding on. It must like you."

"Well, I don't like it. Get that damn thing off me."

"I'm working on it." Smokey was at his computer, frantically tapping the keys. "I set up an emergency remote override, just in case. It'll only take a minute..."

"A minute? This is agony! It's squeezing my spine!"

Fran gathered a handful of bright light, ready to burn the device off. Before she could use it, the legs went limp, and it dropped to the floor.

"Got it." Smokey turned to look at Liam. "Sorry about that. No idea what was going on."

"Of all the reckless, dangerous, irresponsible..."

Liam looked furious, his whole face snarled up in hostility. Fran had never seen him look anything like it before. But after a moment, he seemed to find himself. As suddenly as it had appeared, the anger vanished and his familiar smile returned.

"Never mind. Accidents happen." He picked up the device and placed it on the workbench. "Maybe we shouldn't include this in wider testing, at least until it's under control."

Smokey jumped from his seat to the workbench and prodded the device. A loose wire on its underside sparked.

"Hardware problem," he said. "Maybe you could build it next time, Singar?"

"I suppose." Singar pulled it over to her and opened it. "Never get a programmer to do an engineer's job."

"Sorry about that." Fran patted Liam on his arm. "Aside from it attacking you, what do you think of Smokey's invention?"

"That's quite a big aside," Liam said. "Still, I'll admit, the idea has potential. It's probably in the top half of the concepts we've looked at so far."

"Great!" Fran smiled. "So now what? Time to go away and make more? I'm having so much fun coming up with all of these."

"Sorry, but I think it's time to get serious about some of them. Otherwise, we'll never get anything ready for market." Liam looked around the team. "We should set up an informal focus group to get feedback on these. People you know already so there's less chance they'll share what they learn with a competitor. The more diverse a group of magicals we can assemble, the better. If they have different backgrounds, different powers, different needs and wants, that will help us to understand the devices and their potential market better. So, who can you all bring to the mix?"

"I've got my mom," Fran said. "She's an, um, a, like me. And Josie too, my roommate. Ooh, and Cam from the coffee shop, if we want a mundane human."

"Anyone else from the coffee shop?" Liam asked. "That seems like a good recruiting ground."

There was something in his expression that Fran didn't quite understand, a sort of suppressed eagerness.

"Not really," she said. "Cam was the one who helped us out."

"Okay, what about other friends and acquaintances? Who can the rest of you bring?"

Liam looked around.

"Inventors, mostly," Singar said. "Maybe some other Willens, if you really need them."

"That's good, more perspectives. How about you, Smokey? You seem like you'd know some interesting people."

Smokey narrowed his eyes.

"What do you mean by that?" he asked.

"What I said. You're a shifter and a fairly unusual one. That probably leads to some unexpected contacts."

"You mean like Paws and Claws?" Smokey prowled down the workbench until he looked at Liam from only a few inches away, scrutinizing his face. "Is that what you're asking about?"

"Is that your campaign group?"

"It is, as you well know."

"Then sure, magicals from there would add great variety and a diverse spread of user experiences. I'm interested in unusual magicals with two legs too, and I bet you know some who could give us their perspective."

"Oh, sure, try to put me off my guard, make this seem like it's not about the group." Smokey's tail swished firmly from side to side.

"Sorry, I didn't mean to exclude your group. I only meant…"

"Exclude? Ha!" Smokey turned his back on Liam and strode down the workbench to watch what Singar was doing with the device. "It might not look like it, but we've got an eye on you. Right, comrades?"

He glanced at a pair of crows perched on his monitor. One of them croaked, while the other glared at Liam.

"Okay, there's clearly something going on here." Liam held up his hands. "Whatever I said to offend, I'm sorry. I'll get out of here for a bit, and maybe we can talk about it later." He flashed a quick smile at Fran. "See you this evening?"

"Sure." She smiled back. "Looking forward to it."

Liam headed out of the workshop and up the stairs. The door to Worn Threads *creaked* open, then *banged* shut.

"Okay, Smokey, what was that all about?" Fran crossed her arms and frowned at the cat.

"Isn't it obvious?" Smokey hissed. "He's a spy."

"That's ridiculous!"

"Is it? Then why does he keep asking questions all the time?"

"Because he's trying to understand what we're doing so he can help."

"Now all this going on about who we know? A focus group seems like a convenient excuse to me."

"Really?" Fran hesitated, uncertain. That line of conversation had made sense at the time, but it was a new one. Was something odd going on here?

"Of course! Because he's trying to find out about our associates." Smokey waved a paw, taking in himself and the crows. "He's an agent sent by the authorities, using Mana Wave as a back route to spy on Paws and Claws. He thinks he's so subtle, but I'm onto him."

Fran laughed. She couldn't help herself.

Smokey stared at her indignantly. "What?"

"He's not spying on you," she said. "If anyone wanted to do that, they could turn up to your meetings. They're open to the public, remember?"

"Well, maybe he's trying to find out other things, like the protests we're planning."

"If he wants to know about those, he could read the fliers advertising them."

"Yeah, well, well…"

"Oh, Smokey." Fran shook her head. "Your paranoia was even getting to me there. But Liam's a friend, he's on our side, and he's going to help us out. You'll see."

"Maybe," Smokey muttered. He prodded at the scalp-massaging device again. "Enfield's coming in today to talk about the containment unit. Maybe we can test this on him."

Liam Wade stood outside Worn Threads, checking the messages on his phone while he calmed down. He'd been an idiot back there, pushing things too far too fast, desperately trying to create an excuse to meet more of the Mana Wave crew's associates to track down these Evermores.

Still, the pressure from Howard Phillips was growing, especially after the confrontation with Handar. Liam was determined to prove himself. He would show Phillips he was more valuable than his idiot bodyguard and that ice-cold PA.

A few more minutes of emails, then he would go back in and look for a different line of attack, another way to learn what he needed to know.

He glanced up and did a double-take. A guy was walking past. Not just any guy but the one from the file that Phillips had given him, the runner who Handar had failed to catch. The Evermore.

Liam played it cool, turned his attention back to his phone while watching the guy from the corner of his eye. He was going into Worn Threads. If Liam had been in there ten minutes longer, he would have met him!

Maybe this was better, though. Liam's car was across the street. He could wait there until the Evermore left the building and follow him. If he got lucky, he could work out where the guy was based. Wouldn't that be better, in the long run, than a face-to-face encounter now?

Feeling excited that things were finally coming together, Liam crossed the street, got into his car, and settled down to wait.

CHAPTER TWENTY-SEVEN

"How do I look?" Fran twirled in the middle of the apartment between the sofa and the TV. She hadn't worn high heels for a while, but she managed to spin without falling.

"Stunning." Josie stood by the kitchen counter in her sweatpants, waiting for the microwave to reheat her dinner. "That dress suits you."

"Thanks. And thanks for lending it. Turns out I don't have much for a fancy date."

"It's good for my dress to experience a date or two, even if I don't. That way, it'll be in practice at looking good, so it can show me off when the time comes."

"It hasn't been that long."

"I know. And I'm definitely not jealous of your fancy date with your flashy executive, during which I'll sit at home with my reheated lasagna."

"You shouldn't be. You get to watch cartoons on the sofa. That's not acceptable on a date, but I wish it was."

"I might be spending the time with Proust instead of

Mickey Mouse tonight, but your point's a good one. Time alone is time to do my thing." The microwave *beeped,* and Josie opened the door. "Speaking of which, won't your ride be waiting by now?"

Fran glanced at the clock.

"Oh my!" She grabbed her handbag and rushed for the door. "I've got to go! See you later, Josie."

She dashed out the door and down the stairs, pushed open the building's front door, and walked out into the street with as much poise and dignity as she could manage.

Her mouth fell open. A limousine waited by the curb, and Liam leaned against the door, dressed in a suit even sharper than the ones he wore for work.

"Hi, Fran," he said. "Might I add, wow, you look amazing."

"I, uh, thanks. You too." She drew a deep breath. "Sorry I'm late."

"That's okay. It all adds to the anticipation." He opened the car door. "Shall we?"

The limo was every bit as comfortable as it was elegant. Once inside, Liam opened a bottle of champagne and poured each a glass while the driver headed out into the evening traffic.

"This feels so decadent." Fran sipped her drink.

"I should hope so. You work so hard, I wanted to make sure you got a proper treat. A taste of luxury. After all, you've earned it."

"Maybe once our contracts start paying off."

"They will." He raised his glass. "Here's to you and the dazzling success that you're sure to be."

Fran blushed as they *clinked* glasses and drank their toast.

They chatted about little things as they drove through Mana Valley. Funny incidents at work, some tech items in the news, and the gadget expo coming to town. Then the limo stopped, and Liam climbed out.

"Here we are." He offered his hand, and she took it before climbing out of the car.

Only a few steps from the limo, they walked into the fanciest restaurant that Fran had ever seen. There was low lighting, plush seating, sculptures in niches on the walls, and an elf playing a grand piano in one corner. The waiters all wore vests and ties. The napkins were cloth instead of paper, and there were no ketchup bottles on any of the tables.

"Mr. Wade." The woman at the front desk smiled at them. "Your usual table is waiting."

"Thank you."

Liam led Fran through the restaurant. She looked around in panic at the other diners. They all seemed so sophisticated, the men in designer clothes or sharp suits, the women in elegantly unique dresses. She was sure that they saw through her borrowed dress to the nervous nerd underneath and that she would trip over her feet and make them all laugh at her. The combination of champagne and high heels only added to that fear, but somehow she crossed the restaurant in one piece and slid with relief into her seat.

"I feel like everyone's staring at me," she whispered.

"Of course they are," Liam replied, and for a moment

his fingers touched the back of her hand, making her skin tingle. "You're the most beautiful woman here."

Fran hadn't thought that she could blush any deeper, but it turned out that she could. She tucked a strand of hair back behind her ear, then found the courage to look around the room again.

"This place is amazing," she said. "And they know you!"

"I've been here quite a lot."

"On dates?"

"A few." He laughed. "Honestly, I can only find the time when it's a very special case. Normally, I'm here for business dinners."

"Oh, so is that what this is?" she asked with a hint of mischief in her voice.

"Definitely not. This is all pleasure." He leaned forward. "So far, it's very enjoyable indeed."

A waiter appeared with a bottle of wine and poured them each a glass, then left the bottle in a bucket of ice on a stand. There was plenty of space for that, with the tables widely separated, letting Fran feel like she was alone with Liam.

"They didn't bring us menus," Fran said. "Should I get the waiter back?"

"Oh, Fran, you are adorable." Liam laughed softly. "Places like this don't have menus. Don't worry. The food will be excellent."

"Okay." She took a nervous gulp of her wine. "So, what now? I'm used to going to places where we can color in the back of the menu while we wait to eat. I don't really know what to do in a grown-up restaurant."

She couldn't quite tell how seriously Liam had taken

the joke, but he smiled at her in a way that made her feel giddy, or perhaps that was the wine.

"There's this thing people have invented called conversation," he said. "Why don't we give it a try?"

"Sure, why not. How do we start?"

"Tell me a bit more about yourself. You have a roommate, right?"

It was easy to talk to Liam. He listened so well. By the time the starter arrived, Fran had already told him all about Josie and somehow gotten onto her mom via the awkward question of her almost non-existent Mana Valley social life.

"These are delicious!" she exclaimed as a flaky pastry parcel of goat's cheese crumbled in her mouth. "And they go so well with the chili jam!"

"That's a relief. I'd hate to think that I wasn't impressing." Liam topped up their wine glasses. "Wait until you taste what else they've made."

"Like what?"

"Like wait and see, that's part of the fun." He took a sip of his wine, and she followed suit. "Now, you were telling about what you do for fun..."

"I mostly work and skate," she admitted.

"Don't you meet people skating?"

"Oh yes! That's how I met Bart."

"I like Bart. He seems like a good guy."

"He is! He's been so much help in getting the business going."

"You mean by running the finances?"

"Well, yes, that and..." She sat back while a waiter whisked away their plates, then another placed new plates in front of them. Each of these new plates had a large roasted mushroom scattered with nuts and herbs, a portion of pasta in a deep red sauce, and a neat stack of asparagus and broccoli spears. "Ooh, this looks fantastic. Thank you!"

She dug into the food with enthusiasm. It felt like forever since lunch, and she needed something to soak up some of the wine. Once again, everything was delicious, from the subtle spices of the pasta sauce to the citrus dressing drizzled across the perfectly steamed vegetables.

"You were talking about Bart?" Liam suggested while eating his meal with less speed and more care.

"Oh, yes!" Fran wiped sauce from the side of her mouth. "He brought us…" She looked around to make sure no one could hear her. "He brought us our first contract, you know, the one with the FBI."

"Ah, yes. The one you're not supposed to talk about." He smiled. "The one where you've been waiting for a field test to finish."

"You've been paying attention."

"I should hope so. I like to know who I'm getting into bed with."

His eyes met hers as he said that last part. Fran couldn't help imagining what Liam's bed would be like. She was willing to bet that there were silk sheets and fewer stuffed toys than at her place.

He poured more wine for them both, then held out the empty bottle. A waiter took it and placed a fresh bottle in the ice bucket.

"If you don't mind my asking, do the FBI send people over often to check on your work?"

"Hardly ever. It's probably a good thing too, because…"

Fran hesitated. She probably shouldn't talk about this, should she? She wasn't supposed to mention the Evermores to anyone. Still, this was Liam. He was a good guy. She could trust him. Besides, she didn't have to mention the actual Evermores. She could talk about the thing without doing that, right?

"Don't tell anyone," she whispered, leaning in across her mushroom, "but we've also been providing the containment unit to someone else."

"You've sold your exclusive technology twice?"

"No, no, no!" She waved her fork. "Not sold. It's just that some people I knew were doing something important, they needed a way to contain a powerful source of magic, and it was when we'd been making the containment unit. So I thought, why not? You know? If we're making this thing anyway, why not make two, and help them look after the world?"

"That's very noble of you. And these friends of yours, these…"

"I can't say who they are. You understand, right?"

"Oh, of course."

He smiled, and it was reassuring. There was a glint there that put Fran's instincts on edge. She tried to push that feeling aside, but it kept intruding, cutting through the haze of wine and fine food and gentle piano jazz playing in the background.

For a moment, the jazz caught her attention.

"Listen," she said. "The song."

Liam tipped his head on one side. She smiled, waiting for him to work it out. Maybe he wouldn't know the original hip-hop version, but like her, he should recognize it from the reinvention when Weird Al had sung about the Amish. After all, he'd said that he loved that music.

Liam shook his head. "I'm not sure I know it."

Fran blinked. Maybe she'd gotten confused about which tune it was or about his tastes. It happened, especially when you were tired and contented and getting a little fuzzy around the edges.

"Never mind." She reached instinctively for her wine but then took a sip of water instead. "I think I misheard."

"It happens." He smiled. "So, you've told me about Bart, but how did you meet the rest of your company? They're an amazing bunch."

Dessert was a dark chocolate moose with a lattice of white chocolate across the top and berries on the side. Like everything else about the meal, about the evening, it was wonderful, and Fran ended up scraping her bowl clean. Of course, she knew how to behave in a fancy restaurant, so she didn't wipe her finger around the bowl like she would've done at home. It was a shame, letting that bit of delicious mousse go to waste, but she didn't want Liam to think he couldn't take her to nice places.

"Where to now?" he asked as they left the restaurant arm in arm. "A cocktail somewhere, perhaps?"

"I shouldn't. I have to be up for work tomorrow."

"Early to bed, then." He turned her gently so they faced each other. He looked so handsome in the light spilling through the restaurant window. She could still taste the wine and hear an old ballad from the piano. It would've been hard for the night to be any more perfect.

While they'd been in the restaurant, she'd started to

have doubts. He asked so many questions, which made it easy to talk, but so many related to work, she'd almost wondered if he was really interested in her or only in her business. Standing here now, seeing the way he looked at her, all those doubts faded away. He rested a hand gently on each of her arms and looked her in the eyes.

"Perhaps you'd like to come back to mine?" he asked softly.

Fran looked up at him, remembering soft conversation and laughter, thinking of silk sheets and the taste of chocolate that would still linger on his lips. She leaned on tiptoes toward him...

That sliver of doubt was still there, something cold and hard in the back of her brain. The edge of doubt grew stronger instead of fading as he leaned in too, as their lips were about to touch...

She pulled back, flustered.

"I have to get home." She looked away. "Early start tomorrow."

"Fran?" he asked, and there was frustration poorly hidden beneath his concern. "Is everything all right?"

"Absolutely. It's all fine. I've just... Work tomorrow, you know? There are all the prototypes and an investor meeting, and I really should call Agent Baldwin to check on the secret thing, not the top-secret thing but the other thing, and tonight's been amazing, but I really have to..."

She wanted to kiss him on the cheek, to show that she meant it, but she didn't trust herself if she got that close, so instead, she grabbed his hand and shook it.

"Can I at least give you a lift home?" He gestured at the

limo, that wheeled paradise of soft seats and champagne. She didn't trust herself in there.

"No, no, it's good. I'll get a bus, or a taxi, or walk, even. Yes, I'll walk." She kicked off her high heels, picked up her shoes with one hand, made sure that she was clutching her handbag in the other, then turned and strode off down the street. "I'll see you tomorrow, yeah? Sleep well, and thank you for a great night!"

Her cheeks were glowing as she stalked rapidly away down the street. What was she doing? What was she thinking? She'd made a complete fool of herself and probably put Liam off forever.

At least that cold, hard feeling wasn't pressing on her mind anymore. And at least Josie would be in when she got home to tell her that it was all right.

CHAPTER TWENTY-EIGHT

The streets were quiet as Fran and Enfield emerged from Worn Threads. It was an hour past rush hour, which meant it was more like two hours since most sensible people had stopped working for the day.

Most sensible people weren't juggling the stresses of a startup with trying to improve a containment unit for the powerful Source, work which Fran had now shifted to the end of each working day after Liam was gone. Not that she didn't trust him, but she was worried that she'd already told him too much during their date. While she couldn't undo that, she could at least do better in the future. In theory, at least.

"Okay, so, we understand why the containment failed," Enfield said. "In theory, at least. How are we going to correct that so we can transport it?"

"I don't think we should be correcting." Fran waved in negation. She liked moments like this when there was a practical problem to solve, not an awkward social situation to muddle through. "We should exploit the interactions between the fields to assist us in moving it."

"How?"

"I'm not sure yet, but I have a few ideas I've been considering." She pulled out her phone and glanced at the time. She should get home for dinner soon, but it wasn't desperately urgent, and this was important. "You want to grab a coffee and talk about them?"

"Sure. My run can wait."

"I still can't believe you run every day."

"I can't believe that other people don't. It's so satisfying."

The relative merits of running, skating, and sitting watching TV kept them occupied as far as the Blazing Bean.

"Hi, guys," Cam said as they approached the counter. "What can I get you?"

"Green tea, please," Enfield said.

"Cappuccino with all the sprinkles!" Fran said. "Ooh, and whatever cake's good today. It's been forever since lunch."

"Certainly."

"I'm going to the bathroom," Enfield said once he'd paid. "Can you find us a table?"

"How will I manage that?" Fran gestured at the many empty seats around them. "Sure, go for it. I'll even carry your coffee for you. That's what a good friend I am."

Enfield gave her an odd look. "We are friends, aren't we?"

"Of course we are. Now go, and I'll see you in a minute."

As more customers came in, Fran took her tray of

drinks and cakes to a table by the window. She sank into a padded seat with a satisfied sigh. She should have that coffee and cake quickly before she fell asleep. First, a few seconds of resting with her eyes closed…

"Francesca?"

Fran's eyes shot open, and she peered up at her mom.

"Mom? What are you doing here?"

"You weren't at your apartment, so I thought I'd try the next most obvious place. Is it all right if I join you?"

"Sure, of course." Fran sat up. "Are you okay?"

"Absolutely, I just…" Irene glanced around, sat, and leaned forward over the table. "There's something important I wanted to talk about with you."

"What sort of important?" Fran tensed. "Is it about my dad?"

"No, no, nothing like that, I just…" Irene noticed the second cup and the cake with it. "Oh, I'm sorry, you're here with someone. Am I interrupting a date?"

Fran laughed. "No, nothing like that. So, what did you want to tell me?"

"Well, it's about the E—" Irene looked up as Enfield approached. "Oh, Enfield, you're here."

Her voice became flatter, quieter.

"Hello, Irene." Enfield looked uncertain. "I'm sorry, am I intruding on—"

"No, I'm interrupting the—"

"Because I can—"

"Because really, it can wait until—"

"Guys!" Fran cut across the awkward back and forth. "I can have coffee with both of you at once. Although…" She looked at Irene. "Mom, the thing you wanted to tell me about, will that have to wait now?"

To Fran's surprise, her mom's attention stayed on Enfield, watching him carefully, like she was waiting to see what he would do. Enfield paused too, with one hand on the back of a chair.

"No," Irene said at last. "I hadn't planned for this, but I think perhaps it's something Enfield should hear."

Enfield pulled the chair back and sat, his expression as serious as hers.

"Has something happened?" he asked.

"Not for thousands of years." Irene laughed without much conviction. "Sorry, bad joke."

She slumped in her seat and gnawed on a fingernail while the others watched and waited.

"How old are you, Enfield?" she asked.

"A hundred and fifty," he said.

The words caught Fran by surprise. Of course, she'd known in theory that Enfield was older than he looked, but hearing an actual figure attached to it made it seem far stranger. Especially when that figure was so different from how he seemed. It was easy to forget that Enfield wasn't Fran's age.

"Relatively young then," Irene said. "I presume that no one has told you about the origin of the Source or why it did what it did once it escaped?"

"It's a power that the Evermores bound thousands of years ago," he said. "To provide magic on Earth while that world was separate from Oriceran. It's instinctively drawn to sources of power, which it consumes to make itself stronger."

"So no, they haven't told you the truth."

"What do you mean?"

Irene rubbed her eyes. "This is a conversation that we should have been having in the community years ago. Then maybe things would be different."

"What conversation? Irene, what are you getting at?" Enfield gripped the edge of the table. His knuckles went white from the pressure.

Outside the window, it was starting to rain. Pigeons fluttered away to take shelter. Fran realized to her surprise that there were no crows around. They must be at one of Smokey's meetings. Now they were missing out on this...

"The Source isn't only a force," Irene said. "It's a living, conscious creature made of pure magic power, as smart and sentient as any magical. It lived free until the Evermores trapped it."

"That can't be true." Enfield's voice was little more than a whisper. "It would be appalling, doing that to another living being."

"It is true, and I think you know it. You've heard enough little things, haven't you, seen enough odd details that you couldn't quite explain."

Enfield shook his head but didn't say anything.

"I believe you," Fran said. "It makes more sense like this, the way I've seen the Source behaving. It's not only a force of nature, and it's not merely acting on instinct, no matter what Winslow says."

"Thank you, dear." Irene looked at Enfield and raised an eyebrow.

"What did you mean about when it escaped?" he asked.

"We trapped the Source thousands of years ago. It was

Winslow's plan, and the rest of us, well, we went along with varying degrees of enthusiasm. Some saw it as a sad necessity. Others were excited to find such an elegant solution to a difficult puzzle. None of us talked about the deeper, darker meaning of what we did. We were too busy doing it.

"We bound the Source into a prison at the heart of our home, using our magic. Then we built the kemanas and put a part of the Source's power into each of them to give them the magic they needed. Because if we had the kemanas, there would still be magic on Earth after the portals closed, and we wouldn't lose what we had. Nor would the other magicals living there. Magic would remain.

"We took parts from a living, thinking, feeling creature and used them to give magic to a world. We thought it was worth the price, and for twenty-six thousand years, none of us questioned that terrible bargain."

Irene tugged at the corner of one nail with the fingers of her other hand.

"Here." Fran handed over her cake. "Worry at that instead."

Irene laughed sadly as she looked down at the cake.

"You used to do that when you were little, remember?" she said. "You would distract me when I became anxious. I think it helped keep me sane. Then you moved away…"

"The Source," Enfield reminded, his voice heavy.

"Yes, yes. So, we took the magic for the kemanas from the Source. It was one of the things I became uncomfortable with. Eventually, my conscience grew on me thousands of years too late. It wasn't why I left, but it was part of what caused the rift between Winslow and me, why he couldn't persuade me to stay.

"Then, years later, someone came to meddle with the Source, and it escaped. What followed was inevitable. The Source went to find the stolen parts of itself, to rebuild and heal. It ran from one kemana to the next, not because it was some monster set on stealing magic, but because it needed those lost parts of itself. It was the only way that it could be whole and happy.

"The kemana at San Jose was important because it was where the Source's power had been most twisted by what we did. The Source loves wild places, nature, and growing things. The San Jose kemana turned a part of it into technology, cold wires, and circuit boards, and sensing that distressed it deeply. It needed time to build up to facing that place, so it set out on its path, recovering parts of itself across the country until it had the strength and courage it needed. Then..."

"Then we trapped it." Fran felt sick to the pit of her stomach. "It was trying to heal itself, and we locked it up."

"That's right, dear. I'm sorry, but it's true."

Fran slumped in her seat. She felt wretched. On some level, it had always been obvious that the Source was a living thing. She'd let herself accept the idea of that as an illusion, had accepted Winslow's narrative about a force of nature. What had she done?

"We should let it out," she said.

"Maybe," Irene said. "But maybe not. Think about how much good magic does on Earth. Think of all the amazing things that are possible because of the Source. The lives saved because people have the power to drive back monsters, heal broken bodies, summon supportive spells. Would you want a world without that?"

"It's not fair," Fran whispered.

"What isn't fair, the question I asked, or what we've done to the Source?"

"Both."

"Why do you think I've taken this long to tell you? It's a terrible thing to know, and I didn't want to put this on you."

"Then why have you?" Enfield snapped.

His face was red, and his lips pressed tight together. His eyes blazed with fury, and Fran couldn't tell who he directed it at.

"Would you rather not know?" Irene asked.

Enfield hesitated for a long moment.

"I don't know," he admitted.

"We're all complicit in something difficult," Irene said. "At least now, we're not hiding from it. Now we can make choices. Perhaps I've made mine by telling you. Perhaps this is all I'll ever have the courage to do, but at least I've done it."

She set down the cake plate and got to her feet.

"I'll leave you to think about it. If you have questions, you know how to find me."

She walked out the door into the falling rain.

Fran and Enfield stared at each other in silence across the table. She felt the terrible weight of the knowledge they now shared and what they were part of.

"How do you feel?" she asked.

Enfield picked up his cup and took a long drink of lukewarm tea. When he set the cup down, he did so forcefully, banging it against the table. "I don't know. Confused. Angry. Uncertain how to face the other Evermores. Some of them knew this, maybe all of them, and they didn't tell me. How am I supposed to feel about that?"

"I don't know," Fran admitted. "I don't know what to think or feel or do. I seem to get a lot of that lately. At least this time, you're in the same position as me. Maybe we can work it out together."

"Maybe," Enfield said quietly, staring out at the rain.

CHAPTER TWENTY-NINE

Gruffbar sat at the kitchen table of his small apartment. Pieces of his bike engine were spread out on the table in front of him, along with a soft cloth, ready for a good clean. His shotgun sat next to them, and the tools he would need to dismantle it so he could clean that up as well. He had a glass of whiskey, a cigar waiting for when he finished, and there was a drama on the TV about a dwarf mining clan facing the challenges of ore extraction on an alien planet. Life didn't get much better than this.

There was a knock on the door. Gruffbar frowned. He hadn't been expecting anyone. On instinct, he reached for the shotgun, then remembered that he'd unloaded it ready for cleaning. He had some shells in a drawer in the kitchen. It would only take half a minute to get loaded, but a lot could happen in half a minute, and that door wasn't exactly tough.

He walked quietly to the counter, shotgun in hand. The drawer slid open on well-oiled runners, and the shotgun shells rolled to the front. He picked them up and started loading the shotgun by feel, his eyes on the door.

"Just a moment," he called, bracing himself in case a gunshot or a boot to the lock immediately followed his voice. When that didn't happen, he finished loading and walked to the door.

Of course, this could be a perfectly innocent visitor. A neighbor come to talk about a leak, perhaps, except that the neighbors usually kept to themselves. The only other people with his address were his colleagues and the people who did deliveries.

No one from Mana Wave had ever come to visit him here, and he liked it that way. If he'd wanted guests, he would've had a house warming when he moved over from Earth. As for deliveries, he couldn't remember ordering anything recently, and he wasn't a dwarf prone to impulse purchases or drunken late-night bidding on auction sites.

All of which meant that this was most likely someone with a grudge against him. Not a current legal opponent, as all his work was now for Mana Wave, and the company wasn't causing anyone any problems. Someone from his past. Someone with a vendetta to pursue. Someone looking for revenge, or possibly for justice, depending upon which side of the moral divide he'd been on when he crossed them.

The security chain was already on its latch. It wouldn't hold a determined opponent, but it might slow them down. With one hand holding his shotgun behind the door, he used the other to open it.

Elethin stood in the corridor with her arms folded, scowling at him. He'd been half-right. It was someone with a grudge against him. It was just that they worked together too.

"How long can it take to answer the door?" she asked.

"When I'm answering it to someone who once tried to kill me, I'm willing to take my time."

"That was weeks ago. Besides, we're on the same team now, remember? Why would I want to kill you?"

"To get revenge? Because you owe me money?"

"I'll pay you back when I can."

"Do you mean that about the money or the revenge?"

"Both, but neither tonight." She glanced down the corridor, then back at him. "Look, I wouldn't be here if it wasn't important, so can you let me in?"

Gruffbar considered his options. If she'd wanted to overcome him with magic, she could have done it by now. If she wanted to play a prank, she had easier opportunities. Besides, they had a shared interest in Mana Wave. Sometimes profit made for unexpected allies.

He unhooked the chain, set the shotgun down, and opened the door.

As she walked into the room, Elethin looked around with open curiosity, not bothering to put up a façade for him. Was that a compliment, showing some trust, or was it an insult, showing that she didn't care what he thought? It didn't matter. He was firm that he didn't care what she thought about him.

"Drink?" He shut the door and headed for the kitchen cabinet.

"What do you have?"

"Whiskey."

"Just whiskey?"

"Whiskey's all I need."

"Is it the good stuff?"

"It's not the bad stuff."

"Then I'll risk a drink." It took her a moment to force out the next word. "Thanks."

Gruffbar poured her a glass, grabbed his off the table, and went to sit in his lone leather armchair. Elethin settled on the sofa with her legs crossed. The glass of whiskey rested on her knee.

"What do you want?" he asked.

"I've run into some people who I think are trying to undermine Mana Wave. As the other devious-minded criminal in the company, I thought that I should get your perspective before taking it to the others to check whether this is something real."

"Okay, that makes some sense of you coming here. Though I suspect Singar has dark patches in her past too."

"You've looked into her?"

Gruffbar shook his head. "Sometimes it's better not to know. Makes it easier in court."

He took a chunky metal lighter from his pocket and a cigar from where it rested on the arm of the chair. There was a *click* and a *hiss* as fire flared from the lighter. Once he had the cigar smoldering nicely, he leaned back, cigar in one hand and whiskey in the other.

"Go on then," he said. "Tell me a story."

Elethin talked him through Laurel Anders' approach and her interview at Karmic Charisma. Gruffbar considered it to her credit that she didn't try to hide that she'd considered leaving Mana Wave. That made all the other details seem more plausible. Although if she was lying to him for some reason, perhaps that was the point of that confession. After all, she was a master at manipulating her image.

Then came the last little detail, the one that made Gruffbar lean forward in his seat.

"You're sure it was him?" he asked. "Liam Wade?"

"Positive. He's been around the office a lot lately, and he's a striking man."

Gruffbar snorted. "Maybe if he grew a beard."

"We're not here to compare tastes in men. What do you make of it?"

Gruffbar tapped his cigar over an ashtray and took a sip of his drink.

"You're sure they were digging into us?" he asked.

"Positive. They weren't direct, but they weren't subtle either. The offer was there if I wanted it. Spill what I knew in return for a lucrative and prestigious job."

"Could it have been a coincidence that Wade was there?"

"Theoretically, yes. Karmic Charisma caters to several companies in his range, and it's reasonable for somebody from sales to coordinate on their image with the company's PR firm. Realistically, him meeting with one of my interviewers straight after what I'd sat through, that doesn't feel like a coincidence."

"No, it doesn't." He drained the last of his whiskey, got out of his seat, and refilled both of their glasses. "It puts all the questions he keeps asking around the office into a different light. Less helpful ally, more corporate espionage."

"My thoughts exactly. Which begs the question, why?"

"To gain some business advantage."

"Yes, obviously, I'm not an idiot. What could he possibly think he's going to gain by going after a tiny startup like us?"

"An acquisition, maybe? Looking for leverage so he can take us out before we grow into a real competitor."

"That's a lovely fairy story, but we both know that Mana Wave's too insignificant for anyone to feel threatened."

"The tech then. He caught wind of Fran's new battery, and he wants it for Prestige Craft. They sell magical tech, right?"

"With a strong emphasis on the magic, yes."

Elethin got up from her seat and paced across the small room. As she went, she swirled her whiskey around, watching the golden liquor ooze down the inside of the glass.

"It's plausible that he could've heard about the power source," she said. "After all, it's been a part of our pitch to our investors, and we know that he's connected to at least one of them." She stopped and turned to look at Gruffbar. "You don't think Gabriella Daigle could be in on this too, could she? After all, she sent him to us."

"Not likely. She has a financial interest in our success, remember. More likely, he picked up on the connection and used her to get to us."

"Where he's trying to steal our battery tech..." Elethin frowned and shook her head. "I still don't buy it. The interview questions, Liam's inquiries, they've been more about people than technology."

"Maybe they're trying to be subtle or looking for leverage over us."

"Still…"

"What else do we have that's worth this effort, if not the tech?"

Elethin shook her head. "Nothing."

"Well then." Gruffbar grinned. "By my beard, I've missed this sort of thing. A bit of scheming and skullduggery."

"Me too."

Gruffbar took a last draw on his cigar, then ground it out. He reached for the whiskey bottle.

"There's still one thing you haven't told me," he said.

"What's that?"

"Are you going to take the job?"

She looked at him with a shocked expression, her hand clutched to her chest.

"You think I'd do that to you all, sell you out for my advancement?"

"In a heartbeat."

The shock vanished, replaced by a wry smile.

"You're right. I would." She took a sip of her whiskey. "The question is, what profits me more? If someone on the outside thinks Mana Wave is worth spying on, that says they think we're going places. I'd hate to miss out on the chance to see my initial investment grow into those mythical Mana Valley millions because I was impatient."

"What investment? You have no money."

"My investment of time and hard work, the same as the rest of you."

"You still haven't answered my question."

"I haven't, have I?" She walked over to where the shotgun leaned against the wall and brushed her fingers across its barrel. For a moment, the gun seemed to flicker. "Would you have shot me if I'd been looking suspicious?"

"In a heartbeat."

She smiled. "One more argument for why I should stick with this company. For all of Fran's fresh-faced innocence, we also have the sort of people who will do what's needed."

"You said we. That means you're staying."

"I am." She put her glass down on the table and looked around the apartment again. "Though not here. Your home decoration skills are appalling, and the drinks are tolerable at best."

"I'll have a word with my bartender."

"Please do." She opened the door, then turned to look back at him. "You should tell Fran. She trusts you."

"You should tell her. She trusts all of us. After you considered leaving, doing this will help you to keep that trust."

"You're looking out for my best interests. How sweet."

"My best interests. I want this company to hold together."

"Don't pretend that you're not trying to be a good guy, Gruffbar. It only suits one of us."

She headed out, and the door *clicked* shut behind her.

Gruffbar set the whiskey bottle back on the table, next to his engine parts and the cloth to clean them. He should deal with the shotgun first. If they had people spying on them, the situation could escalate, which meant he needed to be ready. A clean, well-maintained gun was a big part of that.

He reached for the shotgun where it leaned against the wall, and his hand passed straight through it. He frowned and tried again. The same thing happened. He hadn't drunk anywhere near enough to be fumbling this. What was going on?

Then he remembered Elethin's hand on the barrel, that flicker of magic. She'd hid his gun somehow and replaced it with an illusion. One more petty trick, another tiny scratch at her itch for revenge.

He would've laughed, but that was his favorite shotgun. Instead, he flung the door open and strode out after her.

"Hey, elf! Bring my gun back!"

CHAPTER THIRTY

"You look really nice again," Josie said as she and Fran climbed out of the taxi. "I mean, not going on a fancy date with Liam sort of nice, but nice still. It's a very pretty dress."

"Thanks." Fran clutched the bottle of sparkling juice she'd bought from a farmers' market.

"Exactly the right sort of nice for meeting your dad."

"Thanks." Fran looked up from the bottle with worry written across her face. "Do you think he'll like me?"

"He should. You're amazing," Josie linked arms with her friend and led her toward Irene's apartment building. "If he doesn't, that's his problem, not yours, understand?"

Fran nodded, a small, jerky motion. "Okay."

"I mean it. You're Fran Berryman, the one person in all the world I've chosen to live with, the one friend who's been there whenever I needed her, ever since college. Remember when Will dumped me, and you turned up ten minutes later with a bag full of chocolate? Or when I almost got arrested on that trip down to Texas, and you came to bail me out?"

"You did get arrested!"

"Technically, yes, but I never got a record, so I don't think it counts. The point is, you're brilliant. He'll see that, and if he's not willing to admit it, he's the loser here."

"I guess." Fran squeezed Josie's arm. "Thanks."

"Remember, there's another guy who wants to spend time with you, a certain well-dressed man with excellent taste in restaurants as well as women."

Fran blushed. The thought of Liam instantly cheered her up. For all her doubts, that had been an amazing date, and she had high hopes for more to come. Dates that would get her over this pointless doubt and let her enjoy what he represented.

"Hey look, someone else came to give you support." Josie stopped six feet from the door of the building, looking up at a nearby tree. Its branches were full of crows.

Fran stared at the birds in surprise. It was often hard to tell them apart, but some of the ones in the tree looked familiar. She hadn't seen a crow all day, which was unusual for her, and seeing a whole murder of them gathered like this felt even stranger.

"What are you guys doing here?" she asked.

As one, the crows all *cawed*. It was a harsh, discordant sound that lasted only a couple of seconds. It should've been unsettling, but something about it soothed Fran. The crows weren't exactly friends, but they always seemed to be present for her. That made them reassuring, like pulling on an old sweater or eating a favorite dessert.

"Thank you for your support." She waved at them. "I'll see you later, okay?"

With a chorus of beating wings, the crows fluttered into the air.

Two minutes later, Fran and Josie had been buzzed into the building and were standing outside Irene's door. Fran's hands tightened around the bottle again.

"Thanks for coming along," she said quietly.

"Happy to be here. I like Irene, and I have to admit, I'm curious about your father."

"I don't think I could've done this without knowing you'd be here."

"I'm honored that you chose me." Josie looked at her friend with concern. "If you want to walk away, we can still do that. If you're not sure, just say. He waited twenty-three years. He can wait a few more weeks."

"No, I want to do this."

"Okay, but if you change your mind at any point, if it all gets too much, give me the nod and we're out of there."

"Okay. Thanks." Fran straightened her back and raised a hand. "Let's do this."

She knocked on the door.

Footsteps hurried across the apartment, then the door opened. Irene stood behind it, wearing a brittle smile and a dark blue dress. It was a more elegant outfit than Fran usually saw her mom wear, and even though it seemed reasonable for a dinner party, it still cranked Fran's nerves up an extra notch.

"Hello, dear." Irene hugged Fran, both hanging on a little tighter than they normally did. "Josie, it's lovely to see you too. Why don't you both come in?"

"Is he here already?" Fran asked quietly, both nervous and excited.

Irene nodded.

Josie squeezed Fran's shoulder.

"I'll be right here if you need me," she whispered.

Every muscle in her body clenched tight, Fran followed her mom into the apartment. A man was rising from the sofa. He was tall and broad across the shoulders and belly and wore a tweed suit cut in an old-fashioned style with a cravat instead of a tie. His sturdy workman's boots diminished the smartness of the ensemble. His long dark hair had strands of gray running through it. In his hands was a box wrapped in sparkly blue paper and tied with a ribbon.

Fran stared at him. She'd had so little idea what to expect from her father, and she'd pictured him a hundred different ways, but none of them had been as someone she'd already met.

"I know you," she said, her voice knotted with confusion. "I met you at the skate park."

"That's right," he said. The air around him smelled of pine needles and fresh snow.

"Woodrow." Irene was aghast. "You promised me!"

Woodrow shrugged. "I happened to be there."

"You…" It was clear from Irene's face that she wanted to say a lot more, none of it polite, but she held herself back and instead spoke in a calm voice. "Francesca, this is Woodrow, your father."

Fran stared at him. She had no idea what to think or feel. In a way, having spoken before made things easier. Woodrow had seemed friendly and pleasant, so she knew that she wasn't facing some cold-hearted monster. How was she supposed to start a conversation when half her opening lines didn't make sense anymore?

A crow fluttered in through an open window and landed on Woodrow's shoulder. It winked at Fran.

"I brought you something." Woodrow held out the box.

Fran set her bottle down on the dining table, then accepted the gift. With trembling fingers, she untied the ribbon, folded back the paper, and opened the simple cardboard box. Inside was a carving of a pony, painted with a bright green dye that left the wood grain visible.

"I know you don't have this one already because I carved it myself," Woodrow said. "I hope it goes with the others."

The conversation at the skate park. She'd told him about the presents she'd most loved as a child when discussing possible gifts for his daughter. Before she'd known that the daughter was her.

"It's beautiful." She took the pony out of the box. Then her voice hardened, and she looked him in the eye. "You spied on me."

"Forgive an old man his curiosity. I wanted to make sure I did this right."

"Well, you blew that, didn't you?" She looked at the pony again. "It is lovely. Thank you."

She put the present down on the coffee table, then turned to the door. Josie was still waiting there, not wanting to intrude. Fran waved her over.

"Josie, this is my father, Woodrow." She hesitated for a moment over what word to pick next. "Woodrow, this is Josie, my best friend and roommate."

"I'm honored to meet you, Josie." Woodrow shook her hand. "Francesca, you can call me dad if you want to."

"I don't want to. At least not yet. Maybe later. We'll see."

Out of the corner of her eye, Fran noticed that Irene had relaxed, her hunched shoulders settling, her back less stiffly upright. That was good. She didn't want her mom to be unhappy, especially not in her home.

"How long until dinner, Mom?" Fran purposefully turned her attention away from Woodrow.

"We can have the starters now if you like, dear," Irene said.

"That would be great, thanks. Being nervous has made me, like, super hungry."

Woodrow laughed. It was a deep, rolling rumble of a sound, like a melodious form of thunder. "There was no need to be nervous, girl. You'd met me already."

"Without you telling her who you were," Josie said sharply. "That's not a point in your favor, asshole."

Irene gave a small gasp and hid a smile behind her hand. Fran was stunned and strangely relieved to hear someone say what she'd been thinking. From the way Josie glanced at her and the hint of a grin at the corner of her friend's mouth, she thought that might've been the point.

"Fighting spirit." Woodrow nodded. "I approve. My daughter shows good taste in her comrades. But a warning, girl, you only get one free swing at me. Next time, I fight back."

"If you say so." Josie turned brightly to Irene. "What's for dinner? It smells delicious."

They started with a spinach and watercress salad with slices of pear and blue cheese. There was a dribble of balsamic glaze across the fruit, and crushed nuts sprinkled over the top. Fran couldn't remember the last time she'd seen her mom make so much effort. Was she trying to impress Woodrow, and why? As a way of connecting, or of proving she could manage without him? Either way, the food was lovely.

"This is just as good as what I had at that fancy restaurant," Fran said, nearing the end of her salad.

"Thank you, dear." Irene beamed.

"You eat in fine places, then?" Woodrow asked, lifting the spinach with his fork and peering suspiciously underneath.

"It was a date," Josie said. "With a big executive from one of the other tech firms. Very handsome guy."

"Ah, you have a beau." Woodrow looked at Fran with pride.

"It was only one date," she corrected but couldn't help smiling. "Although I think there might be more to come. How about you, are you seeing someone? Or married? Do you have other kids? I mean, that would be totally fine, maybe even cool to meet them, like, if they want to, not that I'm assuming anything, or…" She forced herself to stop babbling. "There was a question in there somewhere. You can find it."

Woodrow laughed. Fran couldn't tell if he was laughing with her or at her.

"No, I'm not married," he said. "Nor in any way settled. I roam, and that is not a forgiving way to live where family is concerned."

"Huh." Fran tapped her fork against her empty plate. "That seems kind of sad."

"Not at all. I live glorious and free."

Josie cleared her throat loudly and glared at him.

"Not that it would have been a burden to be around you, Fran," he added hastily. "But that is not what your mother or I chose."

"Until now," Irene said. Once again, it seemed to Fran that there was much more going unsaid between her parents. "Woodrow, please clear the plates. I'll fetch the main course."

The main turned out to be spiced rice, a stew of Mediterranean vegetables with eggs poached on the top, and a cheese and mushroom quiche so tasty that the smell of it made Fran's mouth water.

"Is that tarragon?" she asked after the first bite. "It goes really well."

"Thank you, dear."

Woodrow dug through his stew like an archaeologist looking for buried remains, then turned to carving his quiche open, staring suspiciously at the contents.

"Where is the meat?" he asked.

"There isn't any," Irene said with slow deliberation. "Not every meal needs it."

"A body needs meat to grow strong."

"You can get all your protein from other things, like the eggs," Fran said. "Vitamins and minerals too."

"But…" Woodrow frowned. "You're not a vegetarian, are you?"

"Would that be a problem?" Fran looked at him, keeping her face straight. His face crumpled further as he struggled with unfamiliar social territory.

"No, you are a strong woman, you can make your own choices, but, I mean…"

Unable to hold herself back any more, Fran burst out laughing.

"The look on your face! No, I'm not vegetarian, but I almost wish I was now, so I could see you try to deal with it." She held out her plate. "Can I have some more quiche, Mom? It's great."

"Really, Irene, no meat?" Woodrow stared aghast at his former partner. "You know how I eat."

"Do I?" Irene smiled. "It's been a long time, Woodrow."

"Not for the likes of us."

"Long enough."

Fran's curiosity was piqued. She knew that Woodrow wasn't an Evermore like Irene, so who was he, if not a normally aging wizard? She set that question aside for another day. For now, she wanted to enjoy her dinner, and winding her dad up about his old-fashioned views on food.

Maybe having him in her life wouldn't be too bad.

CHAPTER THIRTY-ONE

"Are you sure about this?" Josie asked as the taxi settled down outside Worn Threads.

They'd caught a bat cab from Irene's place—a flying basket carried on ropes by a team of giant bats. It was a great way to get a reliable ride at night, as the bats' sonar meant they never missed the dangers in the darkened sky, no matter what strange creatures and machines were flying above Mana Valley.

"I'm sure." Fran opened the door of the basket and climbed out.

"Going to the office at midnight is how you turn into a workaholic."

"I wouldn't normally, but I'm too hyped up to sleep. I mean, I met my dad today, or I learned that I'd already met my dad, and he was…"

"Weird? Intense?"

"Yes, those! I don't know if I like him or how he fits into my life or anything, and I know I can't answer those questions yet, but I can't stop thinking about them, and my brain is like a box full of phones all vibrating at once. If I try to sleep, I'll get more and more worked up and frustrated and tired and—"

"You go work." Josie finally cut her friend off. "I need to sleep. I've got my work in the morning."

"Thanks for being there for me, Josie."

"No problem. I'll see you tomorrow."

Josie closed the door of the basket, and the cab took off into the air, the bats' wings flapping softly through the night.

Fran took her keys out of her purse and made for Worn Threads' front door. When she put her key in the lock and turned it, there wasn't the resistance she'd expected. The door swung open as if it were unlocked all along.

That was weird. Raulo and Gail were normally fastidious about locking up their store. She hoped that nothing bad had happened. Perhaps they'd gotten distracted while on their way out.

She walked into the store, locked the door behind her, and went to switch off the alarm system, but that wasn't on either. Raulo and Gail must have been really distracted. She would have to check in with them tomorrow, make sure that nothing was wrong, and let them know she was happy to help if they needed it. That was the least she could do for the people giving her free work space.

As an Evermore, it was easy for her to summon a small handful of light, which she used to illuminate her path across the store, past big rolls of carpet and sample books set out on low tables. The door to the basement was closed but again not locked, and that made Fran tense. For this to be open meant that it was someone in her team who hadn't locked up properly, not Gail or Raulo. Was everything okay?

When she opened the door and light shone out, she almost laughed in relief. Of course. Someone else hadn't been able to sleep and had come to work instead. She would have to remind them to lock the front door when working after hours, but at least the place hadn't been left unattended. She smiled. It would be nice to have someone to work with, a bit more distraction from the thoughts still buzzing around in her brain.

Whoever was in the basement stopped moving as Fran came down the stairs. The sound of typing stopped, replaced by a midnight silence.

"It's only me," Fran called. "I couldn't sleep either. Figured I'd come in."

She walked past the partitions into the office. To her surprise, Liam sat at one of the computers, looking at her with a fixed smile.

"Hi," he said. "You're working late too, huh?"

"Yes…" She frowned, confused. "You don't have keys."

"I borrowed them from Bart. Wanted to look at some documents he'd been telling me about."

"Huh." She took a step around the desk. This was all a little odd, and that cold, hard, wary feeling she'd had before was trying to push forward. Still, she needed something nice, and Liam was nice to see. After the evening she'd had, she could do with some comfort and reassurance, someone who would tell her how lovely she was. Someone who wouldn't only tell her that but show her, perhaps, like he'd wanted to outside the restaurant.

"You could check with Bart if you want." He apparently

misread the source of her worries. "Although I guess he might be asleep by now."

"You're right. I shouldn't bother him."

That had reminded Fran of her phone and the fact that she hadn't checked it since stepping inside her mom's apartment. Before she let herself get distracted, she should check her messages, just in case.

"Working on something interesting?" She set her bag down on the desk across from Liam.

"Oh, some initial costings for if we took different prototypes to the production phase. I know it's a bit far ahead, but Bart's a thorough guy."

"He really is." Fran pulled out her phone and looked at the screen. "That's odd. Elethin doesn't normally message me after work."

"I'm nearly done here." Liam pulled a thumb drive from the computer and shut down while Fran unlocked her phone. "You want to go get a drink? I know a place nearby that's open all hours and does a great mojito."

"Just a second…"

Fran opened the message from Elethin and read,

Don't trust Liam. He's spying on us. He set up a job interview to squeeze me for secrets, but I'm not going anywhere. Call me when you get this, whatever time it is, and we can discuss next steps.

Fighting to keep her face blank, Fran reread the message twice to ensure she hadn't misunderstood. There it was, clearly spelled out by one of her team. There was a reason for that dark, suspicious feeling she'd been getting.

All Liam's questions, his innocent inquiries, his attempts to be helpful. It was all a lie.

Their date was a lie.

Dinner was a lie.

That almost kiss…

"Fran, are you okay?" He moved slowly toward her. One hand was reaching out, but that hand was a distraction, trying to draw her attention from what his other hand was doing, quietly sliding the thumb drive toward his pocket. A small drive full of what he really cared about— her company's secrets.

Anger flared through her. What was with all these men spying on her, not being honest about what they wanted? Men with fancy restaurants and carved ponies and promises that she mattered to them. She'd had enough.

Without ever consciously choosing what to do, she let that anger focus her magic. Light blazed, intense and righteous, from the tip of her finger. It struck the thumb drive. Liam yelped in pain and dropped the drive as it melted, liquid metal and plastic spattering across the floor.

"What the hell?" he exclaimed. "You crazy—"

He drew a deep breath, and his anger, his true face, vanished behind a pretense of concern. She could see through him now. She knew it wasn't real.

"Fran, are you all right?" he asked. "What did you do that for?"

"What was on there?" she asked. "Blueprints? Patents? Our financial records? No, that wouldn't have any value. It must be something technical."

"I told you, it's financial projections."

"I know you're lying, Liam. I know you're spying on us.

So why don't you tell me the truth before I kick your sleazy ass out of here?"

They looked at each other for a long moment, Liam still keeping up his pretense of concern, despite the fury in her voice and her face. Then he shrugged.

"Address books from all your staff. I don't even care about your pathetic inventions. I care about who you know."

"Yeah, right. You can't help lying, can you?"

"Believe me or not, I don't care. I need the information." He drew his wand. "That means I need to stop you from causing trouble until I've downloaded it again."

He raised the wand and chanted a spell, but Fran was faster. She didn't need her wand. She opened her mouth and unleashed a blast of magical sound. It flung him off his feet and into one of the partitions, which crashed beneath the impact. Liam rolled and came to his feet next to Singar's workbench.

"No wand?" he asked. "Neat trick, but I have plenty of my own. Stupefacio!"

With a snap of his wand, a bolt of magic shot across the room. Fran ducked, and it barely clipped her, but she still felt the effect of the stun spell, her body and brain slowing. She flung herself down behind a desk while she tried to shake it off.

"You think it's that easy?" Liam stalked across the room. "That I'm going to leave you to recover?"

He came around the desk and pointed the wand at her. Fran flung up her hand, and a blast of light melted his ice bolt, filling the air with steam. As Liam waved the cloud away, Fran scrambled back across the office.

"This could've been easy for you," Liam said. "Fun, even. A few more meals, a few more drinks, a little pillow talk. Something memorable for you once you went back to being this weird, single nerd girl with a head full of ridiculous machines."

"They're not ridiculous!" She flung a bolt of light at him, and he deflected it with a protective spell.

"You built a smellophone. That's like a bad joke some toddler would come up with. Your company's never going to come to anything because that's what you are, a big kid trying to play at being a grownup."

He waved his wand, and a string of spells struck around Fran. One knocked a workbench flying, and it crashed into the stacked storage crates, scattering their contents across the floor. Two more spells flashed harmlessly against the floor, but a fourth flung Fran back, and she slammed into the sheet covering the massive mirror on one wall.

She winced and tried to push herself to her feet. She was tired and aching and disappointed at the world, but she wasn't going to let him beat her.

"What a wasted opportunity." Liam shook his head. "For both of us. You really did look good in that dress."

He pointed his wand straight at her. Magic swirled around the tip.

Fran twisted aside, pulling the sheet with her. Liam's spell hit the magical mirror, and while a part of it formed frost across the glass, part of the magic flew back at him. It hit him in the shoulder, and ice formed across his arm, all the way down to the wand.

"What's that?" Liam's eyes were wide as he stared at the figures moving in the mirror.

"Those were the first people to try and ruin my business," Fran said. "Still think I'm ridiculous now?"

Liam started chanting another spell, but he couldn't channel the magic with his frozen wand hand.

"This isn't over," he snarled. "I know where else your friends are hidden. I know what to take. I'm going to make you hurt for defying me."

He turned and ran, heading for the stairs.

Fran got to her feet. The anger was still blazing inside her, narrowing her light power to something violent in its intensity. She pointed at Liam's back, then raised her hand. She didn't want to kill him. Instead, she shot a blast of light across the top of his head, leaving a scorched gap through his perfect hair. Then he was out the door and gone, leaving behind a smell of burned hair.

For a moment, Fran considered running after him. Still, she wasn't out for blood. She only wanted to keep her business safe, and as far as she could see, she'd done that. She sagged. She still couldn't sleep, not with all the adrenaline coursing through her veins.

Maybe it was a good thing that the basement was in a complete state, with partitions and furniture overturned, storage boxes broken, and parts scattered across the floor. That would give her something to do. Possibly too much if she wanted to get things in order before the start of the working day. She did want that. She didn't want Liam to have the satisfaction of slowing Mana Wave down for even a few hours.

She picked up her phone and called Elethin.

"Hi, I got your message, and you said I should call at whatever time."

"Of course," Elethin replied. "Listen, I'm sorry about taking that interview, I shouldn't have—"

"Can you come to the office? I need help tidying up Liam's mess. We fought, and there are bits of workshop everywhere."

"I don't really do tidying up."

"If it helps, you can think of it as penance for almost leaving us."

There was a moment's silence before Elethin spoke again. "I'll see you in twenty minutes."

CHAPTER THIRTY-TWO

"When I stayed up all night, it used to be for glamorous parties full of famous people," Elethin said as she and Fran walked down the street, away from Worn Threads. "Now I'm dressed like the worst sort of college slacker, and I've spent the night doing a cleaner's work. How did it come to this?"

Dawn had broken over Mana Valley, and the city was coming to life, with the first traffic crawling into the streets. A single crow watched them from a lamppost.

Fran examined Elethin's outfit of perfectly fitted yoga pants and a little t-shirt that showed off a hint of her flat belly. "Your idea of dressing down is very different from mine."

"You're wearing a dress and a very nice one. Not my style, of course, but it suits you."

"Thanks, I think. I wore this for dinner. I was meeting my dad about twelve hours ago, or perhaps a thousand years ago, judging by how tired I feel."

"You just met your father? That's... Congratulations or

commiserations, depending on what's appropriate. How was it?"

"Weird. Turned out I'd met him before."

"Life is never what it looks like."

"True."

They reached the Blazing Bean, which had just opened for the day. Cam sat behind the counter with a big old book in his hands and a laptop in front of him. He hastily put the book away as they walked in.

"I wasn't expecting anyone this early," he said. "Certainly not you guys, but I shouldn't be surprised. You always work so hard."

"We've certainly worked hard tonight." Elethin held up a hand. "Fran has reduced me to a manual laborer. I'll get callouses next. I mean, look at this."

"At what?"

"My fingers."

"Um…"

"I've chipped a nail."

"Oh. I'm…sorry?"

"Correct." Elethin sighed. "Now, coffee, please. And a plate of pastries, at least three each." She took a payment card from her purse. "One last act of penance, breakfast is on me."

The two of them slumped into padded chairs by the window.

"These seats are my new best friends," Fran said. "I hang out with them all the time."

"They're fine, as seats go. Could do with better padding."

"Should we tell the management?"

"Not until they've served us. Then I'll know whether to complain about anything else." Elethin took out a compact mirror and a makeup set. To Fran's surprise, the elf didn't start work on her face but instead slid them across the low table.

"What's this for?" Fran asked.

"To fix your makeup, of course. You look like the last woman standing at a dwarf party, and if you don't know what I mean by that, we need to get you out and about more."

"Don't you want to do your makeup first?"

"I look magnificent already. Besides, I'm not the priority here. As well as being our CEO, you're a woman who went through a breakup. It's your duty to look amazing so everyone knows that you've come out on top while he's scuttling back to his hole."

"I don't feel magnificent."

"All the more reason to armor up."

Cam appeared with a tray. He set down two large mugs of coffee and a heaping plate of pastries.

"I added a few extra," he said. "To make sure you got enough." He hovered for a moment uncertainly. "You look really nice, Fran. Have you been somewhere special?"

"Dinner with my mom."

"All night?"

"No, then I had to stop Liam robbing our business. It's been, like, the weirdest night in forever."

"Liam was robbing you?" Cam's hands tightened on the tray. "Where is he now?"

"Licking his wounds." Elethin sipped her coffee. "Let

that be a lesson to any man who messes with the CEO of Mana Wave."

Fran shook her head. "I don't know where he is, but it's all good now. Raulo and Gail are keeping an eye on the place while we get caffeine." She sipped her coffee. "Thanks, Cam. You're the best."

"I try." He looked around as another customer came in. "Got to go serve. I'll be back."

As he hurried off, Fran dove into the pile of pastries. Maybe Elethin was right, and she should make sure she was presenting her best face to the world, but first, she needed to get some calories and caffeine inside her. It was the only way to get through the day after a sleepless night.

"So, Liam." Elethin pulled a croissant apart with the tips of her fingers like she was carefully dissecting some pastry-based corpse. "Without setting a precedent for heart-to-hearts, do you want to tell me what happened?"

"No." Fran stuffed half a pain au chocolat into her mouth in a single bite. It was a whole minute before she was able to speak again. "All right, yes."

"Come on, then." Elethin gestured. "Tell me all about it."

Fran sighed and slid lower in her seat.

"I thought he liked me," she mumbled. "He was always asking about me, and he listened, let me talk. He seemed to care."

"That's far too rare."

"I know, right? That's what makes it worse. So many guys want to talk about themselves or their careers or record collections, but he seemed to care. Except that he didn't care about me. He cared about sneaking into our company and stealing our secrets."

Fran wasn't surprised to hear herself talking so much, but she was surprised to find herself talking about something so personal to Elethin. That wasn't going to stop her from speaking. She was too tired to care who heard.

"It's the disappointment that hurts, you know? Like, not even the betrayal. That's obvious. It's crude. It's what happens when you trust someone you shouldn't—being made to believe that you can find a decent guy like that, only to learn that it's all a lie, a trick, a way of getting into your corporate records. How is that worse than trying to get into my pants? Because it sure feels worse.

"I don't even know if he's the worst. I mean, who spies on their daughter? Spies on her before telling her who they are, even. I don't care if he was nervous or curious or what. That's weird and creepy."

"Liam has a daughter? I didn't know that."

"What? No, this is Woodrow."

"Who's Woodrow?""

"My dad. Can you believe that? I couldn't."

Elethin, with one eyebrow raised and a fragment of pastry halfway to her mouth, sat staring at Fran in fascination.

"You're telling me that both your father and your boyfriend were spying on you?"

"I couldn't call him my boyfriend."

"Still, it's like something out of a soap opera. You don't know anyone in a coma, do you?"

"I don't think so."

"Any evil twins?"

"No. Though for all I know I might have half-brothers and half-sisters out there. He never answered that part."

"Amazing. Please, keep talking. Get it all off your chest."

Fran downed the rest of her coffee. It did feel good to tell someone about all of this. Of course, she would talk about it all with Josie later, but it was good of Elethin to listen to her now.

"I showed him," she muttered.

"Your father?"

"No, Liam." Fran grinned. "I burned his hair."

"You burned his…" Elethin laughed. "Oh, dear. That's going to take some hiding. He was so proud of it, too."

"Yeah, well…" Fran waved. "Don't mess with the magic fingers."

"You might not want to say that on your dating profile."

"No dating for me. Not after this. Work all the way."

"Oh, don't say that. If today is anything to go by, the world would be a far less interesting place without you dating."

They looked up as Gruffbar walked in with a long bag over his shoulder. Instead of going to the counter to order, he came straight to their table.

"Any more sign of Wade?" he asked.

"No, but magic fingers here is ready for him," Elethin said.

"That's right," Fran said. "Fizz, whoosh, blammo! I'll burn the rest of his hair off."

"Are you all right?" Gruffbar looked at her with concern.

"I'm fine. Just very tired. Hey, what's in your bag?"

"Shotgun, just in case."

"Aw," Elethin said. "Were you worried someone might steal it again?"

"Just in case there's trouble with Liam. He went to extremes. I'm not taking any chances for the next few days."

"We're executives, not gangsters," Elethin pointed out.

"You of all people know how little difference there is. Now come on, we should be in the office, just in case."

Fran started to get up. Her whole body felt heavy.

"You stay here and rest," Elethin said. "If we need you, we'll call."

"Sure?"

"I'm sure."

The dwarf and the elf walked out, arguing as they went.

Cam came over, carrying another cup of coffee. "Here." He set it down next to Fran. "I thought you might need this."

"Thanks." She fumbled for her wallet.

"My treat," he said.

"Aw, that's sweet." She rubbed a sleepy eye, then sipped. "Ooh, coconut milk and chocolate syrup! That's really good."

"Thought you'd like it." Cam hovered awkwardly, rubbing the back of his neck with one hand. "I have to admit. I heard some of what you guys were saying. Are you okay?"

"I'll be fine. Not hurt, just really tired. Don't know why."

"Apart from staying up all night?"

"I've done that before."

"And the emotional turmoil, the fight, the cleanup work?"

"I guess, maybe..." She took another sip. "But coffee,

Cam. Coffee normally makes everything better when I stay up all night inventing. Why isn't it working now?"

"You used some pretty intense magic, right? Maybe that's worn you out. It can do that."

"I suppose." She sighed. "Maybe I should go home and sleep."

"Good idea."

"In a minute."

"Sure. Hey, for what it's worth, I never thought Liam was good enough for you. He was too slick and fancy. He wouldn't have stayed up all night watching cartoons or gone with you to the video arcade. I can't see him even trying on a pair of roller skates. You deserve someone who will join in with the things you love, and he would've tried to make you into someone else instead."

"I guess." She sighed. "Still, it hurts, you know? Getting your hopes up, and then…" She slapped her palm against the table, spilling coffee and bouncing pastry crumbs around. "Splat. A hard fall and collide with reality."

"Well…" He hesitated a moment longer, looking down at his hands. "I'm not going to push this now, but I don't want to risk missing my chance again, so, um, once you feel up to it, I'd like to take you out on a date myself." He pushed his glasses up his nose. "No pressure. No rush. I'll understand if you say no. But if you want to, then a proper Fran date, something fun."

She blinked, then blinked again, while her sluggish brain processed what she'd heard. To her surprise—how much surprise could one night take?— excitement stirred through the exhaustion. She smiled.

"Sure, someday." Her eyelids were drooping. "After I've had… I've had…"

Her eyes finally slid shut, and she fell asleep.

Cam stood for a little while, watching her with a fond smile. Then he took the cup from her hand, fetched a blanket from under the counter, and draped it over her.

"You rest for a bit," he whispered. "We can come back to this conversation."

CHAPTER THIRTY-THREE

Josie walked into the Blazing Bean, carefully carrying a bag emblazoned with the Philgard Technologies logo. She always tried to take care of the things she received, but today she had to be extra careful.

"Hi, Cam." She rested the bag on the counter to avoid knocking its contents against anything. "Can I have a green tea, please? Have you seen Fran? She went to work in the middle of the night, and I haven't seen her since."

"She's over there." Cam nodded at one of the window tables. "Haven't you heard what happened?"

The way he said those words immediately put Josie on edge.

"No, what's happened?" she asked. "Is it a problem with Mana Wave, or has somebody done something to Fran?"

"She should tell you herself." Cam handed over the tea.

Josie hurried to the table by the window where her friend was sitting. Fran still wore her dress from the previous night, with a blanket over her knees. On the low table next to her was a heap of plates and cups, so many that Josie didn't think Fran could've consumed all their contents by herself. Enfield sat across the table from Fran, both of them drinking coffee while they talked.

"Fran!" Josie pulled a chair over. "What's going on? Cam made it sound like something bad."

"I was just telling Enfield…" Fran started talking, explaining what had happened the night before. She detailed everything from the moment Josie dropped her off to waking up sitting in the coffee shop with the blanket across her lap and Cam watching over her from behind the counter.

Josie listened in shock, then growing anger, then relief to hear that Fran had come out of it almost entirely unscathed. "What are you going to do now?"

"Not much, for now," Fran admitted. "Elethin says we're going to the press but that she needs a little time to set it up right, to work out the story and provide extra evidence. She thinks we can do a lot of damage to Liam and his company, which he deserves after this, but it doesn't make things any better for us unless we phrase it carefully, you know?"

"Do you know what he was after?"

"Not exactly. I mean, the battery's the main thing. It's a shame, if he'd worked with us, we could have put it out together, but he had to get greedy, and now it's all a mess."

"At least you weren't hurt."

"That's what I've been saying to her," Enfield said. "Not that he stood any chance against Fran and everything she can do."

Josie smiled at that. She hadn't talked with Enfield much, only met him in passing as they both hung around with Fran, but it seemed like he was the sort of support her friend needed.

"Do you know what Liam's doing now?" she asked. "I mean, could he be going to the press as well, trying to tell them stories to discredit you, so people won't listen when you talk about him."

"Elethin says she's got that covered." Fran laughed. "I've never seen her like this before. She's like some warrior of words, all pumped up and out for blood. Bart said he would talk to some people as well, but I think he mostly said that to make me feel better. It's not like the people he knows run news sites and TV stations."

"They might spread the word around other executives, though, make people less likely to work with Liam."

Fran sighed. "I should do something. The others all say that I should take some time off work, get rested, recover from what's happened. If I sit around, I'm going to think about it, and I'm going to drive myself nuts. Maybe I could go home and get my skates or head down to the place with all the retro video games."

"Or maybe I could provide a distraction. I brought something to show you..."

Josie reached for her Philgard bag, then realized in alarm that she didn't have it anymore. She looked around, trying hard not to panic. The design team had only let her have the new Manaphone prototype reluctantly, with a lot of pressure from Julia. Before letting her take it, they'd stated over and over again how important it was to keep it safe, not to let it get into the wrong hands, and she'd already let something happen to it.

At that moment, Cam walked over, carrying the bag. Josie let out a deep breath of relief.

"You left this on the counter," Cam said. "Sorry, my fault for distracting you."

Josie grabbed the bag and held it close. "Thank you so much. I almost gave myself a heart attack there. I was so worried."

"Happy to help. Is it something important?"

"For my career, maybe."

Josie took a box out of the bag and set it down on the table, then removed the lid. Inside was a magically enabled smartphone. "The latest prototype for the new Mana-phone. Refined and improved based on a whole load of testing, feedback, and novel ideas, all of which started with Fran and her mom."

"Really?" Fran leaned forward, peering at the phone. "They used my ideas?"

"And then some. Tell me one of the things that you and Irene came up with."

"An aura filter."

"Okay."

Josie unlocked the phone, opened its camera function, and tapped a couple of options. She pointed it at Fran, who smiled while her friend took a photo, then at Cam, who merely raised an eyebrow.

"Here we go." Josie held the phone out so they could all see, then flicked back and forth between the two photos. "See, the picture of Fran has captured her magical aura. It's really bright, full of light, with wavy lines. It's all her chaos and excitement and energy, in magical form. Then you look at Cam, and there's almost no magical aura at all, barely even a hint of anything there, only the background magic of any living thing."

"Thanks for the reminder of my inadequacies," Cam said.

Josie looked up, about to apologize, but then she saw the mischievous look on his face.

"It's okay," he said. "I came to terms with being a dud years ago."

"You shouldn't call yourself that," Fran said. "You're awesome, just not in a spells and powers kind of way."

The smile that put on Cam's face reassured Josie that she hadn't offended him.

"What else did you and Irene talk bout?" she asked.

"Turning it into a magical projector."

"Oh, yes. That part's limited in what it can do, largely because of the phone's limited store of magical power. But still…"

Josie tapped the screen again and set the phone down. The picture of Fran appeared in the air above the phone, projected in light and magic onto nothing at all.

"That's so cool!" Fran exclaimed and waved her hand through the image.

"It's small, and the picture quality's not great," Josie said. "You can't put it up for long without completely killing the battery. Still, it's a fun novelty, and that should get us some extra publicity when the phone launches."

"It's like one of the things we're working on, only our version does more, and it's not in a phone." Fran took the phone and started scrolling through its app icons, looking for new and interesting options. "Ooh, did you put in the magic device detector?"

"Yes, but again, it's limited, at least for now. We were trying to cram the technology of an entirely separate device into a small corner of this, so we were never going to get the full function. The range is lousy, and sensitivity's not great, but it's better than nothing. There, it's the one with the finger symbol."

Fran tapped on it, then held the phone out in front of her. The screen had turned white, with a green patch at one edge.

"That's a weird color scheme," she said.

"We carried it over from the previous device. I expect that they'll make the colors more appealing before it goes on sale."

"How does it work?"

"Move it around, you'll see."

Fran did as instructed. The green at the side of the screen grew in intensity as she moved the phone closer to her handbag.

"Oh, it's changing as it gets near something! It's found my wand."

"Exactly."

"Now it's finding your wand." She waved it around Josie. "And something on Enfield, about waist level. Are you wearing a magical belt?"

He pulled up the bottom of his sweater, revealing a row of tiny potion bottles with different colored liquids.

"Not quite," he said, "but after some of the trouble I've seen recently, I'm carrying more of these."

"What do they do?" Josie leaned forward, curious.

"Different things for different occasions. This one is for

healing. This one restores magical power. That one creates a flash of light when it's smashed."

"I didn't know you did alchemy."

"I'm a man of many talents."

"Clearly."

"Ooh, ooh, ooh!" Fran waved the phone around. "What about the remote controller? Did you get it so you can use it to control other devices?"

"Fran Berryman, do you really think I'd give you some sort of magical universal remote control?" Josie asked. "Imagine the chaos you'd create."

"Aw." Fran slumped, her enthusiasm waning a little. Then she noticed the gleam in her friend's eye. "You did do it, didn't you?"

"Oh yes, we did." Josie pointed at another icon on the screen. "Tap on that, then see what you can do."

They all watched as Fran waved the phone around again, more purposefully this time. At her remote command, her wand rose out of her bag and hovered above the table.

"That's so cool." She turned the phone to point at Enfield's potions. "Aw, nothing's happening."

"They're not sophisticated enough to control remotely." Josie looked around. "There must be some other magitech devices in here you can try."

"The coffee machine," Cam said. "The manager added a new magical filter to help keep it clean."

Fran waved the phone at the machine behind the counter. Sure enough, steam started shooting out, and coffee poured from one of the spouts.

"This is brilliant!" she said. "Although I probably should've put a cup there first. How do I stop it?"

"How did you start it?"

"I'm not sure. I was pressing things and waving things and…"

Cam ran over to turn the coffee maker off, while Josie reluctantly took the phone from her friend's hand, locked the screen, and set it down in the box.

"That's enough for one day," she said.

"I suppose." Fran smiled. "Thanks, Josie. For listening to me and for bringing along such a cool distraction."

"Thanks for your ideas. They've really helped."

"Cool. You're not allowed to steal my smellophone idea."

"No risk of that."

The whole time, Enfield had been watching Fran's antics with the phone. Now he picked it up himself and turned it over in his hands, not trying to access its abilities, just studying the object itself.

"These things can do so many tricks," he said, "but there's one trick they do that everyone overlooks."

"What's that?" Josie asked.

"They give people the illusion of control, that their lives are their own to command. Let them speak to their friends, look up trivia, keep track of their steps, and they feel like everything is under their command when that's so far from the chaos of reality and the structures society imposes."

"How incredibly portentous." Josie took the phone from him and closed it up in the box. "You sound like the worst sort of Russian novelist, ranting about the horrors of society and the misery of the human condition."

"The worst sort, or the best? Dostoevsky had a lot to say about the society he was living in."

"He also spent a lot of time treating self-indulgent, angst-ridden men as the most important people in the world."

"I suppose they were to him. Some people might say that he was one."

Josie tilted her head, looking at him from a new perspective. "I didn't know that you read Dostoevsky."

"I've had a lot of time to read. Not much going on where I come from."

"Hm. Interesting."

Fran tapped the Manaphone box. "This is brilliant, Josie. I think you've got a real hit."

"You were bound to say that. You're my ideal target audience." Josie allowed herself a moment to bask in her success. "I think you're right. We've helped make something that people are going to love."

CHAPTER THIRTY-FOUR

Julia sat at her desk outside Howard Phillips' office, working through the vast heaps of emails that filled his corporate inbox. There were plenty she could simply delete. Others required only a brief acknowledgment in his name. Some she knew to leave for him or to flag as urgent. To her left, the door to his office was closed while he took calls and dealt with virtual meetings.

The elevator *dinged*, then opened. Josie emerged.

"Hi, Julia." She held out the box holding the Manaphone. "Thanks for arranging this for me. I showed it to one of my friends who helped with the feedback, and she loved it. I think we've got this right."

"You've definitely got it right." Julia took the box. "Thanks for bringing it back so promptly. Howard wants to have another look at it later. Was there anything else?"

"You know a lot of people in the industry, right?"

"I couldn't do this job if I didn't."

"Do you know Liam Wade, from Prestige Craft?"

Julia kept her expression fixed as an alarm bell went off

in her head. Why was Josie bringing this up? Had she over-heard something that she shouldn't have?

"I've met him once or twice. He's their head of sales, isn't he, and part of the senior management team."

"Something like that." Josie rubbed her temples. "He did a shitty thing to one of my friends, messed with her business and her personal life."

"That's awful."

"Yeah, she's been pretty hurt. She thought they were dating, but he was spying on her and trying to steal her company's secrets."

"It wouldn't be the first time, sadly."

"I feel even worse because I encouraged her. I thought that she was onto a good thing, and he was only trying to grab technology from Mana Wave."

"Mana Wave. That's your friend's company?" Now Julia had to fight to keep her surprise from showing. How had she not realized this connection between Josie and the company Howard was interested in? How could she exploit it?

"That's right. They're only a little startup. I have no idea why he picked on them."

"Some guys want to break what others have. I'm sorry for your friend."

"Thanks. Anyway, I guess I was wondering if there was anything you could tell me about Liam and his company, gossip around the Valley, that kind of thing. Fran's PR elf is going to the press with this, and the more she has, the harder she can bring this dirtbag down."

Julia leaned back, thinking carefully. Sure, she knew some

things about Liam Wade, and she would love the chance to help take him down. However, the things she knew weren't things she could share, not without endangering her boss and her position. On the other hand, some facts were a matter of public record, ones that Howard Phillips would have to face if Liam Wade's reputation suddenly turned sour.

"Sorry, I can't think of anything," she said. "But I think there are shares in Prestige Craft in Howard's portfolio. I could ask him about it, see if he knows anything I don't. Maybe even give him a nudge to sell, try to encourage people to think that something's wrong."

"You could do that?"

"No promises. Howard won't do anything that hurts his financial position, and I'm not his financial adviser. But I'll plant the idea and see what happens."

"Thanks, Julia, you're the best."

"No problem. You get back to work. I should go have a chat with Howard."

When Josie was gone, Julia knocked on Howard's office door.

"Enter!" he called.

She walked in, closed the door behind her, and laid the Manaphone box on the desk. "You wanted to have another look at this."

"I did." He looked up from his list of calls. "Is there something else?"

"We have a problem with Wade and Prestige Craft."

"What kind of problem?"

"He blew it at Mana Wave, got caught snooping around. They think he was trying to steal their technology. Reading between the lines, I think he slept with someone there as well, and that's added to the upset."

"He told you this?"

"No, I heard it elsewhere."

Phillips leaned forward. "Where?"

Julia considered her priorities. On the one hand, there was loyalty to her boss, who she ought to tell about all of this. On the other hand, there was protecting and building up her position. Josie was a valuable asset, one she didn't want drawn into Phillips' intrigues, at least not yet. Knowing more than her employer gave her some power of her own if she ever decided that a change was needed.

"It's going around the rumor mill," she said. "I picked it up from a PA at another firm."

That should add urgency to the situation, making Phillips think that this was something others had heard about, something he needed to act on fast. If he acted, Josie would appreciate it, which would tie her more closely to Julia. Wheels within wheels.

"What is Mana Wave doing?" Phillips asked.

"Going to the press. They're building up their case first, but I don't think they'll delay long."

"Hm."

Phillips got out of his seat and walked to the window. With his hands clasped behind him, he looked out across Mana Valley with its towering office blocks and the sprawl beyond them reaching out to the mountains. For a minute he stood silent and thoughtful.

"The Silver Griffins are taking more interest in white-collar crime," he said. "Cracking down on magical businesses that cross legal lines, however petty those lines might seem. I don't want us getting caught up in that, not when there's so much more at stake."

He turned from the window and looked at her.

"Can we cut the connection?" she asked. "Avoid Liam's downfall coming back to hurt you?"

"That's why I used him. Plausible deniability. He can't prove that I asked him to do what he did, and if he makes claims to the Griffins, it will look like he's lashing out, trying to hurt me. Especially after I sell all my shares in Prestige Craft and brief the press against them. His claims will seem like a lie made for revenge."

"You're going to sell the shares?" Julia allowed herself a small smile. She hadn't even had to steer him hard in the direction she wanted.

"Definitely." Phillips strode over to his phone. "Even if we weren't part of this, I'd want to get rid of them before this story diminishes their value. Of course, my sale is going to kill their worth completely."

He scrolled through his contacts until he found the number for his investment manager.

"Is there anything you'd like me to do?" Julia asked.

"Get me a press appearance as soon as you can. TV, perhaps. Who's that one with the red ties?"

"Don Karelsky?"

"Right. He's always chasing me for interviews. Tell his producer to clear their plan for this afternoon's episode. I'm going to make his day and cut my losses in the process."

"Very good, Howard."

As Julia walked out of the office, he was already on the phone, ordering the sale of the stocks. She smiled. There was a real power to serving at the foot of the throne.

Liam Wade stood over a table in a meeting room at Prestige Craft. He felt absurd, wearing a baseball cap indoors like some sort of redneck mechanic, but it was all he'd been able to find to cover his missing hair and the scorched stretch of scalp. At least his arm had thawed out. He would need it for what was coming.

Around him, members of Prestige Craft's security team were preparing for action. Some of them were readying weapons, others checking their wands. The squad leaders were looking at the map on the table. It showed a certain house in the Mana Valley foothills where Liam had followed the Evermore after seeing him leave Mana Wave.

The time for subtlety was over. They would grab the Evermore and this novel power source that Fran had mentioned over dinner. Then they would use that leverage to keep Mana Wave quiet. Hell, Liam would probably use the power source himself if it was any good. Prestige Craft could do with an upgrade to the tech they were selling.

He looked around the room. Some men had started to relax, watching Don Karelsky's business show on a screen on one wall. That was fine. There was a reason why Prestige Craft hired former mercenaries for corporate security, quite apart from their moral flexibility and willingness to do whatever Liam told them. These were people who could spring into action in a moment. They were always ready, even when they looked like they weren't.

"I'm going in with the first wave." Liam ran his finger over the map along the road that led up to the house. "I want first sight of whatever's in the house and to make sure no one damages it."

"Yes, sir," one of the security guys said.

"Take some of the men around the back, in case our magical target tries to get away. I don't want to…"

His voice trailed off as the TV show caught his attention. What was Howard Phillips doing giving an interview to Don Karelsky? That was the sort of thing that should've been announced in advance, that Karelsky's team would've used to get extra eyes on the screen. There would've been a lot of anticipation for an appearance like this, but Liam hadn't seen any publicity for it. What was going on?

He walked over. The men around the screen parted to let him closer. The interview was already well underway, with Karelsky in his usual form, sucking up to the guest.

"You've done so much to support good causes in the Valley," Karelsky said. "Today I'd like to talk about the flip side of that, about when businesses take a dark turn."

Liam snorted. As if Karelsky had decided this was what they should talk about. He'd been given his talking points by Phillips' people and was happily regurgitating them.

"That's right, Don." Phillips put on a serious expression and leaned forward in his seat. The camera zoomed in, catching the angles of his face in the bright studio light.

"For every company like ours that takes corporate responsibility seriously, there are others for whom honesty and integrity are hollow words. They bring down the industry's good name and do terrible damage to people's faith in us and our products. That's why it's so important that, when we identify a bad player, we don't leave it to the authorities. Business has to show that it can keep its own house in order."

"Could you give me an example, Howard?"

"Of course, Don. Up until recently, I was heavily invested financially in Prestige Craft."

In the meeting room, every single security guard froze. None of them turned to look at Liam, but he could feel their attention, could see them watching him from the corners of their eyes.

His hands clenched into fists. What was that traitor Phillips doing to him?

"Then I learned through a trusted source that a senior executive at Prestige Craft, Liam Wade, had been indulging in some unsavory and potentially illegal business practices and that the company had done nothing to restrain him."

"What sorts of things had he done?"

"That's not my story to tell, Don." Phillips leaned back in his seat. "Although I think you'll hear more over the next few days. The point I want to make is this. As soon as I heard what was happening at Prestige Craft, I sold off my investment in that company.

"I don't want to support a business like that, financially or any other way. I don't want my money to send a signal that I approve of their behavior, that I think it's acceptable or even profitable. We have to send a message to bad companies that we won't take their money, we won't give them ours, and we absolutely will not work with them.

"I don't know this Liam Wade well, although I'm sure I've met him once or twice. That's how the Valley works. But I know his type, and that type cannot be allowed to—"

Liam slammed his fist into the screen, which shattered

in a shower of sparks. Now the security guards were staring openly at him.

Phillips had set him up and now was abandoning him. Well, screw Phillips. Liam knew things that Phillips didn't. He knew where the Evermores were, whoever they were. He knew about this power source. Once he had those things, he'd use them to prove that Phillips was the villain. He'd bring that smug asshole down and that Mana Wave witch with him.

"Everybody grab your wands," he growled. "We're going now."

CHAPTER THIRTY-FIVE

"If you're such a big reader, how come I've never seen you with a book?" Fran asked as she and Enfield approached the Evermores' house.

"Why would you? Reading is for when I'm alone." Enfield opened the door and let them both in. "Why would I lie about something like this?"

"To impress Josie. Guys lie to girls sometimes, to talk them into dates or to infiltrate their companies for financial gain."

"One of those things is not like the other."

"Well, they both suck."

"I agree. Even if I did want to impress your friend, I'm a hundred and fifty years old. I've outgrown telling lies she'll quickly see through."

"OK, then where are all your books?"

"In my bedroom. Do you want to see them, or does that sound too much like I'm trying to chat you up now?"

"Ooh, no! No offense, Enfield, but you're practically family. I don't think about you like that."

"The feeling is mutual. Shall we get to work instead?"

They walked through to the room where the containment unit held the Source. Fran connected measuring devices to the containment unit, then recorded their readings as Enfield summoned small portals in different places around the field.

While they worked, Fran kept looking at the Source, remembering what they'd learned from her mom. Enfield seemed able to keep working despite it, but Fran found it increasingly difficult to concentrate on what she was doing now that she saw the Source as a thinking, feeling being, one that could be hurt and frustrated by what it was going through. She didn't want to leave it trapped like that, but what else was she going to do, leave the whole of Earth without the magical power it needed?

"Fran?" Enfield snapped his fingers.

"What?" She looked up from her laptop screen and realized that she hadn't registered the figures on it.

"You were miles away. What's going on with you?"

"Nothing, I'm just…"

A movement caught Fran's attention. Through the window, people were running up the driveway, people in black clothes and body armor. They carried wands and guns. Liam was leading them.

"Look out!"

She flung herself at Enfield, knocking him to the floor as a steel cylinder smashed through the window and clattered to the floor, streaming smoke. A gun made *popping* sounds, and tranquilizer darts flew past, burying themselves in the wall.

"Attack!" Enfield yelled at the top of his lungs. "We're under attack!"

There was a *crash* as someone smashed the door open, then voices raised in anger and alarm. Guns fired, fists *thudded*, and spells *crackled* somewhere in the thickening smoke that filled the house.

Fran got to her feet. A black-clad figure was running at her. She held up her hand and launched a concentrated wave of sound. It hit the attacker in the chest, and they stopped, clutching their chest as they sank to their knees.

"Get out!" Fran pushed Enfield toward the door.

"But the Source…"

"It can take care of itself."

She ran for the door, or where she thought it must be. A couple of figures fell past, wrestling with each other. Light blazed from one's hand.

Another of the black-clad attackers loomed in front of Fran. She was an elf, tall and muscular, with long ears and a shaved head. She pointed a gun at Fran.

The same sense of tension and panic Fran had felt facing Liam in the basement swept over her again. She raised her hand and pointed a finger straight at the gun. A pencil-thin beam of bright light shot out and melted the end of the barrel. The elf pulled the trigger, but instead of firing, the gun let out a muffled *thump* and bucked in her hand.

"Stupid ." The elf flung the broken gun at Fran, who dodged aside. The elf summoned a ball of sparkling magic and threw it.

Fran flung up a shield of sound, which deflected the magic. The elf changed her chant and tried again. This time, instead of throwing the spell, she kept it in her hand as she swung it at Fran. The fist plowed through the protective wall of sound and hit Fran in the chest. The physical blow knocked her back while the wave of numbing magic swept through her.

She stumbled and slumped against the wall as a wave of drowsiness took hold. She had to fight back against it, had to keep on her feet, had to keep going. It had already been a long day, and she was so tired, and the magic was almost irresistible.

The elf came closer, pulling a thick cable tie from her belt.

"Guess you're one of these people we're after," she said. "There's a nice little room ready for you, hidden under HQ."

Then Enfield strode out of the smoke. His fist hit the elf in the side of the head, and she fell to the floor. It looked like a restful place to be.

"Here." Enfield handed Fran a potion. "Drink this."

With numb hands, she unscrewed the lid and tipped the contents down her throat. Immediately, the magic that had hit her vanished, and she felt her energy replenished. She was buzzing as though she'd just drunk the biggest, sugariest coffee in the world.

"Woohaa!" she exclaimed. "Let's go kick ass!"

Together, she and Enfield walked out of the smoky house into the back yard. Several Evermores lay sprawled on the grass, two of them with their hands bound behind them. Armed security guards stood over them. Others were fighting the remaining Evermores, using magic as much as weapons. Winslow was in the center of a whole crowd of attackers. He'd taken down six or seven, but the rest kept coming.

As Fran and Enfield appeared, Liam turned to face them. He wore the same black body armor as the security guards but with a backward baseball cap covering his head.

Fran snarked, "I'd say you looked better in a suit, but I don't want to inflate your ego again. So let's just say that you look like the biggest idiot I've seen all day, and it's been a really long day."

"I told you already." His sneer turned his face ugly. "You could've made this fun, but instead, you've forced me to go the other way."

"Nobody forced you to do anything. You chose to behave like this." Fran gestured at Winslow. "Enfield, go help him. I've beaten this guy once already. I can do it again."

"Like hell, you can." Liam rushed at her with his wand outstretched. A blade of magic emerged from its tip, lashing out at Fran. She flung up a sonic shield again. It blunted the magic knife's edge and sucked its momentum so what hit her was only a slow-moving stick.

She grabbed hold of his wrist and twisted, hoping to get the wand out of his hand. He clung on tight to the wand, but she turned his arm around, and he grunted in pain.

"Not so full of yourself, are you, now that you're not throwing spells at me," Fran said.

"I don't need spells."

He kicked her in the shin with a heavy boot. As she winced and stepped back, his hand came around. Once again, her magic shielding caught part of the blow, but the punch was still enough to hurt and throw her off balance.

Liam pivoted, broke her lock on his wrist, and hit her in the face with his elbow. Fran stumbled back, trying to summon the magic she'd burned him with before, the power of light funneled through her righteous fury. Again, he was ahead of her, knocking her arm aside so the light scorched the ground. Then he had hold of her wrist, twisting her arm up behind her back. Her shield couldn't help her this time. Her shoulder burned with pain.

"Do I take you captive like your weird friends?" Liam hissed in her ear. "Or do I kill you to stop you from spreading rumors about what I did?"

"Those rumors are the truth."

"Truth, lies, who cares. It's power that counts, and I have power over you."

He yanked on her arm, and she cried out in pain.

Wings fluttered, and a pair of black shapes appeared: crows. They clawed and pecked at Liam's face, angrily *croaking* as they did it. He let go of Fran's arm and thrashed his hands around, trying to beat the crows back.

"Flying fleabags," he said.

The crows kept pecking and scratching, maintaining the frenzied assault. Still, they were a fraction of Liam's size, and he knew what he was doing in a fight. He snatched one of them out of the air and squeezed. There was a *crunch*, and a sad bundle of feathers fell limp on the ground.

The surviving crow flew back, out of reach. The attack had cost it, but it had bought Fran time.

"I get it." She faced Liam with her feet braced and her hands outstretched. "You know how to fight. I don't. But I have a few tricks of my own."

She opened her mouth and summoned magic through her hands, turning her scream into a sonic blast. It hit Liam and flung him through the air, tumbling end over end like a discarded doll. He crashed through a window and into the house.

Fran ran after him. She jumped through the window, careful not to touch the broken glass, and landed in the shifting smoke.

"Where are you?" She peered through the haze. "You can't hide from me forever."

"Not forever." His voice seemed to come from everywhere at once. "Just long enough to get the jump on you, and …"

Magical chains shot out of the smoke. Fran flung herself aside, and the chains slammed into the wall, then clattered to the floor. She grabbed one and flung it into the smoke, where the magic had come from, but Liam had moved. The chain hit another wall.

"Nice try," his voice said. "Like everything about you, not good enough."

She heard the movement behind her a moment too late. As she turned, his kick hit her in the side. She fell, landing in front of the containment unit.

Here, the smoke was brightened by the light shining from the Source. It filled the whole room with a strange, pale glow, out of which Liam's black-clad figure appeared. He was panting, one arm badly bruised, drained of power and energy, but fury still flared in his eyes.

He drew a knife.

"I don't need you alive, Fran." He pointed the knife at

the Source. "Not now that I have your friends, and whatever this is."

He grabbed Fran's hair and hauled her up. The knife moved toward her throat.

Fran raised a finger. Liam flung his head back to stop it from pointing at him. Instead, she aimed at the knife and let fly. White-hot light struck the blade, which glowed like it was on fire.

"Argh!" Liam dropped the knife and clutched his burned hand.

Fran flung a sound blast, knocking him into the wall. He slid to the floor.

"You… you…" Liam muttered. His eyes crossed and his hand trembled as he tried to raise it.

"I got you." Weary and aching, Fran crawled over to him. There were cable ties on his belt. She would use one of those to tie him up. "After this, the Griffins will have you, and they'll find out what you're all about, and they'll throw you in Trevilsom, and, and, and…"

"Wasn't my idea," Liam mumbled. "Someone else. Working for them."

"Who?" Fran asked. "Who's behind it?"

Liam whispered something. Fran leaned in closer, trying to hear.

There was a flash. A burning hole appeared in the middle of Liam's forehead, and he fell dead.

Fran looked around. The Source was looking at them, one hand pressing against the containment field, straining to weaken it enough to get that blast of magic through.

"Why?" Fran stared at the Source in horror.

The Source pointed, and Fran looked down. There was

another knife in Liam's hand, only inches from her ribs. He'd been about to stab her.

"It was a lie, wasn't it?" she said. It shouldn't have been a surprise, after everything. "There was no one else. He wanted me close enough to stab. You saved me…"

She pressed her hand against the containment field and felt a tingle of energy as the Source did the same.

"Thank you," she said.

The Source nodded at her, then sank to the mirrored floor of its cage, weary from the strain of breaking through, even for that brief moment.

"There you are." Winslow walked into the room with Enfield at his shoulder. "Are you all right?"

"Great." Fran barely had to force her smile. It would be hard not to be happy, seeing Liam get what he deserved.

"We've dealt with the rest," Winslow said. "Thank goodness, the Source didn't get out."

"Thank goodness."

Fran looked at the Source, the creature that had saved her life. It hadn't gotten out this time, but one day it would be free. She made that promise inside her head. She would find another way to power the kemanas, to power all the magic on Earth. Then the Evermores wouldn't need the Source, and she could let it go.

One day, this ancient creature would be free.

CHAPTER THIRTY-SIX

"It's quite a story, Fran." Don Karelsky put on an excessively shocked face for the TV cameras. "While a lot of people have accepted the allegations of spying you've made against Prestige Craft, others are asking, where's the evidence?"

"Oh, we've got, like, a ton of evidence." Fran held her arms wide. She could mug for the viewers as well. "Two tons. Three tons. Four tons."

Elethin, sitting in the studio's other guest chair, gave a small laugh.

"To put it in slightly more prosaic terms," the elf said, "we have records of all Liam Wade's comings and goings at our company's premises, as well as CCTV footage from the area. We also have computer logs from when he interfered in our systems and witnesses from when he took Fran out to dinner and tried to seduce secrets out of her." Elethin shook her head solemnly. "Honestly, does it get any lower than that?"

Across Mana Valley, female viewers shook their heads in angry camaraderie.

"A despicable tactic," Don agreed. "Of course, now that Mr. Wade has disappeared, he can't answer your accusations."

"A sure sign of guilt, running away as soon as the truth appears." Elethin frowned dramatically. "Our story might not be the worst part. Half of his company's security team has vanished with him. Who knows where they've gone, or what trouble they might cause, this band of armed mercenaries led by a man with no scruples."

"Who indeed. At least the residents of Mana Valley can sleep better for knowing that they're gone." Don turned to the camera. "That's it for today's show. A huge thank you to my guests today, Fran Berryman and Elethin Tannerin of Mana Wave Industries. We'll be back tomorrow with…"

Fran stopped paying attention as Don went through the show's closing spiel. She was glad it was over. Fun as it was to denounce Liam on live TV, she'd been worried that she would say the wrong thing and let a secret slip. It had taken a lot of effort to hide the attack on the Evermore house and to cover the trail as Winslow carried their captive attackers off to wherever he was keeping them, as well as getting rid of Liam's body. If she'd said the wrong thing, she could've exposed the Evermores, the Source, and the whole story they were spinning. Some lies were necessary, but that didn't mean she was good at maintaining them.

The lights dimmed, then came up again once the cameras turned off.

"Come on, Fran." Elethin unfastened the microphone from her lapel and handed it to a producer. "Time to go."

"I can't tempt you ladies to a drink?" Don asked.

"No, thanks," Elethin said curtly. "We have another appointment."

Fran handed over her microphone, and they headed for the door. Outside, a limousine was waiting for them.

"That looks familiar," Fran said.

"One of the remaining board members at Prestige Craft offered it to us," Elethin said. "He knows that the company's doomed, but he still wanted to make some sort of gesture, a hint of apology for sending Liam our way. It seemed rude to say no."

"And it's a coincidence that this is exactly the sort of thing you want?"

"A happy coincidence, perhaps."

They climbed into the back of the car and Elethin tapped on the partition.

"Driver, take us away," she said.

"Only if you ask nicely," Gruffbar said from the driver's seat.

"Take us away, and I'll let you play with the limo's engine later."

"Doesn't get nicer than that." He started the car, and they headed off.

As they rolled through the streets of Mana Valley, Fran leaned back in her seat. There was a lot more space in the car without Liam, even though Elethin was as tall as him, taller even. Maybe it was about personality, or perhaps ego.

"I could get used to this," Fran said.

"Good. Keep that in mind. Let it motivate you to keep pushing this company to better things."

The vehicle halted in front of the Blazing Bean.

"Driver, get the door," Elethin called.

"You can get your door," Gruffbar called back.

Before the argument could go any further, someone opened the door from the outside. Singar climbed in, carrying a sturdy bag. Smokey jumped in after her, tail swaying from side to side as he paused to sniff the new space. Last came Bart, who closed the door behind him.

"Thank you, Gruffbar," Bart said. "We can go now if you're ready."

"See, that's how you talk to a driver," Gruffbar said. "Remember who's in control of the fast-moving lump of steel and flammable liquid."

Once again they headed out through the streets while the team settled in among the plush seating and explored the drinks cabinet.

"There should be milk in here," Smokey said.

"It'll give you indigestion," Singar pointed out.

"Fine, oat milk. Something for cats, that's what matters."

"I promise, if we keep the car, we'll put in something for everyone," Fran said. "Did you watch us on TV?"

"You were great," Bart said. "Really showing the professional face of the business. We've already had calls from some other companies interested in licensing the battery technology."

"First we prove its value." Singar tapped the bag. "Then we start licensing it."

"No, first we get them to pay a fee for possible future licensing, then we prove its value, then we set the price for those licenses. Get their money both ways."

"We can decide those things later," Fran said. "Did you finish it?"

"We did." Singar opened the bag. "Here it is, the prototype that beat all the other prototypes, the one device to hang our fortunes on. The very first Mana Wave Industries Fun Delivery System, or FDS for short."

She held up a bright orange box the size of two people's hands, with controllers down both sides.

"Is that the name we're going with?" Smokey asked. "FDS?"

"I like it," Fran said. "Elethin, what do you think? Can you market it as FDS?"

"I'll think about it," Elethin said. "First show me that it works."

"Of course."

Singar set the device down and tapped a button. A hologram of a cartoon mouse appeared in the air. It was brighter, clearer, and stronger than the image from Josie's Manaphone prototype. It was also three-dimensional and moving.

"There's more," Singar said. "Sound." She hit a button, and the hologram mouse started making squeaking noises. "Magical aura." Another button. Now the car's magically inclined inhabitants could see a faint glow around the hologram as if it was a real living creature. "Of course, in tribute to one of Fran's greatest creations, smell." Another button. They all drew a deep breath.

"That's…" Fran hesitated. "It's weird."

"Yeah, well, mice don't smell great, and that part isn't working quite right yet. But we're so close that it seemed like time to celebrate."

Singar hit another button, and more mice appeared.

They picked up tiny top hats and started dancing while singing a show tune in high-pitched squeals.

"It's adorable!" Fran clapped.

"It's twee and derivative," Elethin said. "Which is good because twee and derivative sell."

"Almost there," Gruffbar called from the front of the car.

They'd been heading out of the city toward the foothills. Now they pulled off the road and up a dirt track that strained the limousine's suspension. They stopped at a clearing, and all got out.

Several witches and wizards in suits were standing in the clearing. In their center was a wizard in a well-fitted black suit, with a white shirt and black tie. There were gray streaks through this short black hair, and he smiled the sort of smile that TV hosts used to put people off their guard. Fran reckoned that he might've made a better TV host than Don Karelsky if he'd ever wanted to go down that path, but it would have meant a serious change to his line of work.

"Hi there, Agent Baldwin," she said. "How are you doing?"

"Very well, thank you, ma'am." Baldwin shook her hand. "And you?"

"I've just been on TV."

"I saw. You did pretty well. Just relax a bit. People like listening to you talk."

"Thanks, I think." She looked around. "Did you bring the prototype back?"

"In a manner of speaking."

At that moment, two more magical FBI agents emerged

from the woods. One of them had his wand out, levitating the containment device that Mana Wave had built for them. The device was on, and it was full of blue squirrels.

"Ten minutes exactly." Baldwin looked at his watch. "How many did you get?"

The agents let the squirrels out of the trap one by one, counting them as they went. Fran was impressed with how well they controlled the containment field, only letting down a small part at a time, keeping the other squirrels inside.

"We've found this is a good exercise," Baldwin explained. "Makes sure the agents think about how they're using that there device."

"Seventeen," one of the agents called as she let the last squirrel go.

"A new record," Baldwin declared. "Congratulations. Your drinks are on everyone else tonight."

The victorious agents cheered while their colleagues laughed and groaned.

"It's working okay, then?" Fran asked.

"Working okay?" Baldwin chuckled. "Oh, it's more than okay. What y'all have built is one of the most useful devices my team has had since magicals came into the open. It's a game-changer. The field tests have been a huge success." He took a sheet of paper from his pocket and handed it to her. "This here is a proposed extension of our contract, commissioning you to go into mass production straight away."

Fran stared at the paper.

"You want how many?" she asked, mouth hanging open. "By when?"

"Is there gonna be a problem?"

Gruffbar grabbed the paper and looked over it. "I'll talk to your legal team about the details before we sign," he said. "I'm happy to hear that you've decided to go ahead."

"Thank you so much," Fran said. "This is great, really it is." She shook Baldwin's hand, then laughed. "I can't believe I'm doing this for real."

"Word to the wise, ma'am?" Baldwin said. "Maybe don't tell customers that in future. They want to know that you know what you're doing."

"Oh, I do, it's just…" Fran looked at her team, assembled in front of their company limousine with Singar holding the FDS. "It's all so exciting."

"I get that. You want to burn off some of that excitement with a squirrel hunt, maybe? Seventeen in ten minutes is the score to beat."

"Yay, that sounds like fun. Who else is in?"

"I don't chase things." Elethin shook her head.

"Looking after this." Singar patted her bag.

"I don't like the taste of squirrels," Smokey said.

"Just no," Gruffbar growled.

"I'm in!" Bart stepped forward and rubbed his hands together. "It's always worth trying something new when you have a chance."

"You can talk contracts with Gruffbar while I'm gone," Fran told Baldwin as she picked up the device. "Who's timing us?"

An agent held up her hand.

"All right," Fran said. "I've had a stressful week, but now it's time to play. Ready, steady, go!"

Off they ran.

Get sneak peeks, exclusive giveaways, behind the scenes content, and more. PLUS you'll be notified of special **one day only fan pricing** on new releases.

Sign up today to get free stories.

Visit: https://marthacarr.com/read-free-stories/

AUTHOR NOTES - MARTHA CARR

DECEMBER 8, 2021

It's finally 2022 and I am refusing to say what kind of year it will be. I am entering this one cautiously, whispering, tip-toeing in with a smile plastered on my face, hoping to go unnoticed.

I said to Michael back in December of 2019, I think this next year is going to be great and, well... you know. And then, for some wild reason I did it again – same words in December 2020. One broken arm, bunch of surgeries and some chemo later and I'm catching on.

Only wink at the New Year as you pass by. Holy Toledo, no, I take that back. Maybe don't even do that. Just mind my own business and walk on in with no expectations, no cautious optimism either. Just a blank slate, whistling past the graveyard kind of thing, while I try to take deep breaths.

Maybe I will even pretend that there are now some extra months in a year. Nothing to see here. It's still the same year.

Oh, hell with it. I'm way too much of an optimist to

start doing that. Fine, I'll throw out some resolutions here and see what wild ride there is in store for me in 2022. Who knows, maybe this one will be full of good news.

Come to think of it, I did build that garden (that Michael calls a Forest) in the backyard. An oasis that makes everyone breathe deeper when they're in it. And there was the Post Ranch Inn on the cliffs of Big Sur, or the Thousand Waves Spa or Wild Rice Retreat. Clearly, I got my spa on in 2021. I already have plans to do at least one more of those in April at Miraval. Before 2021 I had never been to a spa and boy, am I making up for lost time.

Okay, so resolutions. Well, more spa time. Sitting in my garden more. Throw a few fireballs and let a certain troll run wild. Lose weight – rarely has there been a year when that one hasn't been on the list. Avoid doctors whenever possible. (Even my doctors understand at this point.) Learn how to use my digital camera. (I was a whiz at a SLR and had my own darkroom but this computer stuff.) Draw more cartoons. Get back to painting. Go hear Jackie Venson perform. Swim, do yoga, box, ride my bike (and hopefully stay upright). Play with Bluebell and the good dog Lois Lane. Outdo my neighbors with my Halloween decorations. A very high bar to meet. One neighbor hired a legit mariachi band. A band! But I am determined to at least compete. Grow out this bad haircut that was a result of a recommended hairdresser hacking away and laughing as she did it. Big red flag. Plant wildflowers in the front yard. Have everyone over again for crawfish.

That's about it. A pretty doable list except maybe the Halloween one unless I truly bring it.

Maybe get a bunch of full-sized skeletons and set up a

yoga class in the front yard. Nope. That's funny but can't compete against a Halloween tunnel of lights that led to a haunted house set up in someone's front yard. Okay, enough about Halloween, wrong holiday.

Back to the turning of a new year in a strange time that has not ended.

There's so much about what's going on all around me that I have no control over, but whether or not I keep on showing up for friends and family, doing the best I can for myself, and have a good time is all up to me. Even in the strangest of times, in years where I enter with extreme caution there can be good times. It's not so much about what is happening, but what I choose to do with it. Happy New Year everyone! More adventures to follow.

AUTHOR NOTES - MICHAEL ANDERLE

JANUARY 3, 2022

Thank you for not only reading this book but these author notes as well!

So, when Martha...

Said she was just going to waltz into 2022 and ignore saying anything about goals, I was rooting her on! Then she went and made plans anyway, laughing at the cosmos and daring it to screw with her.

She's more brazen than I am.

But since she started this, I'm going to admit that I read an article that suggested not making goals but rather stating what type of year you'll go for. Do you want a peaceful year? One with more adventure than the last? Do you want romance this year? Perhaps exploration? That kind of stuff.

I'm truly befuzzled.

LMBPN Publishing (my company) is implementing a couple of really large projects and a couple of mid-range projects that are taking a while to complete.

So, maybe "completion" is my mantra for 2022? That would work, I think. I'd like to COMPLETE stuff.

Like…tomorrow, we will complete a book series called *The Kurtherian Endgame*. BOOYAH, BABY!

That brings an end to the Bethany Anne mega-series (comprised of thirty-two books between *The Kurtherian Gambit* and *The Kurtherian Endgame*) and allows me a bit of breathing room on what I'm going to do next.

Which is probably going to be a short series about Bethany Anne's alter ego Baba Yaga. We are going to do three covers and plan out three books. If we get enough interest, we will build out the series as a trilogy, and depending on the response, maybe do a few more.

I can complete a weight loss plan to lose ten pounds this year. I'm NOT setting a goal, just a simple downward trend. That doesn't break any rules, right? Maybe I shouldn't say ten and just leave it with "Eat a bit healthier" or something?

I might need a little slack on how I'm operating this year of completeness thing I'm contemplating. Stick with me here, and I'll update you (I hope) from time to time!

Have a fantastic weekend or week, and I look forward to talking in the next story you read from us!

Ad Aeternitatem,

Michael Anderle

JOIN THE ORICERAN UNIVERSE FAN GROUP ON FACEBOOK!

BOOKS BY MICHAEL ANDERLE

CONNECT WITH THE AUTHORS

Martha Carr Social

Website: http://www.marthacarr.com

Facebook: https://www.facebook.com/
groups/MarthaCarrFans/

Michael Anderle Social

Website: http://lmbpn.com

Email List: http://lmbpn.com/email/

https://www.facebook.com/LMBPNPublishing

https://twitter.com/MichaelAnderle

https://www.instagram.com/lmbpn_publishing/

https://www.bookbub.com/authors/michael-anderle